LOVELY GREEN EYES

Arnošt Lustig was born in Prague in 1926. In 1942 he was sent by the Nazis to Theresienstadt and later to Auschwitz, where his father died in the gas chambers, and finally to Buchenwald. He left Czechoslovakia after the Soviet occupation in 1968. He settled in 1970 in Washington D.C., where he is Professor of Literature at the American University. He is the author of *The Unloved*, *Diamonds of the Night*, *A Prayer for Katerina Horovitzova* and *Night and Hope*. He is a two-time winner of the Jewish National Book Award.

Ewald Osers has translated more than a hundred works of prose and poetry from the Czech, German and other languages. He has many honours for his work as a translator, most recently the Medal of Merit from the Czech Republic.

ALSO BY ARNOŠT LUSTIG

Waiting for Leah

Arnošt Lustig

LOVELY
GREEN EYES

TRANSLATED FROM THE CZECH BY
Ewald Osers

VINTAGE

Published by Vintage 2005

1 3 5 7 9 8 6 4 2

Copyright © Arnošt Lustig, 2000
English translation © Ewald Osers, 2001

Arnošt Lustig has asserted his right under the Copyright,
Designs and Patents Act, 1988 to be identified as the author
of this work

First published with the title *Krásne zelené oči* by
Peron, Prague

First published in Great Britain in 2001 by
The Harvill Press

First published by Vintage in 2003

Vintage
Random House, 20 Vauxhall Bridge Road, London SW1V 2SA

Random House Australia (Pty) Limited
20 Alfred Street, Milsons Point, Sydney,
New South Wales 2061, Australia

Random House New Zealand Limited
18 Poland Road, Glenfield,
Auckland 10, New Zealand

Random House (Pty) Limited
Endulini, 5a Jubilee Road, Parktown 2193,
South Africa

The Random House Group Limited Reg. No. 954009
www.randomhouse.co.uk/vintage

A CIP catalogue record for this book
is available from the British Library

ISBN 0 09 948354 8

Papers used by Random House are natural, recyclable
products made from wood grown in sustainable forests.
The manufacturing processes conform to the environmental
regulations of the country of origin

Printed and bound in Great Britain by
Cox & Wyman Ltd, Reading, Berkshire

FOR EVA AND ALL WHO ARE
AND WILL BE WITH HER

A.L.

To the memory of my mother,
one of the millions who perished
in the Holocaust.

E.O.

How many people have secrets
that no-one ever discovers?

Part One

Chapter One

From early morning, units of the Waffen-SS had been arriving. They had demanded an extension of the shift until 4 p.m.

Fifteen: Hermann Hammer, Fritz Blücher, Reinhold Wuppertal, Siegfried Fuchs, Bert Lippert, Hugo Redinger, Liebel Ulrich, Alvis Graff, Siegmund Schwerstei, Herbert Gmund, Hans Frische, Arnold Frey, Philipp Petsch, Mathias Krebs, Ernst Lindow.

For the past three days the frost had been severe. The pipes in the former agricultural estate had burst when the water in them froze. The girls had been provided with two new tubs, but the water froze rock hard in these too. The river had frozen over. Iron rusted, steel fractured. Once or twice a train halted by the bridge because its engine's boilers had burst. Inside, the plaster in the building developed mould and the walls of the cubicles turned black with soot from the stoves. The waiting room and the canteen, with its long table for 60 people, were no better. The living quarters resembled a bacon-curing shop.

Overnight the walls had acquired a crest of snow, like a chef's white hat pushed up from his forehead. At dawn, when the blizzard was over, when the wind had blown away the clouds and it was no longer snowing, it looked as if what lay on the ground was blood. For a few minutes the snow was steeped in purple and ruby red. An invisible silence hung over the landscape.

Inside, along the corridor, an inscription in spiky Gothic letters (the flashes of the SS insignia were ancient runes) declared: *We were born to perish.*

The silence was broken by a truck or a bus making for the field brothel. From the distance, from between the sky and the ground, came the rumble of artillery.

She had woken in the middle of the night. She had pain between her legs. Before her eyes and in her ears was the Pole who'd stood at the ramp in Auschwitz-Birkenau when they'd stumbled from the trains – the deep, chesty voice of a broad-shouldered soldier of the Kanada squad who, over and over, had ordered the mothers to give the children to their grandmothers.

"Don't ask why. Do it now!"

Having passed the doctors at the end of the long line who sent people either to the left or to the right, she had arrived at the Frauen-konzentrationslager and there understood the meaning of the order.

"Give the children to their grandmothers".

The old women and the children had gone straight from the ramp to the gas chambers.

This is the story of my love. It is about love almost as much as it is about killing; about one of love's many faces: killing. It is about No. 232 Ost, the army brothel that stood in the agricultural estate by the River San before the German army retreated further west; about 21 days, about what a girl of 15 endured; about what it means to have the choice of going on living or of being killed, between choosing to go to the gas chamber or volunteering to work in a field brothel as an Aryan girl. It is about what memory or oblivion will or will not do.

I fell in love with Hanka Kaudersová's smile, with the wrinkles of a now 16-year-old, with the effect her face had on me. What saves me, apart from the uncertainty of it, is time. There are fragments out of which an event is composed, there are its colours and shades. And there is horror.

On that last day before the evacuation of No. 232 Ost, before they put Madam Kulikowa up against the back wall a few steps from the kitchen, and the first salvo shattered her teeth, she'd said that deep down she had expected nothing better.

Twelve: Karl Gottlob Hain, Johann Obersaltzer, Wilhelm Tietze, Arnold Köhler, Gottfried Lindner, Moritz Krantz, Andreas Schmidt, Granz Biermann, Carolus Mautch, August Kreuter, Felix Körner, Jorgen Hofer-Wettermann.

In my mind I can hear Madam Kulikowa introducing Skinny Kaudersová to No. 232 Ost on that first Friday morning . . . Anything that is not specifically permitted is forbidden. (This was something Skinny already knew from the Frauenkonzentrationslager at Auschwitz-Birkenau.) Regulations are posted on the cubicle doors. The soldier is always right. Kissing is forbidden. Unconditional obedience is demanded. You must not ask for anything.

"Any perks we share equally," Madam Kulikowa said, with both uncertainty and cunning. "A man is like a child and generally behaves like one. He expects to get everything he wants. He will expect you to treat him unselfishly, like a mother."

She urged her to think of pleasanter things.

Oberführer Schimmelpfennig had ordered the following notice to be posted on the doors of the cubicles, in the waiting room and in the washroom.

> With immediate effect, it is forbidden to provide services
> without a rubber sheath. Most strictly prohibited are:
> Anal, oral or brutal intercourse;
> To take urine or semen into the mouth or anus;
> To re-use contraceptives.

During roll-call one day, Oberführer Schimmelpfennig threatened to import Gypsy women to the estate. He knew of at least five brothels in Bessarabia where they were employed. "No-one here is indispensable," he said.

Twelve: Heinrich Faust, Felix Schellenberg, Fritz Zossen, Siegfried Skarabis, Adolf Seidel, Günther Eichmann,

Hans Scerba, Rudolf Weinmann, Hugon Gerhard Rossel, Ernst Heidenkampf, Manfred Wostrell, Eberhardt Bergel.

In the evening, as they were sweeping by the gate which carried the German eagle, Skinny arranged the snow into symmetrical piles, and wondered whether she was punishing herself for being alive. What had become of Big-Belly, from whom she'd inherited Cubicle No. 16 and a pot for heating water and a small cask? Where was Krikri? Or Maria-Giselle? The first two had gone to the wall, the third to the "Hotel for Foreigners" at Festung Breslau. Here, as Oberführer Schimmelpfennig put it, Skinny was serving her apprenticeship. What kind of girl was Beautiful? Or Estelle, Maria-from-Poznan, Long-Legs, Fatty, Smartie and the others? What was the name, or the nickname, of the girl who died at two in the morning three days after Schimmelpfenning's botched attempt at an appendectomy?

"If you don't sleep you'll feel like death warmed up in the morning," said Estelle later that night. "You won't change anything by not sleeping."

There was fresh snow. A train with troops on home leave rattled across the steel bridge over the river.

"This is what it must be like in the Bering Straits," Estelle said. "Except for those wintering, there isn't a soul about."

Skinny had never heard of the Bering Straits.

"Twenty-four hours of darkness every day. An ocean of ice," Estelle said.

"How deep is it?" Skinny wanted to know.

"Never mind. Go to sleep."

Suddenly Estelle said: "Do you think anybody knows the truth?"

"About what?"

"About you. About me. About the Oberführer or Madam Kulikowa."

"My head is spinning," said Skinny. "I have to get some sleep."

"My memory is failing me," Estelle said.

6

"You should be grateful."

"Why?"

"Because."

Skinny's eyes were falling shut. In a moment she would be asleep. It was cold and she would be frozen stiff by the morning. In the cubicle, with a soldier, it was at least warm, but the Oberführer did not allow the girls' dormitories to be heated. They could nestle up to each other, he'd said. Skinny fell asleep thinking of the Frauenkonzentrationslager at Auschwitz-Birkenau, when she was still with her mother and her father. Before her father had thrown himself against the high-voltage fence and her mother was taken away at a selection parade. Her brother had gone to the gas chamber straight from the ramp.

Sometime before dawn Estelle said to her: "Did you know that you wake up, say something about your father and then fall asleep again? You sit up, half comb your hair, but you lack the strength to finish."

"Do I talk in my sleep?"

"Only about your father. You turn about a bit."

"I'm tired."

"That's all right."

Chapter Two

Oberführer Schimmelpfennig corresponded with a doctor in Mauthausen in Austria. His friend was learning to amputate limbs, measuring the time before an amputee could walk again. Did he think of Helga, with whom he had been at University? She was training at Buchenwald. They were due to start at an army hospital together. They were thinking of getting married before they were transferred to the front, where they would have to operate in earnest.

For her part, after three tots of liquor Big Leopolda Kulikowa would return in her mind to the Odeon and the Gloria in Cracow. The fairytale of the frog that changed into a prince after a single, generous kiss should be rewritten, she felt, so that no-one was misled – those single girls in civvies who saw every possibility as love, for example. That's how unmarried mothers pay for a single love-making . . . those girls don't take account of their own worth, they give themselves away cheap, mostly for free. To the soldiers, a girl is like a spring of water in the desert.

Twelve: Gustav Habenicht, Sepp Bartells, Hanan Baltrusch, Fritz Puhse, Heinrich Rinn, Otto Scholtz, Heini Baumgarten, Fritz Heindl, Wilhelm Kube, Johannes Kurfürst, Rudolf Weissmüller, Hans Ewing.

There was an icy wind blowing, and freezing fog. The truck driver wiped his nose on his sleeve and muttered a few obscenities. He stacked the huge boxes he had stolen from a wooden Orthodox Church before setting fire to it in the office of the Oberführer, Dr Helmuth Gustav Schimmelpfennig.

*

I was still in Terezín at the end of September when I lost sight of Skinny. She was put on one of five transports going east. In the Frauenkonzentrationslager at Auschwitz-Birkenau she and her mother were put to work, at first, repairing the sides of rail wagons, sweeping roads and carrying stones to and from the Auto-Union plant. Eventually she found herself as a cleaner in the hospital block of Sturmbannführer Dr Julius Krueger, who sterilized her.

The day after Dr Krueger was promoted to Obersturmbannführer he performed an urgent operation on a frostbitten Waffen-SS Obergruppenführer, transplanting onto him a large patch of skin cut from a Jewish subhuman. For this, Dr Krueger was instantly transferred to the eastern front. He only had time to retrieve his medical diploma from the wall and one proclaiming him to be a doctor of philosophy and biology.

Skinny finished cleaning up the surgery. With a damp cloth she wiped blood from the tiles and polished the used instruments. Dr Krueger's departure had left her at her wit's end. She didn't even dare contemplate what would happen in the morning. They would get rid of her as a compromising witness. She was alone in the surgery, perhaps the whole block, probably by mistake. She switched off the light, and the surgery windows were engulfed by the night. It was one of those nights at Auschwitz-Birkenau when the darkness seemed to mean the end of the world, the end of the last human being, the last tree, the last star.

Life at the Frauenkonzentrationslager was simply the opposite of how people had lived before they got there. She was faced with the deadening knowledge of what was an everyday occurrence: the medical experiments, the killing of people on a conveyor belt, the processions towards the basement undressing rooms of the five crematoria. And then the flames licking up from the low chimneys, exhaling in the form of soot and ashes the remains of what an hour previously had been living beings. From Monday, when the selections were held, to Sunday, and again from Monday to Sunday – again and again. In her mind she tried to tell somebody about it, just to convince herself that she was still sane. She clung to memories of people who had long forgotten her, but whom she once knew. The teacher at her primary school, who had commended her for drawing so well, or the music master who had tactfully told her that whatever she was going to succeed at when she grew up, it would not be a career in opera.

The surgery smelled of carbolic acid, iodine, blood and water. It was a smell Skinny had grown used to. Through the window she saw the fires of the No. 2 and No. 3 crematoria. While working for Dr Krueger, she wore an apron and didn't have to endure what the other girls from the block had to undergo. She had a pass through the Postenkette, past the sentries. It expired that night. Even though she didn't think of it for more than a second, everyone at Auschwitz-Birkenau could picture themselves in the basement undressing room, pulling off their clothes, stepping under the showers before the airtight door without an inside handle closed on them and the crystals of greenish Zyklon B began to drop from the shower-heads, turning to gas on contact with the air.

As well as the smell of the surgery, the greasy smoke which penetrated through every crack hung in the air. This was how she might live her final moments, though she had never harmed a soul. This was how she might rack her brains without ever finding an answer. Auschwitz-Birkenau was the final station for her. In her mind's eye, she saw the inoffensive German word, the compound noun *Endlösung*, final solution.

She felt tense, like a mouse caught in a trap. Only yesterday she had been reassured by the presence of Dr Krueger, in his smart uniform with its silver epaulettes and silver-trimmed buttonholes. He could pick up the telephone and call his wife, or his grown-up children, just as he had called his daughter in Alsace. There was a question of what he would do on Sunday. But not now.

Skinny was hungry and thirsty, and knew it would be worse by morning. She was cold too, so she kept her headscarf on. The previous week she had had toothache. The girl she had replaced in

Dr Krueger's surgery had not received any special treatment either. Anyone here was alive at the expense of someone else.

She heard a noise in an office at the far end of the corridor that was rarely used. A door creaked and then slammed. Someone was going to the lavatory. She heard the door again and then water flushing. A girl appeared.

"Hello," Skinny said, moving into the passageway.

"What is it?" the girl asked in Polish.

"Do you belong to this block?"

"No."

The girl was about 18. She was dressed as if she were somewhere in Warsaw: a knee-length skirt, a blouse with short, puffed sleeves of a bright washable material, warm woollen socks and high lace-up boots – not at all what the female inmates looked like. Her hair was brushed into a quiff, the way boys used to wear it in Prague at the beginning of the war. The girl told her that the doctor who was to replace Krueger (she didn't know his name) was choosing girls for a field brothel further east. With lightning speed Skinny considered what this could mean for her.

"If we're lucky they'll turn us into whores," the girl said. "What do you think? Am I suitable?"

"Is it a selection?" Skinny asked.

"What's that, a selection?"

"*Sortierung*. Sorting out."

The girl didn't know the camp jargon.

"There are 60 of us and they'll choose 30. He's already told us. The rest can volunteer for nursing."

Suddenly the light went out in the block, the outside lights as well.

"You have power cuts here just as in Warsaw?" the girl said.

What kind of girls had they brought here? From the far office came a voice shouting into a telephone:

"What? Half an hour to an hour? *Scheisse*. This is Hauptsturmführer Schneidhuber – Lucian Schneidhuber. Block 21."

Then came the sound of him groping for the telephone and

putting down the receiver. The instrument tinkled for a while before clicking and falling silent.

"Is there anybody else in this block? I need candles!" he called out.

Skinny knew about the candles. "Here," she shouted into the dark, over the head of the girl. She picked up a flat box of candles, locating it from memory. Groping her way, she carried it to the far end of the corridor to the Hauptsturmführer. He gestured to her to wait by the wall, with the as yet unselected girls. Did he take her for one of the Aryan girls crowding the room? She had nothing to lose. In the morning she would be going up in smoke. The Hauptsturmführer lit the first candle with his lighter, then clicked it shut and with the burning wick lit another. With a candle in each hand, he let a few drops of wax fall on a black, cloth-bound, record book – the kind that Dr Krueger had also used – set the candles into it and held them in place for a moment.

A draught blew through a crack in the door, which Skinny had left ajar, and the flames flickered until she closed it. She stood by the wall, the last in line, trying not to look around too much for fear of being conspicuous; but at the same time she observed the girls who had already been selected, about 15 of them. They wore civilian clothes – blouses and skirts and shoes, and had coloured jackets hanging on hooks. The girls must have been fresh; they had only just been brought in. They were all around 18. The room was beginning to smell of sweat and perfume, and of clothes and underwear not changed for some days. Skinny was preparing herself for the Hauptsturmführer's questions. She didn't suppose that those the doctor didn't choose would become nurses.

She felt as she had on the 28th of September at the ramp at Auschwitz-Birkenau – at the mercy of whatever might happen, a lump of clay that could be moulded into anything. Was it to be her good fortune that Dr Krueger could not bear cleaners in prison outfits and had ordered some civilian clothes to be brought for her from the store, with long sleeves and lace-up boots and thick woollen stockings?

The girls were standing casually against the wall, legs crossed.

Either they did not know they were at Auschwitz or they didn't realize what that meant.

Now and again the Hauptsturmführer shouted: "*Ruhe!*" Quiet!

Then he said: "*Schweinerei.*" He called out three German names from his list: "Mathilde Seiler, Brunhilde Bausinger, Helga Burger." He had dark rings under his eyes.

At that moment Skinny knew she would deny that she was Jewish. There was no mistaking the pointed questions of the Hauptsturm-führer as he verified the racial origin of each girl. She would lie. If he asked her she would say she was Aryan. If he asked her religion she would answer as though she were her drawing teacher from primary school. They'd all known which church she belonged to. She composed her answers in her head, trying to guess what the Hauptsturmführer would ask.

She had been 18 days in Auschwitz-Birkenau. Her head had been shaved. The girls by the wall did not yet have the prescribed mascu-line crew cut. They had slides, ribbons and combs in their hair.

The girl with the quiff failed to answer the Hauptsturmführer's questions satisfactorily and joined those not selected, along the wall. The girl probably thought she would become a nurse. How come so many people believed the Germans? Probably because it was more comfortable to believe; it was not so easy to disbelieve and terrible not to trust in anything. What qualities would a girl need to have for the Hauptsturmführer to choose her?

Skinny wondered how Kowalska in Block 18 would deal with her absence. Would she assume she was dead already? Unless they had been looking for her in the evening, they wouldn't bother looking for her in the morning. Even with the meticulous organization of Auschwitz-Birkenau, people got lost for a day, for two or three days, even for longer.

What were her chances? No-one knew that she was only 15. On the advice given to her by some Poles at the ramp as soon as she had arrived, she had added three years to her age. In the twinkling of an eye she was 18. After a day and a night at Auschwitz-Birkenau she wouldn't have been lying if she'd declared that she was 1,000 years old. Children under 15 went straight to the chimney. And most of those over 40 went as well.

She listened carefully to the Hauptsturmführer's questioning of each girl, how he moved from one question to another, what he wrote down. He was in a hurry. That was good. The girl with the quiff had accepted her fate lethargically. What did it matter that she would have to carry bedpans around in a sick bay?

The air was getting thick. The candles were smoking. The gaunt Hauptsturmführer was eating porridge from a soup bowl next to his bulging briefcase, washing it down with mineral water from a bottle with a German label. He had searching, tired eyes and short blond hair. His cap with its skull and crossbones was perched on the edge of the desk. On his questionnaire he ticked off the characteristics of the girls he selected. He was not looking for office workers or cooks. If he didn't like a girl, or if he suspected her of lying, he made no secret of his annoyance. Next one. Another *Schweinerei, fort mit dem Dreck*. A few times he swore, *scheissegal*. He spoke carefully and acted in a businesslike manner, severely. His vocabulary was almost coarser than Dr Krueger's, and he was not exactly prissy. From the ceiling, on a two-foot length of wire, a light bulb, extinguished, swayed in the draught.

It was Skinny's turn. He looked her over quickly, head to toe. Did he remember that she was the one who had brought him the candles? He picked up his riding crop and lightly smacked the open palm of his hand.

"Oh, it's you," he said. "Let's get on with it then." He put the crop on the desk and picked up a pencil. He wrote something on the top of the sheet and cursed when the lead broke.

"Aber jetzt nur die Wahrheit!" he said. Only the truth. Without knowing why, he'd decided in advance that he would take her, but she did not know that. She was the last needed to make up the prescribed number. He fumbled among his papers to find the 30th question-naire. He told her to answer only *ja* or *nein*.

14

It was not the first time her life had been in the balance, but each time felt like the first time. She hung on to what had so far always helped her. Something that made her rely on herself and hope she would be lucky. It was not quite rebellion, but there was a touch of rebelliousness in it.

Perhaps he sensed in her a will to live; and this didn't affect him the way it did the Waffen-SS who killed people in order to kill that very will to live.

She didn't wear glasses. Hauptsturmführer Schneidhuber had been told that female prisoners with glasses weren't suitable for field brothels.

Skinny had already lost everyone she could lose; but she had not yet lost herself and did not wish to. It was a primitive instinct, but it was the only thing she could hold on to. She refused to let it distort her outward appearance: the Hauptsturmführer mustn't suspect what she was feeling. Pity was not a Nazi characteristic. She was going through a selection, of the kind they had at Auschwitz-Birkenau every Monday, morning and evening. At every selection her life was in someone else's hands. Whether she lived or died would be decided, as always, by someone who did not know her, who was seeing her for the first time, perhaps with only half an eye. For her brother, Ramon, his first test had been his last. And at one unexpected selection at Block 18, Skinny had lost her mother. In some recess of her brain were all those, acquaintances and strangers, whom she'd last seen at a selection. There must be no uncertainty about supplies to the crematoria. When there were too few sick people, more healthy ones went into the gas chamber. In the commandant's office they had detailed quotas according to which selections were performed. If there were no Czechs, they took Hungarians. On the Tuesday morning when they selected her mother, a story went around that the Sortierabteilung truck would take them not to the crematorium but out through the gates of Auschwitz-Birkenau.

She thought all this in the instant between nodding her head and raising it again. *Ja, nein.*

"Name, day, month, year of birth. Place of birth."

The Hauptsturmführer was sharpening one of his pencils with a pocket knife. He stifled a belch and took a sip of mineral water.

"Last place of work."

Those were easy questions.

"Dr Krueger's surgery."

"Is that so?" said Hauptsturmführer Schneidhuber. "Have you any Jewish relations?"

"No."

"There was never talk in your family about anyone, no matter how distant?"

"No. Not that I remember."

"Good. You're sure that you only have Aryan blood?"

"I have Aryan blood," she replied, in the firmest voice she could manage.

There was no way back now. She gave her old Prague address to avoid making a mistake later on. She heard herself speaking as if the voice were not her own. Her blood was no longer throbbing in her temples as it had while she was waiting her turn. She tried not to think of their Prague flat which had been taken over by the Zentralstelle für jüdische Auswanderung. The Germans had made sure that the flat would go to a German.

"What's your height? You don't look short."

She told him, not sure whether to straighten up or make herself shorter.

The Hauptsturmführer was anxious now to pack up his things and lie down. He had come from Hamburg by fast train, but because of enemy air-raids they had been held up eight times. He was exhausted. He went through her questionnaire quickly, but he didn't skip anything. Nor did he recognise that what confronted him was concealed stubbornness. What he had seen during the day had been mostly resignation rather than defiance. As Skinny stood facing the doctor she heard within herself only one voice out of the many she was suppressing. Hers was a small lie compared to the German lie:

16

that the gas chambers were only shower rooms where they could freshen up after their journey.

The Hauptsturmführer heard only eagerness, willingness, perhaps a keen and ambitious desire to serve Germany. Her voice was hoarse with excitement and resolution. The doctor knew that in Krueger's surgery she had become used to working with the human body. She would be prepared for touching the bodies of German soldiers.

Skinny had not anticipated the questions for which the Hauptsturmführer had a long column and to which he now turned.

"If you had to choose between a rat and a rabbit, which would you choose?"

"The rabbit," she said.

"Why?"

"For its soft fur."

"Between an ox and a cockerel?"

"The cockerel."

"Why?"

"I don't know."

"Between a pig and a horse?"

"The horse. It's cleaner, faster and cleverer."

"Good. What about between a lamb and a snake?"

The Hauptsturmführer might – for his own amusement – have enriched the questionnaire, but he didn't feel like it. It was getting late. And it was dark. Very well, we shall see, he thought. A whore did not have to brim over with intelligence. He was thinking of the paper he would write about lymphatic glands.

Dr Schneidhuber finally ordered her to lift her skirt. She knew about this already from the ramp, from when they had arrived. Legs apart! She obeyed. She had long legs, childish thighs, yes, but that shouldn't be a problem. At that moment the Hauptsturmführer's voice sounded almost genial. He had not said yet that she had passed.

"*Ich bin unfruchtbar.*" I'm sterile.

"How do you know?"

17

"Dr Krueger used x-rays on me. Twice. From the front and behind, with my legs apart."

She was beginning to interest him.

"How sure are you of this?"

"As sure as there's a God above me."

"Suppose he's below you in hell?" Dr Schneidhuber smiled.

"*Gott macht die Nüsse, aber er knackt sie nicht auf.*" God makes the nuts, but he doesn't crack them. It sounded to him as if she were boasting that she was blind, deaf and dumb. He felt more at ease with an Aryan than he did with Jewish subhumans, on whom he would start his experiments the next day. He signed her questionnaire at the bottom. She followed every one of his movements wordlessly. He put the questionnaire into his briefcase. That someone else would go into the gas chamber in her place in the morning so the numbers would be right – this she did not think about. The doctor drank some mineral water and picked up his cap.

"You'll have to grow your hair," he said. "You haven't got much now. Why? Did you have lice?"

He told the girls it would be for a year. To serve frontline soldiers was an honour. Duty to Germany came before all else. Cleanliness, order, obedience. They would wash and sew their own underwear. There would be enough time for needlework. Embroidery, crocheting, knitting sweaters and woollen face-masks for themselves and the troops.

He left some porridge at the bottom of his bowl. It was cold now. He picked up his riding crop. Its handle was made of African hippopotamus hide. He allowed one of the girls to finish his porridge. She licked out the bowl and the spoon, not knowing when she would get her next meal. He picked up the telephone. They would leave under escort at once. Yes, they were all ready, things had moved fast. When would the light come back on? Five minutes? All right, better late than never. They could take their coats with them. Skinny did not have one and didn't know whose she could take in the next 15 minutes, so that she wouldn't have to travel in just a dress. She mingled with the girls; it was always better to be in the middle of a crowd than at the head or the tail.

Those he had not picked for the brothel would find plenty of work as nurses, Dr Schneidhuber added. *Morgen gehts los*, he thought to himself. Tomorrow they'll be off.

The guards were bored. They were not allowed to have any dealings with the prostitutes, though some did. This was an infringement of the prohibition for both parties and if they were caught, it meant punishment. The guilty SS man would go to the front, to join an Einsatzgruppe, or be sent to prison. The army whore, if she was lucky, would go to Festung Breslau, to the "Hotel for Foreigners" which they knew only by reputation. In any case she would get a thrashing on her bare bottom.

By the wall where the executions took place when the quarry was too deep in snow, the previous detachment of guards had organized dog fights. They would catch stray dogs on the wasteland, keep them hungry, then choose three of similar size, one of them a weaker one. The two stonger ones would tear the third to pieces and lick up its blood. The guards had another trick. They would take a pair of dogs and by giving them nothing to drink, even snow, they became so dehydrated that their blood would not run so much. They would bet their wages on which dog would win the fight. The dog that survived would drink the blood of the defeated one to quench its thirst.

In November the guards had invited Madam Kulikowa to a dog fight. A sheepdog which had won two fights let itself be torn to pieces in the third. It had no strength left. Its blood splashed all the way to the wall, mingling with the dried bloodstains of the executed.

Oberfülrer Schimmelpfennig saw a confirmation of the laws of nature in the brutality of the dog fights. The ancient Germanic tribes were instinctively right when, instead of praying, they relied on the flight of birds, the behaviour of horses and dogs; the mirror of lakes, the whiteness of hoarfrost. He didn't need the whores to confirm his conviction of the closeness of human and animal behaviour. The soldiers confirmed it too. Consciously or unconsciously he felt close to his distant ancestors. Did not the wasteland with the quarry resemble a giant emerging from frozen mist? The rats in the snow with their ravenous teeth reminded Schimmelpfennig of squirrels fanning quarrels according to the wisdom of the ancients, spreading dissension.

He was suffering from insomnia. At night he reflected on the Nazi Movement. The cold and the loneliness stripped from him the veneer of civilisation his medical education had given him. He was reverting to nature, to what perhaps he once had been. It thrilled him to watch animals fighting to the death.

"When dogs have an all-out fight they teach you what's good and what's bad," the Oberführer said to Madam Kulikowa. "They remind you of what's happening all around you, of what you must do to win. Every bark, growl or bite affirms to me that what I'm doing, what we are doing, is good. You should teach that to your little tarts."

"Is it the fight that makes you shiver?" he asked her.

"It is the cold that is slow death to me," Madam Kulikowa replied. And to herself she added: "And you Germans, you, Oberführer Frog, are my rapid death."

She did not even attempt to clean off the gobs of spit and excreta that had splashed onto her legs. She would have to change her clothes. She washed everything three times. This was not the first time that Big Leopolda Kulikowa had been sick with horror.

The guards chased the victorious dog out through the gate, where the wolves, faster and stronger, would catch him. The guards were keeping themselves warm with tea from thermos flasks. With frozen fingers they were paying their bets and sharing out their winnings. The girls watched from the window.

The commandant of the new Waffen-SS guard detachment, Hauptsturmführer Peter Hanisch-Sacher, who arrived on the last day of November, did not care for dog fights. He brought his Alsatian,

Fenti, with him from Bremerhaven and assigned a place for him in the kennels. Stray dogs reminded him of Gypsies: they had no business among the pure-bred dogs in the kennels. Among quadrupeds Fenti was what the Hauptsturmführer himself was in his own eyes. They both had their reputation, race, honour and fame. Dead dogs, savaged and bled to death, reminded him of Jews. In that respect he and the Oberführer understood each other. It was love or at least understanding. The fight itself somehow reminded him of the field prostitutes, though he could not have said why. He turned a blind eye to his men's contact with the prostitutes – so long as they kept within bounds – because, as he would remark over a glass of schnapps, boys will be boys. He did not question the logic of his superiors who would send one lot of SS men here and forbid the same practices elsewhere. He was not interested in the prostitutes himself. They disgusted him, though he couldn't stop talking about them.

The fight of the sheepdog, Austri, lasted 35 minutes. Austri cost Sturmmann Ruhe his pay. The dog that killed Austri was torn to pieces by wolves within five minutes. The entrails of both dogs were devoured by rats.

It was 2 a.m. when Madam Kulikowa got to bed, having first sent four girls to the kitchen to peel potatoes for the morning soup. Before pulling up her blanket she went over the day's events.

When the war was over I would sometimes converse in my mind with Big Leopolda Kulikowa, just as if we were having a chat. Even the best person – never mind the worst – will in the end do what suits them best. Danger merely enhances everything. That was why she felt no qualms at stealing bread, margarine and salami from the girls' rations. But she gave them underwear, perfume, make-up or costume jewellery when the Germans brought in a crate of what they had stolen or confiscated from the troops.

*

"It's hard to go to sleep with cold feet," Long-Legs said to Skinny.

"Mine too," Skinny said.

"I feel as if I have a brick in my belly."

Long-Legs began to tell Skinny that she had once been with an Italian who wore puttees. Then she said: "The first day I came here I saw wolves gnawing a naked body in the snow. What the wolves didn't eat, the dogs did."

The Madam did not cry when Oberführer Schimmelpfennig hit her with his walking stick. He had struck her elbow so hard that she couldn't bend her arm. She would have to massage the major with one hand. A few tears did freeze on her cheeks and she wiped her face with her sleeve. An echo of the 60-year-old lover she'd had when she was 14, who had never hit her, drowned in her silent lament. She cursed the Oberführer.

During the roll-call he had shouted: "I regret nothing. You remember that!"

Chapter Three

"No regular duty for you today," Madam Kulikowa said to Skinny. She told her to have a bath, tidy herself up and wait. It would be an officer – Wehrmacht Captain Daniel August Hentschel. She was to put a saucepan of water on the stove. She would be issued with perfume, oil, fresh clothes, underwear and shoes. She would have extra time for him.

The Madam examined her for a while with knowing, grey eyes.

"You're still like a cat who's afraid even of the person who feeds her. If you weren't in a camp you'd see the Germans like the rest. Anyway, when it comes to it, from the waist down they're all the same."

"You haven't got much light in here," said Captain Hentschel. "We won't even have to put it out."

As he walked in she thought that he had a slight limp in his left leg. The flame of the candle flickered and almost died in the draught from the open door. He saluted with gloved fingertips at the peak of his cap, then took it off. She glanced up at him. An officer, she thought, what did this mean? She must not betray how nervous she felt. He had a thin but big face, a narrow aquiline nose and widely spaced, deep blue eyes. Dark brown hair.

"Absolute hell, driving here, my word! Like skidding on snow and ice into hell." He sensed her reserve and put it down to shyness.

"Last week the car in front of my Horch ran over a mine," he continued. "I was half-conscious and I saw a nurse bending down over me. She couldn't have been any older than you. I was dying with my eyes on her throat, her breasts, and her cleavage. When I came to, another nurse was bending over me, one with glasses, older than my mother."

He was talking to her easily, as if they knew one another. She breathed in the smell of his greatcoat with its sheepskin lining and thick fur collar, the smell of mothballs, gunpowder, sweat and wet snow. She imagined his weight on top of her. He was broad-shouldered, tall and looked strong. He had shaved before setting out; his hair was cut short, lighter at its ends, like the hair of the soldiers she had known during her past six days of service. She had a few seconds to look him over. With each soldier she felt like one animal assessing another. She did not want to stare at the captain, the way Fatty would, nor kneel in front of him like Ginger or Maria-from-Poznan.

He was frozen through. With a stiff hand he closed the wooden latch, then pulled off his gloves. His glance swept over the iced-up window. He carried a pistol in a holster. If he knew that he was here with a Jewess he might pull it out. Or kick her out into the corridor. Then they would hang her. On her chest they would pin a notice that read *I concealed that I was a Jew* as they did at Auschwitz-Birkenau.

She reminded herself to be careful. She lacked the coquetry of Ginger and the Marmalade Cat, and she was incapable of offering what Maria-from-Poznan, The Toad, could offer.

"How are you?" he asked.

"Fine, thank you," she replied.

"You look sad to me," said the captain. "Are you?"

"No."

He glanced at his watch. It reminded her of the morning at the ramp at Auschwitz-Birkenau. Her first, girl's wristwatch. She had lost it within an hour, like all the things they had to leave behind in the train. They had arrived at four in the morning and by eight nine-tenths of the transport had their lives behind them.

The captain had tears in his eyes from the cold. He stood, legs apart, waving his arms awkwardly like a frozen bird. His holster seemed tiny on his massive body. Although he had kicked the snow from his boots in the corridor outside, he was leaving marks on the floor. He might be 30 or 35.

He stepped in front of the stove, rubbing his hands. He was speaking with some difficulty, his jaw still stiff with cold.

Captain Hentschel believed that war changed a woman. That she became part of the man she was with. That a man in wartime needed his body to fuse with a woman's soul – that this excited and satisfied a man. At that moment nothing would repel the woman. He could come to her before or after battle, caked in mud, sweaty and dirty and with blood on him. With burnt or tattered clothes, worn-out boots, a torn undershirt or no shirt at all, stubble-faced, ragged and dishevelled, reeking of sweat and gunpowder and blood and mud, smeared with enemy guts. She would restore his confidence and strength. She would give him a sense of achievement, which he could find with her alone. He would straighten up, grow in his own estimation, discover again what he'd feared he had lost. At this moment a woman regarded a man like a child, like a mother capable of giving her life for her child.

She felt that he was taking stock of her. For her part she was weighing up his words. Puffy snowflakes were settling on the window pane.

"Can you imagine what the first people here must have felt?"

The window was almost opaque. A whitish dusk filled the room.

She would have been glad to change places with those first people.

"You're a pretty girl," he said.

Snow was still clinging to his eyelashes, eyebrows and chin. His face was purple from the wind and the cold.

"I could have driven here blindfolded."

The wolves were howling, answered by the barks of the dogs in the kennels. They would come right up to the walls of the estate.

She breathed in the smell of his greatcoat again, his uniform and boots. Shadows played on the floor of the cubicle, on the walls and ceiling beams, twisting with the flickering flame of the candle. Its wax ran down into a small plate on the table. There were stains on the walls: the tiny remnants of insects not eaten by the spiders, frozen in what was left of their webs.

"I hope you're not mute," the captain said. "Or are you still learning to talk?"

"I used to believe in dreams," he said into the dusk. "Now I'm afraid of them."

He was not the first to murder whatever came within reach in his dreams. These were the dreams he feared. He tried to forget them. He did not think of himself as a murderer: he fought because he had to. In its way it was beautiful. He had also dreamt he was dead. He was not afraid of that dream. He woke from it alive.

"Do you know the country here?"

"I've never been further than the railway station."

"Have you ever been to Festung Breslau?"

Why had he asked her that? Did he know about Festung Breslau, the "Hotel for Foreigners"? She waited for him to ask her about Auschwitz-Birkenau. She hoped that as a Wehrmacht officer he would not know about it.

"What question would you say yes to?" He smiled at her with his frozen lips.

"I don't know."

As soon as the captain had warmed up a little, the cubicle with its ceiling beams and walls with blackened plaster seemed cosier to him. He could make out the cars arriving and departing in the courtyard. The fire roared in the cylindrical stove. He was studying his new prostitute, enjoying her slender girlish throat, with its swanlike whiteness and her gingery hair, which had not yet grown back to its proper length. He wanted to have his pleasure, but he wanted to have a friendly talk as well. He did not want a bitch that just lay down and opened her legs. She had pale skin, he liked that, and she had bloodshot, slightly scared eyes. He had asked for her especially from Madam Kulikowa and Oberführer Schimmelpfennig. For a change he wanted the youngest prostitute in No. 232 Ost.

Was Madam Kulikowa trying to do her a favour by sending her an officer after only six days of full service, each day twelve men and on one occasion fourteen and on another fifteen? Did it mean she would have no-one else for the rest of the day? Would she be relieved of a further eleven bodies, faces, hands and feet? Hairy chests and bellies?

"You look fine. You're a pretty girl. Would you believe that this morning, as I was driving here, there was a red dawn? And look at the blizzard that's come out of it."

She was thin, not surprisingly. They had a very strict diet here. Once he had seen one of their helpings on a tin plate – potato salad with carrot and kohlrabi; a thin slice of salami; and a little tub of jam the size of perhaps three thimbles – a breakfast ration for the troops.

He was thawing out. And a good thing too, he thought. At least it was dry here and relatively warm. An idea came to him about the universality of women. Yes, universality, all-world-ness, was the correct concept. A little light in the gloom of the east. The fact that one half of humanity belonged to the same club as the other half – at least in a certain sense. He smiled. It was easier for the girl to adjust to him than for him to adjust to the girl. The war had not changed him in this respect. She was very young, which confused him a little. Almost too young. This was not India or Japan or some Pacific island. The commanding officer of the SS units in the region had spoken of the Kinderaktion, the Children's Programme – though of course from the viewpoint of the SS.

"Have you had a child yet?" The question caught her unawares.

"No."

"Do you occasionally smile?" He was still hoping to hear a friendly word from this young prostitute – he intended to be friendly.

It was not impossible, he thought, that she got here through some similar Kinderaktion.

"You're new here?"

"My seventh day."

"Yes, somebody told me about you – the Oberführer, I think, or the Madam. What's your name?"

"I haven't been given a new name yet."

"I see they've already tattooed a number on your arm."

"Yes." She blushed.

"I doubt they would have sent you here without a name."

She did not know what to say.

"Do you like it here? Got used to the job yet?"

27

"I've got used to the job."

"Am I your first officer?"

She nodded.

"Today?"

"Ever."

She didn't give the soldiers in her cubicle more attention than she had to. It was an indifference with which she armed herself and which deadened her. She was glad the officer was taking his time to get warm; she wouldn't have liked him to touch her with frozen hands. She reconciled herself in advance to what he would want from her. What they all wanted. Twelve times a day, six days a week, making the most of their time.

"How come you speak German?"

"I learnt it."

"In army courses? At home?"

"At home and at school," she replied.

"Everything's a school," he said. "Do you know any German proverbs?"

"Like which?"

"Unkraut verdirbt nicht." Weeds don't perish. *"Aller Anfang ist schwer."* Every beginning is difficult. *"Ende gut, alles gut."* All's well that ends well.

She did not want to explain her knowledge of German. Her father and mother had gone to German schools under the Austro-Hungarian Empire. Besides, both were born in Prague, where every other person spoke German.

"My favourite proverb is: *Das Hemd ist uns näher als der Rock.*" Our shirt's closer to us than our jacket.

Was he going to teach her German proverbs? He couldn't hurt her with proverbs, could he? She blushed again. Maybe it would be better if the captain pounced on her and stopped asking questions.

"Most of the foreign words I know I learnt in bed," he said. "How about you?"

"I don't know."

"Have you got used to this place?"

"I have."

"Where were you born?"

"Prague." The flush left her cheeks only slowly.

"I know of one of your famous countrymen – Rilke. Life is heavier than the sum of all things. We keep only what we love. I have Ernst Jünger's *Marble Cliffs* in my pack."

She had no idea what he was talking about.

At last the captain began to unbutton his greatcoat. On his tunic she saw the Iron Cross. Candle wax was running into the plate on the table and as it cooled it stabilized the candle.

He walked over to the table with his coat open, bent down and blew out the candle. A pale light still shone through the window.

"Do you know why I did that?"

She did not answer.

"It'll be cosier like this, we'll be closer. Don't you want it to be better rather than worse for you?"

She was thinking – as so often, without really knowing why – of the bodies of the drowned that, together with other girls from the Frauen-konzentrationslager, she had pulled out of the mud of the Harmanze pond near Auschwitz-Birkenau, so they wouldn't poison the air the Germans breathed. Of the girls in Terezín and their arguments about what was improper for a girl in relationships with boys. Of the girls at Auschwitz-Birkenau who would dress up as men in order to get past the sentries, so they could see their fathers, brothers, husbands or lovers, or sometimes just to convince themselves that they were still alive. She had seen many others who were worse off. The more courageous took considerable risks just to see their loved ones for a few seconds by the wire. The risk seemed greater because what they took it for was so little. At the Harmanze pond she had envied the wild ducks. She had collected gulls' eggs for the SS men, as she watched the flight of the wild geese. The eggs had a brittle shell and sometimes they broke in her hand. She had secretly eaten a few.

The captain was listening to the blizzard and, distinct from it, the sound of artillery fire. The units fighting were not his.

"Somewhere around here there's supposed to be an officers' mess. Also a distillery."

"I don't know the area."

"I've driven here from Festung Breslau. There are a number of small concentration camps along the road. I stopped at the biggest one, at Auschwitz, to collect greatcoats like the one I'm wearing, for my battalion. Also boots, scarves and gloves, winter equipment. I stopped there for the night."

She pressed her lips together, not what Madam Kulikowa had advised her to do. It was part of her job to listen to the captain talking. She sensed danger. He had spent the night at the camp as if it were a hotel. Didn't it worry him that his coat came from there? That his men would keep warm in pullovers, gloves and socks taken from murdered people? Perhaps he didn't realize.

He was looking at her clothes, which were tight across her chest.

"You're not exactly dressed in something light and airy."

She did not understand.

"It fits all right."

She could see him assessing her breasts.

"How old are you?"

"18."

"When will you be 18?"

"I am 18 already."

"Why not 30 or a 120?" Captain Hentschel laughed. "You look 15."

Again she blushed. She felt the blood in her cheeks.

"I'll soon be nineteen."

"You look 15," he repeated.

He was taking off his tunic. She almost felt relief. Soon he wouldn't ask any more questions. There was a fresh noise outside. A larger unit had arrived, several cars, or perhaps buses. The captain unclasped his holster belt and hung it up, along with his tunic, on the hook by the door.

"Don't you want to take your things off?"

"As you wish."

"Make yourself comfortable. With your permission I intend to stay here for quite a while."

She did as he said, feeling his eyes on her. In his voice and gaze she read something between condescension, contempt and curiosity. A girl was a bottle into which they emptied themselves. She did not want to go over what she had told herself a dozen times the previous day and a dozen or more times on each of the preceding days.

Her gaze was full of fear. He had not come for anything that could threaten or hurt her. And it was one of his principles, where sex was concerned, to share his pleasure as far as possible in equal measure.

"I don't want you to be sad," he said.

"I'm not sad," she said. She couldn't pretend that he hadn't put this very nicely. What would not be nice was what was to come.

Was she pleasing him by undressing quickly? She was losing the last shred of her privacy. She was losing her sense of shame, and that sense of shame was different now. She ought to be glad that she was with a German officer. But her brother and her father were watching her from somewhere above.

Skinny felt Captain Hentschel's presence without looking at him. She was undressed now, her head hung as she looked at her toes. Was she clean? She had scrubbed herself in icy water. She knew that the captain was watching her in the way that soldiers looked at a girl, in admiration, with a touch of contempt, with a desire in which there was some condemnation.

"I'd say you're making yourself older, my girl, though in a few weeks or years you'll be making yourself younger again." He smiled briefly. "Are you concealing your age?"

"No."

"I wonder if you're doing this for your benefit, or for mine."

Instead of waiting for an answer the captain began to undress. He placed his clothes tidily on the chair, as if he were already thinking of his departure. He put down the items one by one. She closed her eyes, hearing the familiar sounds, the clink of his belt and buckle on his trousers, the rustle of his shirt. He wore double winter underwear, a white and a grey set, both clean. Underpants with a tie-string. She lowered her head again. This moment always embarrassed her. She was not just ashamed for herself, she knew that this was pointless. For some reason, as the soldiers undressed, she thought of the sick at Auschwitz-Birkenau. Of the four castrated boys her own age, on whom Dr Krueger had operated with the assistance of two Jewish doctors who knew perfectly well that before long they would themselves be turned to ashes. She had been aware throughout of what was going on, just glad that it did not concern her. She had collected the boy's underwear in a basket. It was not ridiculous, it was pitiful. They would no longer need it.

At Auschwitz-Birkenau she could return to Block 18 at the Frauenkonzentrationslager, where she would find her mother and friends. Here she was alone, with no-one to appeal to, nor any wish to.

The water in the pot on the stove had been bubbling for a while.

"That's for me?" the captain asked.

"We're ordered to heat water."

"You're slim," he said. He thought of the resilience, freshness and flexibility of everything that was young, like springtime grass, an autumn breeze or the smell of pine. His glance passed over her crotch.

He was treating her like an Aryan man would an Aryan girl. It changed her voice, made her more forthcoming without wanting to be. The captain was undressed now. She avoided looking at his body. He was big, everywhere. Big feet, hands, stomach and chest. In a moment he would begin to explore her with his hands like a blind man, or like an animal tasting the flesh it was about to tear off the bone. She was aware of his size, of his giant's hands. His chest was overgrown with short fair hair. The skin around his genitals was reddish, almost purple.

"Do you like the dark?" the captain began to whisper.

"I don't mind it," she said softly.

"You can blame me for everything." His voice was already a little hoarse. "Just do with me what you do with everybody."

She straightened up so that she could look into his eyes.

She poured hot water into the basin, glad that she could do something other than what she was about to do. She added some cold water from the jug and tested the temperature with her fingers to make sure it was right.

"Do you want soap?"

"You think I should?"

"I don't know."

"How did you do it with my predecessor? How do you like to do it?"

She smiled to avoid an answer. Would he regard her smile as a promise? In matters she knew nothing about she was guided by instinct. Her mother had been right. She soaped him, washed him and dried him. She closed her eyes as if some soap had got into them. He let her wash him, not saying a word. He had not touched her yet; he let her touch him.

"You're very young," he said. "You've got good hands. Good fingers."

She knew that this wasn't true – she had calluses on her hands. But she couldn't tell him what they came from. The ropes of the boats on the Harmanze pond, repairing the roads in the Frauenkonzentrationslager in Auschwitz-Birkenau, gravelling the paths to the houses of the SS.

Madam Kulikowa had urged her girls not to underrate the importance of the first touch of their hands. If a girl were nervous her hands would be sweaty and cold. Talking too much was also off-putting; to know when to shut up was an art.

His next question took Skinny by surprise.

"Where did you go to school?"

"In Prague."

"When did you leave?"

"Three years ago," she said.

"Did you sit at the back of the class?"

He was teasing her! Did he expect her to tease him?

"You're tall," he said.

"I don't know about that."

He looked at the bed. "Won't you sit down?"

"If you wish."

She sat down, folding her arms over her chest and crossing her legs. She was unable to cover her crotch.

"Are you ashamed in front of me?"

"No," she replied.

"Not a little bit?"

"A little bit."

She blushed. He thought it rather funny that she should be ashamed. The smell of the coal enveloped the cubicle. It was burning slowly because it was damp.

"You're pale", the captain said.

"I haven't got any disease," she said. "I'm healthy."

"I hope so. Do they let you out to get some fresh air?"

"We sweep the courtyard and clear the snow by the gate."

"Your skin's almost translucent."

"We don't get much sun."

"That's for sure."

He stepped up to her. He seemed like a giant.

"Permit me," he said. He sat down next to her. Sitting, he did not seem quite so huge.

The captain touched her behind with the palm of his hand. She was afraid of crying out in pain. She had a festering sore there where she had been whipped by an SS man for not getting off the train quickly enough on the night they had arrived at No. 232 Ost.

"Who did this to you? Does it hurt?"

"Not so much now."

"Looks like a wound from a whip. Or a cane. You don't see what they flog you with?"

Could his mood change from one moment to the next? There was almost anger in his voice, a new shade, the irritation of a soldier who could not avoid seeing who was firing at him. He had not missed how she'd flinched. Had his voice become more severe? At that moment she could visualize him as a commanding officer or the father of an adolescent girl.

She was waiting for the captain to pull her to him and to roll on top of her. She almost wanted it now. She was not afraid of him, she was afraid of giving herself away. He had so many questions, and every one of them was uncomfortable because it meant too many answers.

The captain lay down beside her, although she was still sitting. Was he waiting for her to lie down beside him? She didn't know what to do. He stretched and she could hear his joints click. He seemed to her like a tree, like a block of wood. He lay there as if he had known her for a long time.

"In the officers' mess you'd look good at my side. You're pretty."

A little bony though, he thought.

She still had her arms crossed over her chest, rigidly. He let her sit there, legs crossed. Did he want her to uncover herself, to drop her hands and open her legs? Madam Kulikowa had said that she was all arms and legs. And it was true. The captain raised himself on his elbow.

"Permit me," he said again and what she had thought an unfriendly tone had now disappeared from his voice. He gave her his enormous hand.

"You shouldn't look at me like this," he said hoarsely. Alarmed, she forced herself to say: "I'm not."

She half turned so as not lie on her wound. The captain understood.

"Did they do this to you here?" he asked.

"I had a fall."

"Where?"

She hesitated with her reply and was afraid the pause between question and answer might be too long.

"On the ramp, by the siding, when we got here a week ago. It was still dark. There was a rush."

"They brought you here at night?"

"Yes. Loaded us up in the dark, too."

"If you ask me, it looks like a hunting crop. At the Kriegsschule in Potsdam we had riding lessons. At home I was taught how to ride and handle a horse by my father and his groom. We kept horses. I don't just drive a Horch or a tank."

He told her in a whisper that her childish voice reminded him of a distant holiday in the Alps, when he was twelve and was seduced by his first prostitute. Then he told her of a prank at his officers' school. As cadets they had blown pepper into the nostrils of Colonel-General von Lothar-Jünger's horse. The horse, inevitably, had thrown him as soon as the general mounted. Later, over cards and wine, the cadets had argued about whether it was right to torture a horse like that.

The pillows in all but Madam Kulikowa's cubicle were of tow-cloth sacking, filled with sand. The sand grated.

"That's not the prettiest sound," said the captain. "Know who you look like? Our first Hungarian maid. She was 14, getting on for 15. Heaven knows what's become of her."

"First they look at your feet, then at your eyes, and next at your breasts. It's a good idea to stretch, that way they look fuller," Madam had told her.

She was lying here with a German officer. Nothing to be proud of. A week ago it would never even have occurred to her to imagine this. Then she had been dead even though still alive. Since that day her flesh had proved to twelve soldiers each day that she was still alive. She thought of the engineer who had complained that she was lying there like a frightened cat. She did not wish to punish her body for what she could not change. She forced herself not to resist. She was nervous, and had forgotten the oil. He saw her glance towards the bottle. She tried to free her hand and reach for it.

"You think we need that?"

He was watching her. Over the past days she had learnt how a famished soldier encounters a body, his body meeting hers, and how that made her struggle with herself. She felt a distance growing inside her, a distance produced by closeness.

He was dissatisfied.

"You're acting like a virgin."

"I can't do it otherwise."

"You can't do it at all."

"I want to."

"Go on, want it then," he said hoarsely. "You should want what I want."

With his palms he parted her legs. He half opened his mouth. She could see his strong white teeth. He was breathing hard. He pressed down on her with his chest so that she felt the wood of the bed against her back and her hands. She knew he would manage even without the oil. She knew by now what the strength of a man meant, multiplied by anger.

Twelve times a day – by way of exception today only once with the captain – she let a stranger do with her body whatever he liked. She felt ashamed not only for herself, even though there were no witnesses. She must not show it. She must not think of whose turn it would be next. The second, the third, the twelfth man. She concentrated on the fire in the stove, on the firewood she had put on it. She had diarrhoea and a headache. Fatty had thrown up from a headache that morning.

"You smell rather nice," the captain said. "You're clean. I appreciate this. You make me think of a bed of heather in the forest."

He was listening to the artillery fire.

"I hope you're not afraid."

"No." She had learnt to differentiate between lies and lies. The best lie was the simplest – almost the truth.

"I'd like you to want what I want."

She did not have a high opinion of her body. She thought of an ocean, deeper than anyone could fathom. Of a night so dark that the day would never dawn. Of fog, with wolves emerging from it, close to the walls of the estate. She could hear the squeaking and scurrying of the rats as they disappeared into the dark corners of the corridor. The captain's features grew tense. It was beyond seriousness, almost a grimace. It took her breath away. She didn't know what would happen next. She was falling into a void, into darkness, into a chill that was different from the outside air. She felt a pain in her crotch, a swelling of her skin. Everything was the captain's body and then her body. Behind her she heard the voices of her father, mother, her brother. She did not want that. She shut her eyes, but she could not shut her ears. She thought of Big Leopolda Kulikowa's advice. The soldier is a snake; the girl is a gullet. She felt in herself water, emptiness. Then fire, friction, pain.

She understood something she had not understood about her first drop of menstrual blood. At 15 she realized that there were things she would not confess even to God.

The captain's breathing was getting louder and faster. She thought of steep slopes, of flat fallow fields, of the abandoned mines at Auschwitz-Birkenau. She thought of the bloody skin of animals.

"You are like a humming bird." the captain whispered.

"Would you like some oil?"

"No."

She shut her eyes. She felt ashamed. She was like the gate of the estate No. 232 Ost with its imperial eagle and swastika, a gate entered by whoever chose to, whenever they chose to.

With his lips close to her ear the captain murmured something about a sun-drenched shore on the Arctic Ocean. Of marble cliffs he had read about the night before. Of the language in which their distant ancestors communicated in Paradise. Of giddiness that rose and fell, of communication without words.

He regarded her as one of them. Exactly what she both wanted and did not want. She heard shouting, something beyond words. What did he get the Iron Cross for? For what had he been proposed for the Knight's Cross, and for what did he, by way of reward, obtain permission to visit No. 232 Ost? She thought of his pistol. Had she reconciled herself to being embraced by a German officer?

"Do I seem too big to you?" he whispered. "Too rough?"

He seemed to her like a hunk of raw meat. She knew that she was acting like a bad whore. In Germany it was better to be a bad whore than a good Jew.

Her stomach ached. She had long known that life was a trap. Most of them were caught in it. Had she ever been free? Yes, she had, when she was at school. But what were you to do once you were inside the trap and did not want to die? She did not want to think of why she did not wish to die. Everything was a trap – her breathing, the captain's breathing, the light, and the sounds from outside. The wolves, the crows and the rats. She was scarcely aware that she was naked. Her body, too, was a trap in which she herself was caught.

The captain had satisfied himself. It did not matter to him who it was. But it was she, the youngest girl in No. 232 Ost. Not that bad really, but not all that good either.

"You're not very good, but you're better than bad," he said.

It was something between a commendation, a reproach and a warning. She did not know what she could have done better. She had simply been there, letting him maul and grind her body. She was with him, he was with her. That was what was keeping her alive, just as her work in Dr Krueger's surgery had done at Auschwitz-Birkenau, or the work on the railway carriages, or catching fish, collecting eggs from gulls' nests, or pulling drowned bodies from the Harmanze pond. She wondered if it was worth the price paid for it, but she was better off than tens of thousands of others. She kept repeating this to herself. She was better off. She was paying for her life with her crotch, her thighs, her arms, legs, lips, fingers, tongue – and her soul.

That was what it was like, and she knew it could not be otherwise because that otherwise meant the gas chamber, the crematorium and ashes. Suddenly she hated Captain Hentschel, the German army captain and son of a prominent, blue-blooded family, for whom, as to so many other Germans, war was merely a job. A job, just as auditing the books of business people had been a job to her father – business people who had envied his mathematical talent, his analytical skill, his friendly nature and his piety when they met on Friday evenings in the synagogue.

The captain had come inside her in three convulsions that shook his whole frame and twisted his features into a grimace that suggested the final exertion of a dying man.

After a while he asked, "What was your first time like?"

"It was here," she breathed.

"You were a virgin?"

He took her silence as assent.

"Was it strange?"

"Yes," she said.

The captain asked no further questions. She was almost grateful to him.

"It's cosy in here," he said. "War is beautiful. After all."

His words surprised her. There were things she did not understand, but she was glad he was talking. All he wanted from her was to listen. He began to tell her about a woman named Lilo.

She was a nurse. One night, after her 18-hour shift, he had taken her to a gutted farmhouse. She smelt of disinfectant, of the blood of the wounded, of medicines. They lay on their backs, close to each other. He kissed her hair.

"Close to her, I sensed life as strongly as when I went into battle the first time. She whispered to me that together we would kill death."

He paused.

"You know, we Germans are in love with death."

He was talking to himself, to his dead lover. For her, death had been neither the sister nor the mother of beauty.

She remained silent. His words seemed ridiculous, nonsensical.

"It was late August and we watched the showers of meteorites. A rain of shooting stars in an August night. Lilo called them laurel tears. It was the 9th of August, Saint Laurentius' day. Fireflies."

"She knew more about war than she wanted to know. That was her second year out east. Kursk, the great tank battle, was in her bones."

He paused, then continued.

"I too know more about war than I would wish to. The beautiful side and the merely necessary one. What about you?"

"I'm new here," Skinny answered.

"Who initiated you?"

"We aren't supposed to talk of anyone we've been with."

"I can see we're not suited to polite conversation," he said. "I only talk to you, but you don't talk to me."

"I answer you."

"When I was a little boy our parents took us to the Savoy Alps in France for a winter holiday. The mist in the valleys had a similar colour to this fog here. It was beautiful, unattainable and sad. At lunchtime, as we sat in the dining room, the sun lit up the snow-covered trees and shrubs so fiercely that for just a few moments it was as though they were made of glass. They had an almost surreal brilliance. Father pointed it out to us. He loved the snow, the mountains, winter. In the evening, at the Golden Court Hotel, father showed us Mont Blanc in the moonlight. He had tears in his eyes."

Did it amuse him to confide in a little tart who did not have much to say for herself? She realized that he was treating her as if he wanted to make her a friend, or create something memorable between them.

"I'm feeling lonely. I feel lonely wherever I am." Then he said: "I kill in order not to be killed and I experience life most intensely with people like you."

Suddenly Skinny felt like telling him that she was 15 and Jewish. But only for a hundredth of a second. Instead, she walked over to stoke up the fire. She thought of her race and his. Of her legislated uncleanliness alongside his immaculate race. The things the captain had told her were intended for the ears of a pure-blood. If he knew that she was Jewish he would treat her like a diseased person whose skin was covered with impurities. He would shrink from touching her, he would let her be exterminated.

"We lost 20,000 men," the captain said. He did not say when.

At Auschwitz-Birkenau as many as that died in a single day and night, 20,000 people were the cargo of a mere four or five trains, each with 50 wagons, arriving from Prague, Warsaw, Copenhagen or Paris, from Bordeaux, Oslo, Berlin or Bremerhaven.

Soon none of this would interest anyone, anywhere. The victors would remain, the vanquished would disperse like vapour, blown by the wind to the Arctic Ocean. She knew everything about what she was not supposed to speak of. She no longer wondered how much of it was illusion. She took in what he was saying; she no longer asked herself why.

Chapter Four

On one occasion 50 girls from Block 18 had been driven to the No. 2 crematorium to clean up whatever the SS ordered them to. Skinny had found herself in a large underground room with three light bulbs in wire frames on the wooden beams across the ceiling. On the walls, where the concrete was cracked, there were brownish stains, just as there were on the floor and ceiling. No-one said that it was blood. It could have been blood and probably was. At first they felt a vague sense of relief at the thought that they were in a shower room. The door with a small window, of glass so thick that it seemed like translucent concrete, stood open against the wall so it wasn't possible to see if there was a handle on the inside or not. The outside handle was of massive steel with a lock and a bolt. They understood that they were in a gas chamber. They were scrubbing the floor of a gas chamber. Skinny saw before her the rough concrete on which the bare feet of children, women and old people had stood; all of them together. Now the chamber was empty and there was no smell of gas, only an odour of decay, of a subterranean place. Under the ceiling, along the beams, ran the electricity supply in steel conduits, half sunk into the concrete so they couldn't be torn out. The walls looked as if someone had emptied countless vats of water from above, water that had run down the sides and left stains, perhaps from sweat, or fingerprints, or torn skin. Or perhaps someone had hosed the walls down with a water jet. None of the women or girls said a word. They were overcome by a horror they dared not show.

An SS man watched them clean up, then said, enough, that would do. They were marched upstairs with their buckets, rags and mops. Possibly they were the only humans of their race who had been in a gas chamber and emerged alive.

For Skinny the concrete floor was fixed in her mind's eye; she saw the little hollows she had noticed in the floor. What had caused them? They could have been made by hobnailed boots, but she knew that by then people were barefoot. What had caused those countless little grooves in the floor, like footprints? The image of the gas chamber was imprinted in her mind and would remain with her, she knew, for as long as she lived.

It was said that in Bordeaux a rail traffic controller wondered why the trains that left packed with thousands of Jews (as he had worked out for himself) all returned empty. In Vichy they had the exact numbers and the papers. They knew that 75,000, including thousands of children, had been rounded up with the help of informers who were lining their own pockets. All the French Jews were picked up by the French police. The Germans only looked on. An NCO who had come from France had told the traffic controller that the Red Cross workers there had recorded 50,000 children without parents. The adults had disappeared as early as the time of the evacuation of Paris, or they had been killed.

"We have sex to convince ourselves that we are still alive," Captain Hentschel said. "Isn't it the same for you?"

"I don't know," Skinny answered quickly.

"I like it to be nice. I don't like to feel like an animal. Or if it has to be like an animal, then an agreeable animal. And this must apply to both sides. Even from the waist down you don't have to be an animal.

"Ludicrous, isn't it," he said, "that my ancestors took their wives, daughters and children with them into battle. When things got tough, the wives bared their breasts to remind their warriors of what the enemy would squeeze in their hands if they let them win. We didn't lose even against the Romans. If you want evidence, look at the fair-haired and blue-eyed Italians. I often look back to the days when we occupied lands beyond the Elbe."

He mentioned Prague. It gave her a small jolt. In the cubicle, with

Captain Hentschel, Prague seemed to her more remote by a dimension that could not be measured in miles any more than her experience could be measured in light years. Prague to her was a vanishing image, a dying echo, a star fading in the night sky. She did not want to think about the city that had been her home, a city that continued to live regardless of what had happened to so many. Prague was vanishing in darkness and mist, beyond a snow-covered wasteland by the River San, distant and unreal like the destinies of the nameless.

Then he spoke of the front near Moscow. The Germans had hoped to seize the Russian capital by a lightning campaign as early as the autumn of 1941. Their machine guns had mown down the enemy troops, wave by wave. But there were always more, like locusts. The Russians had to step over the mounds of their own dead. Suddenly Captain Hentschel's troops had stopped firing. They understood the signal the enemy was sending them and they were seized with horror. The Russians had more men than the German army had ammunition.

He had given orders to open fire again. His men did not obey. He had drawn his pistol, ready to pull the trigger. The massacre continued. They could go on killing the enemy's troops indefinitely, but they could not defeat them. And now they were retreating.

"It's difficult to fight an adversary who doesn't care if he wins or loses."

Captain Hentschel again embraced her childish body, intoxicating himself with her, as he did with his own words. He squeezed her girlish breasts with his cobra-like hands. He tasted the trembling in her that stemmed more from her fear of an attack of diarrhoea than from his excitement. With the tips of his fingers he stroked the tattoo on her belly, a belly that was already a woman's. He didn't mind the blue letters that spelt *Feldhure*.

In the waiting room Madam Kulikowa put on another record of Strauss waltzes.

"When I was a little boy," the captain said, "my mother sang sombre German songs to me. They were songs about vampires who

45

drank virgins' blood, about the ash from which we Germans have sprung and which we revere, about the black steed which draws the night from west to east, and about the eagle which lets loose the wind at the northern end of the sky. There were songs about the goddess Freya, and about the spring under the tree of the world. She believed these tales like the Bible; they were in her blood. She regarded me sternly, lovingly and mournfully."

He paused.

"My mother believed that no woman got the husband she deserved. Her own mother died young. She hadn't been married long. When a woman couldn't find a husband the matter wasn't discussed. And they all acted as if children were brought by the stork."

She did not know yet that Wehrmacht Captain Hentschel's visit would serve to erase any future negative reports from Madam Kulikowa's book – complaints by rank-and-file servicemen, not by officers.

She tried not to look at his greatcoat on the door. The captain had thrown his khaki pullover with its suede-patched elbows over the back of the chair.

"You're looking at my pistol?"

She flushed. "No. At your pullover."

"Officers up to captain have a Luger; from captain up, a Parabellum. Would you like to hear about my first year in service?"

She tried to turn on her side, so she wouldn't press the sore on her buttock.

"When one of my comrades is killed I go to let his wife know. One day, a fellow student from the Kriegsschule in Potsdam – he'd been mortally wounded – asked me to tell his wife how he fell. I rang the bell, she opened the door, and immediately she knew what had happened. She threw herself round my neck. Her child was with his grandmother in the Lusatian region on the Spree, and within a few minutes we were in bed together. It was an animalistic moment, the magnetism of the body – older than you or me."

He was visiting some other corner of the world, even though he lay next to her. He was fitting the curves and hollows of her body into his memory – that childish body she had made older.

She could not guess what the confidences of a Wehrmacht officer could mean for her.

He was watching the skin on her temples. Her tired eyelids. The blue and purple veins on her breasts. The white frostbite patches on her cheeks. Her short, gingery hair. He could see her pulse on her temples. He watched the arteries on her throat, wrists and the inside of her thighs.

"We're not allowed to kiss," she objected weakly.

"You're not much good at it. I'd like this a thousand times every day. Ten thousand times."

What could she or should she talk to him about? About her twelve soldiers? Out of the question. Was she to tell him that, during the act, her blood hammered at her temples? That she had continuous pangs of conscience and moments of panic about being found out. That at each act of intercourse her father, mother and brother were present? They watched so that she should not forget them – and to judge her.

"Some things we ought to be grateful for," said the captain.

He did not expect a reply.

"How often do you cut your toenails?"

"Every third day," she lied.

"You scratch."

"I'm sorry."

"You're good when you're bad," he said. "You're good even when you draw the worst out of me."

Then he asked her if she liked anything of what they were doing. The captain's whisper was again becoming more intimate. He was stronger than strong, she thought. He did not himself deny what he had come for.

"My adjutant says, 'I kill, therefore I am.' For me, my existence is confirmed when I am with someone like you. I do it, therefore I am."

He was inhaling her smell. It reminded him of a little warm calf he had seen in a shack in Russia, tied to a post which held up the roof.

He was aroused by the girl's youth, rather than by her skill. She must know that she was an incompetent whore. He savoured the slope of her shoulders, the arches of her arms when, at his request, she lay on her stomach, her breasts pressed against the sheet. Her concave stomach formed a curve which reminded him of his mother's Venetian glass. He perceived her body as an ear of young grain, still growing, springy, soft and firm at the same time. When she half turned the way he wanted, her back was like the smooth shiny parquet floor in their drawing room at home.

She did what he wanted, it was more comfortable and less painful for her than lying on her back, rubbing her wound.

He kissed her wherever it occurred to him to kiss. It was shameless and, to her, unaccustomed; was it normal for him? She was terrified that she might not be clean enough. She curled up into a ball like a hedgehog, wishing she could retreat into a shell. He handled her like a new-born child. He could not get enough of her.

"Don't we, in a whore, love what we love in ourselves?"

She felt what was bringing her closer to him and what made her hate him. Was it possible to admire him for one thing and to pity him for another? She was confused. She was afraid of something immediate that she could not overcome. He was the first person that had made her feel sorry for German soldiers killed in battle and for their wives, their children, one of them somewhere on the Spree, where barges and freighters were carrying coal. The captain was enormous, handsome, a stranger, and she wished he would remain just that. She wanted to keep a cool head. She did not move at all. The captain provided all the movement. He rolled away from her. He was relaxing, satisfied. He let her hand him the towel.

We're all fools, he thought. He was lying there, still embracing her.

"Green eyes, ginger hair," he said. "I know what I'd dress you in and from what I'd undress you again."

"Do you know why a soldier most wants a woman before battle? Or immediately after battle? It's a reward, or a token of a reward, the one thing that frees him from his bonds. You know, to his mother, his father, or to his children, his wife and family, his country and all his worries."

From the army kitchen came the signal calling the guards to a midday meal – a spanner being struck against an iron bar like a gong. She was hungry; she had visions of food – hot soup with fried pieces of bread and bacon, boiled beef with gherkin sauce and potatoes.

"How did you get here?"

"Via a camp." She thought it safer to tell him the truth. She held her forearm with the tattooed number out to him. "Where you got your winter equipment yesterday."

"Is that so? Why did they send you there?"

"There were a lot of arrests in Prague after the assassination of Heydrich."

"That was in '42."

She froze, but kept her presence of mind as in all moments of danger. She knew this side of her temperament – she would tremble with fear up until the very moment of decision. At that instant some unknown force liberated her from it, from all unnecessary thoughts, hesitation or doubt. A fraction of a second when she made her decision. So far things had gone well. Now she had to wait for his reaction. She wondered if he was trying to prove her a liar. Had she already made a mistake that would cost her dear? She felt his questioning eyes on her. He was wondering.

"What happened to your parents?"

"I think they were killed. They took us to the camp and then they sent me here, along with my papers. They're with Oberführer Schimmelpfennig."

"What did you do at the camp?"

"They did x-ray experiments on me. They sterilized me."

His expression told her that he understood. She came from that Czech region where, as Obergruppenführer Reinhard Heydrich had declared, the Czechs had no business.

"Did your parents have anything to do with it?"

"No."

49

"You'll never have children," he said slowly. "Maybe that's a good thing. For them and for you."

He was running his fingers through her hair. She hated those wandering fingers, but she lacked the courage to flinch.

"If war is a game, then we've lost already," he said. "We started something we can't finish – others will finish it for us. It will not be what we'd planned. If we had won, our victory would wipe out the mistakes and obliterate the crimes we have committed. As it is, we'll be remembered only for our mistakes, our excesses. Only the complete picture determines the value of everything. We have sentenced ourselves to prolonged insignificance. Perhaps for ten, a hundred, a thousand years. Then we shall be known again for what we are good at. Manufacturing motor cars, cameras – anything. My father knew August Horch, I even think he named me after him. Horch began as a foreman at Benz & Cie. They entrusted him with the production of cars. You probably aren't interested in a universal joint or in chrome steel gears. My Horch is a 1939 model. They no longer make it. If we're blown up – my car and I – we'll both end up in a museum."

He laughed. He pushed the blanket off, feeling warm, and fell silent.

She listened to the wolves on the plain, to the footsteps in the corridor, to the bell of Big Leopolda Kulikowa.

"You don't have to say anything you don't want to. I don't wish to interrogate you, that's not my business. I'm only asking out of curiosity. Have you got any brothers or sisters?"

"I had a brother. They separated us when we got to the camp. I never saw him again."

"What age? You've no idea where he is?"

"No. He was 13."

"Perhaps they put him with a family that had lost a child."

"It's possible," she said.

"Would you like that?"

"I'd like to believe he was alive."

"They could have put you with a family too." He wondered how she would get on in a German family. Would his family accept someone whose parents had been killed for the assassination of the Reich Protector? Was she really as old as she said?

"Did they teach you anything after school?"

"Hairdressing," she said quickly.

She had a sudden vision of Slavomír Sláma from their block of flats in Prague, and just as quickly it vanished. In 1941 Mr Sláma had begun to learn German so that he could cut the hair of Wehrmacht soldiers. He ordered German colour magazines for his salon, including an issue of *Der Adler* with pictures of airmen, planes, balloons and Zeppelins. The airmen on the cover were laughing. Her brother Ramon had stood outside the window, looking at the pictures. They were all still alive. Lying here naked in bed with a German captain, she could not reproach Mr Sláma. For the past eight days she had concealed her Jewishness. A few clever questions would be enough to make her give herself away.

The captain began to speak again.

"Funny, at the beginning of the campaign the enemy hardly interested me. I was only interested in how much Germany was growing. I experienced the friendships that war offered, it stripped me of all worldly ties and money questions. How willing women were in wartime. How everything tested you: were you up to it or not, what effort could you make? What you would eventually return to. And what would never be the same again."

"On my last home leave in Berchtesgaden I went to the home of a fellow officer. I couldn't find his father or mother, his brothers or sisters, to tell them that their boy, recently awarded the Iron Cross, was well, in good shape and happy. I couldn't even find the house. There was only a big bomb crater there and they were still clearing up. There are more of those craters in Germany than mouse holes."

It occurred to her that this was where they were now retreating to and where they would end up one day – a day she would like to live to see.

"Would you mind if I had a short sleep?" the captain asked.

He was full of that tranquillity which comes only after sex. That was how sleep, death's sweeter sister, came to a man when he had tired himself with what he'd wanted to do. Perhaps one day the captain would wish to die the way he now wished to sleep. He thought of the dignity and indignity of death, of not having to ask when his hour would come. It was with him all the time.

"You look after the stove meanwhile, or else have a nap yourself. Or if you don't want to, wake me after an hour or so. You can look at my watch. Just shake me by the shoulder."

The captain was dozing already, only vaguely aware of her unease. She had been uneasy ever since he had arrived and he had attributed it to her inexperience and her youth, and to his rank. He noticed her relief when he told her he would sleep. It neither irritated him nor gave him particular pleasure.

The fire in the stove and in the flue lit up her face and shoulders, her breasts and hands. He liked her. Captain Hentschel thought sleepily that she was young and that he would be able to train her given the chance.

He fell asleep thinking of Auschwitz-Birkenau, where she had been sterilized. He had spent the night there out of necessity. It was not a place he was curious about. He accepted that it was one of those historical inevitabilities, the primeval face of war – of this war, which was a total war. For a moment he wondered how his wife was managing without him, and what his children were doing. Thanks to the family's considerable assets he did not have to worry too much.

The captain's face brought back a memory. A woman, the mother of four Wehrmacht soldiers, had been brought to Terezín from the Reich the previous year. Her four sons, one after the other, had been killed in battle. When the last one fell she had lost the protection of the law. The young men had mixed blood on their mother's side. They had all worn the same uniform as Captain Hentschel. They also wore the same uniform as the two Wehrmacht officers who were brought to Terezín when it was discovered that they had Jewish grandmothers, and who were sent east inside a week. Like the mother of the dead soldiers, they had dissolved in the Jewish ocean, in the ocean of ashes from which Skinny had escaped to No. 232 Ost, so she could gaze on the purplish, sleeping features of Captain Daniel August Hentschel. She looked at his huge hands, his neck, his greatcoat on the door, at the flashes of his rank.

She waited fully an hour, and then he began to cough a little. Her father had coughed just like that when he woke from his afternoon siesta. She could see him in her mind's eye, returning from the Aschermann café on Dlouhá Street with the news that the Germans were beginning to transport Jews to Terezín.

At that time mobile x-ray units were making the rounds of the schools. On the pretext of the fight against tuberculosis, the Germans were collecting data on the racial composition of the population of the Protectorate of Bohemia and Moravia – on the percentage of the population suitable for Germanization and subsequent assimilation. The family had been almost glad to escape by being sent to Terezín. SS and SA men were photographing girls aged from thirteen upwards in the nude. Later the photographs were sold in nightclubs.

"Dropped off for a while. What's the time? How long did I sleep? Come to me. Why are you so far away?"

The captain was wide awake. It was after midday. She returned to the bed. His body and the bedclothes smelled of sleep. He sweated a little. If she understood his expression, she knew what it meant.

"Are you here?" he asked after a while.

"Yes," she answered.

"I wouldn't swear to it."

She lay down by his side, closing her eyes. He could do with her whatever he wanted to. She didn't want to have a part of it other than with her body. She heard him say that she was looking at him as if she were looking into water. But she was anxious not to make him angry.

"Do you always keep your legs together so tightly? Do you never relax? Or have you got cramp?"

He didn't like the way she pressed her lips together either. Her youth he accepted; but stubbornness, or what he thought might be stubbornness, he would not. He couldn't and didn't want to admit that she might feel an aversion to him and he could see no reason why she should be afraid of him.

He wanted her to sit on him. It was pleasant to look into her face.

A few cinders dropped, spitting, through the grate.

"It's warm here," he said.

They heard the door of the next cubicle open and close. The captain got up as he was and walked over to the window. The blizzard had moved off beyond the river. She looked at his huge body.

"Soon we shall be defending ourselves on the Oder," he said. "An hour or two from Berlin. Many hounds – death of the hare. We're a tough nut; they haven't got an easy run with us. But we don't have an easy run with ourselves. We're a big country, even if we're small. A mere ninety million Germans. But we're our own worst enemies. I could explain to you why we're withdrawing, if you're interested. As Frederick the Great said: He who would defend everything will defend nothing."

He knew that army whores didn't concern themselves with the technicalities of warfare. They did not care about strategy or tactics, positional fighting, or defence in trenches protected by minefields, let alone about Operation Barbarossa or the Blue Plan which replaced it because the original Blitzkrieg did not allow for retreat. It was ancient history by now that at the beginning of the campaign the men didn't get winter clothing or boots because it was believed that they'd be home before the winter. Was it true then that pride came before a fall? If you want to know what winter means, he thought, you should spend a day in the east. That's what the pious old women on his mother's side used to say. *Wer andern eine Grube gräbt, fällt selbst hinein.* He who digs a hole for others will fall into it himself. He smiled.

"War or no war, millions of women throughout the world get pregnant each day. More than those killed on all fronts. Added to this there are five times as many men crippled as killed. Think how many broken families that means. Good manners command the cripples to make room for their rivals and withdraw with their tail between their legs. I see them terrified of dusk, of the approach of night, of the expectations of their wives."

He was watching the wolves in the half light.

"The worst thing is the frosts."

For her the worst thing in Poland had not been the frosts.

He turned away from the window to face her.

"You'll have pretty hair when it grows again. I like redheads. Do you get it from your mother or your father?"

She took a second to think of a reply. "From my father's mother." Captain Hentschel began to dress. "Light the candle, will you? I can't see my boots."

He was thinking that the enemy had approached within artillery range. Today it was heavy guns; tomorrow it would be machine guns. Gone were the days when they'd advanced with the wind behind them. Now they were retreating. They were being chased back to where they had come from.

"The fog is at home here."

She noticed that he had not put his pullover on. It was lying on the chair.

"Keep it, I have another."

"Thank you. Shall I get dressed?"

"Put it straight on next to your body. That's what Lilo used to do."

From the pocket of his greatcoat, which he had put on but not done up, he produced a flask. He unscrewed the cap. His holster was still on the hook.

"Yes, you can get dressed," he answered, "but you don't have to if you don't want to. You're a feast for the eyes when you've nothing on. You haven't got much of anything."

"No," she said, almost against her will.

Again she thought of her father. If he were to see her like this, with a Wehrmacht captain, and this enormous pullover over her naked body . . . It went down to her thighs. Would this be a greater dishonour to her father than if he saw her dead? It was her body she had killed, not the religion of her ancestors. To her father, as a whore she would be as good as dead. Should she be glad that her family no longer existed? She felt the coarse bulky wool on her; she was warm and realized how welcome the pullover was. Did she know where the captain had got it? She knew where he had got his greatcoat. She might make the excuse to her father that she had not been with the captain; he had been with her. Would her father believe her if she lied and said she would rather be dead? It would only be half a lie. Had she committed a sin by wanting to live?

"Will you have a drink with me?" the captain asked.

He poured himself a thimbleful and drank it in one go. He poured out another. She expected him to drink that too, but he handed it to her. He was treating her as no-one in the brothel had treated her before.

She stood by the bed in his pullover, no longer wondering whether it came from the store at Auschwitz-Birkenau. She knocked the drink back in one gulp, like the captain, and started coughing. The captain laughed, it was a chesty laugh, deep and grating like his voice.

He poured himself a second shot and drank it in one gulp.

"Yesterday I killed a Russian who'd killed a comrade before my eyes. I grabbed a rifle and struck his head, perhaps 15 times. You can't control yourself when your blood is up. What can be worse than seeing a comrade killed at your side?"

Did he assume she was on his side? The SS men in the camps had expected total submission. They believed that the conquered should feel honoured, should appreciate and admire their conquerors. It was the only glory, reflected glory that could fall on them before they perished.

Beneath his greatcoat she could see an Iron Cross. Who knew what he'd got it for? He had been to Auschwitz-Birkenau for a share in the loot held in those huge stores of everything that her father, mother, grandmothers, aunts and uncles and untold others had regarded as indispensable to life, and of which they had been stripped. That, in her eyes, made something cling to him, as it would cling to Germany to the end of all time.

As he poured his third shot he said: "Even a German sometimes forgets that he is a German."

She did not know what that meant.

"Do you have a shop here for the troops? They do at some brothels."

"Not here."

"I'm leaving you a few marks. 30 enough?"

She was overcome with shame. The same kind of shame as when she stood before him naked.

"You've already given me your pullover."

"So?"

"We're not allowed to ask for money."

"As far as I know you're not under orders to refuse it."

He put three ten-mark notes on the chair. It was obvious that he didn't want to offend her. He didn't say what had been on the tip of his tongue: Anyone going with a whore is a bit of a prostitute himself.

"Next time I'll bring you a bag of millet. Your stomach must be rumbling. I've no intention of cooking food for myself."

She was thrown by the words "next time". He smiled. He touched the tip of her nose. If it was possible, he said, he would come again.

She dressed quickly.

He put on his belt, closed the buckle and adjusted the holster. Her eyes were tired and worried, as they had been when he arrived. If he stood up straight the ceiling was too low for him. He touched one of the beams. He might come at Christmas.

"Would you like to see the New Year in with me? I'll let off a red signal flare outside the estate. To let you know I've arrived."

He looked at her more carefully.

"What is that in your eyes? Hatred?" He bent down to her, his legs wide apart, his face very close.

"We're not allowed to kiss," she said once more.

Suddenly he didn't look so huge or so polite as he might have wished. He said he didn't care what he was or wasn't allowed to do. For a few seconds, before he pulled himself together, he looked at her more as he would a lover than a prostitute. She didn't recognize this. She had had over 70 experiences as an army prostitute but not a single one as a lover. She dared not pull away from his hand behind her neck, kept there so he could kiss her.

"I must stoke up the fire or it will go out," she said.

She did not find it agreeable to be kissed by him. Every touch reminded her of who he was.

He was still putting off his leaving. She was getting impatient. He produced a cigarette case from his pocket and with his lighter lit a slim Juno.

"Alight and drawing," he said. "At least something's functioning. Do you smoke?"

"No."

"Never tried it?"

"As a child."

"Would you like one?"

"No, thank you. Really."

He looked at the hot flue as if he was seeing it for the first time in his life. He was reminded of something, and smiled.

"You won't believe this. In our camp we have a stove with a flue just like this one, and in the flue there's a mouse. When we stoke the fire, the mouse hides. It's got some hiding place in the wall, no-one knows where. As soon as the flue cools, the mouse begins to scratch. Bound to be a Jewish mouse. It's not enough to have a will to live, or to dodge being burnt. This mouse must also be clever and lucky, or else it wouldn't survive. Should humans learn from mice?"

He saw her blush but went on.

"I like it when you blush. As you can see, I find it hard to say good-bye to you. I'd love to take you out for a beer to the railway pub. I'll see if they'll let you out with me. They have Czech beer there. Tell me, are you corresponding with anyone?"

"No."

"Would you like me to take a message to anyone? Give someone news of you?"

"Thank you, but no," she said.

She dropped her eyes. She felt herself trembling. Why had he said "a Jewish mouse"?

He put his finger on her lips. He saw her alarm, her sudden start and her step back, but he didn't show it. He didn't want to frighten her even more. He was asking himself why it was so important to him to make a prostitute whom he had already had like him. Did she think that every Wehrmacht officer reported to the Gestapo?

"Would it break one of your private rules if you were to kiss me goodbye?"

She did so.

Then he said: "Anyway, it's all *scheissegal*. Farewell."

He picked up his yellow, elbow-length fur gloves. These probably hadn't come from the Auschwitz-Birkenau store. He was suddenly irritated. He pulled on the gloves. So he was not going to shake hands with her? Had he gone too far? Had it just occurred to him how many dozen soldiers this thin, mournful little whore would lie with tomorrow, and then again, and after her Sunday break, on Monday, Tuesday and so on? Was he already thinking of his armour plated Horch? Of the provisions in its boot? Today he was here, tomorrow who could tell? That was the fate of an officer in wartime. To live from one hour to the next, from one day to the next. Exactly the way a whore lived.

She shrank. Her shoulders and head drooped. The hollows in his cheeks reminded her of how he had come to her cubicle, frozen. He was, she could see, already somewhere else in his mind. Before he closed the door she experienced a moment of panic at the thought that he might still trap her, surprise her or accuse her of something.

But he just said: "You've got lovely green eyes."

He must have told Madam Kulikowa that because it remained with her. At No. 232 Ost they called her Lovely Green Eyes.

*

Fresh snow fell during the night. Black flakes were floating down to the ground; in the morning they would be white. Who could tell how Captain Daniel August Hentschel would get back to his unit in his bullet proof, four-seater Horch with chains on all its tyres? The snow glistened in the darkness. The water in the tubs no longer melted. The wood began to spit in the stoves.

Chapter Five

"You're crying?" Skinny asked.

"Not because of that," Beautiful said.

This was the third day that Beautiful had diarrhoea. It was the first time she hadn't talked about her mother.

"I'm thinking the same as you," Skinny said.

"I'm thinking of my mother," said Beautiful.

Twelve: Erich von Eicken, Albrecht Domin, Karl Osten, Varin Arp, Horst Torberg, Theodor Eisenbach, Herwart Kopf-Eschenbach, Hans Seidel, Endos Bredel, Berthold Wupperthal, Berndt Uhlstein, Max Edell.

They could tell the voices of the guards apart. The deep and even deeper ones, and the high and higher ones, like a children's choir. Was it a sin that she thought of her young brother?

There had been a snowfall. Ginger and Maria-from-Poznan had started yard duty at 5 a.m. to clear the drifts around the latrine.

Skinny and Estelle climbed into one tub at the end of the corridor. Skinny sometimes had the impression that Estelle was avoiding her and at other times that she was seeking her out. She leant against the side of the tub, feeling the rotten wood against her back. Her body was aching, she felt as if she had been run over. Absentmindedly she splashed her face, then licked her lips.

"Don't drink it," Estelle said.

It was almost dark.

"I've had enough of it," Estelle continued. "Haven't you? Did you have that officer yesterday?"

Surely Estelle knew who she'd been with? Why did she ask? She had learned to lie. Her voice was matter-of-fact, but she was keeping something hidden.

The soap was coarse, rectangular double bars for laundry work, with grains of sand. The soap repeatedly slipped through her fingers and she had to retrieve it from the bottom of the tub. The Oberführer had told them that it was the same as was used by the troops. She got a splinter in her hand and immediately pulled it out. They were large splinters, and the larger they were the easier they were to get rid of.

"Aren't you cold yet?" Estelle asked.

"Not really," Skinny lied.

Was Estelle blaming her for having had only one man yesterday? Did the others have to make up the numbers? She did not make these decisions herself; Madam Kulikowa decided who was sent to her.

"I've learned to count the time, not the number of bodies," Estelle said. "How many hours I still have left."

That didn't sound like a reproach.

"Yes," said Skinny.

"It's a shift, like the laundry women, coal miners, or the girls in the weaving shop. Like the girls in the bakery kneading dough."

"Perhaps."

"If somebody asked me what I've learned here, I'd say: To lie and to die."

"We aren't dead yet."

"Twelve times a day," Estelle repeated. "Today fifteen times. I don't know where my family are or what has happened to them. My father, mother and sister. I drown it all in a lie."

The water splashed. Estelle was not lying now. Skinny began to suspect what was behind Estelle's confidences.

"I'd like to be able to handle it like going to work."

Skinny looked at her. In Estelle's voice rang an echo of what she heard within herself. Estelle had never spoken in this way about her family. Was it better to know that they were dead or to be tortured by the uncertainty that she heard in Estelle's voice? No-one knew who they killed, who starved to death or who was lost somewhere. She had been putting off her questions and her doubts from the first day she got to Auschwitz-Birkenau with her family. Now this seemed far away and long ago, but it was neither.

The tubs stood about three yards from each other. It didn't matter where each had come from, from what country or what region. Things vanished under a sea of ashes, of mud, of snow and ice, like abandoned islands in some nocturnal icy ocean. She washed herself thoroughly, everywhere, even the soles of her feet. Who knew what she had stepped on when she came to the tub barefoot?

In the sixth tub someone was singing. Ginger?

Estelle washed herself with a large natural sponge which the truck from the Wehrkreis had brought. The men used them for washing the Oberführer's car. Skinny's ears were full of water. Estelle offered her the sponge.

"Thanks."

"This soap is like sandpaper."

In the yard outside, the troops, ready for departure, were singing a song about Hitler. She could hear the shout *Heil* three times, and again three times.

"They are pigs," Estelle whispered.

Skinny was anxious not to catch something from the water when she had so far avoided infection from contact – or so she hoped.

"They think that we are the pigs. Me and you," she answered.

"If someone accused me of stealing your nose and we both knew that it wasn't true because you have a nose on your face, I'd still feel guilty."

Estelle had never said anything like this to her before. She felt again that an inexplicable closeness to her, which she felt even when her friend was withdrawn. Skinny knew what it meant to feel guilty for what she had not done but would perhaps be capable of doing, though – fortunately or unfortunately – the opportunity would not arise. The idea seemed to bind them together, quite apart from what they had in common. They were also bound by what Estelle had said about her family, who were missing somewhere.

"It's what the cold and the snow are doing to us," said Skinny.

"I don't know what the snow is doing to you. I heard they're going to send us Italians. Men from Sicily have never seen snow. They've already had Slovaks, Estonians and Hungarians here. The girls before us had Frenchmen and Flemish." Estelle paused.

"Right to the last moment I didn't know they were sending me here. There was talk of the 'Hotel for Foreigners', of some knocking shop for workers on 'total employment'. Sometimes they have Waffen-SS brothels directly in the camps. I'm almost glad I don't have to make my own decisions about myself. They told me I'd be an entertainer. I didn't know what that meant. I thought it wiser not to ask. It was enough to be alive, the Oberführer said. His assistant was a whore they'd discharged from Spandau prison. How are you feeling?"

"How do you think?" Skinny asked. "Fine."

"Like me," said Estelle. "Before or after?"

"I close my eyes," said Skinny.

"That helps?"

"I don't want to see anyone."

"Is that possible?"

"Perhaps."

"I didn't know what eyes the devil had. Or his brothers. It never occurred to me that the devil had a military rank, from Obersoldat to Oberführer. Or that he wore a smelly uniform and didn't wash his feet. Perhaps I should learn to shut my eyes like you."

It was said of Estelle that she was waiting for two gunners who shared her. The fact that the story came from Maria-from-Poznan was enough to make people doubt its truth. Maria was known as "The Toad" because she had cold lips and, as one soldier put it, everything that should be the very opposite was as cold as a dog's snout. As for passion, she could at best talk about it. She was both cunning and stupid, as Long-Legs described her. She made up for her lack of beauty with perfidy. Beware of ugly people, Long-Legs insisted.

The worst thing, though, was to fall for one of the soldiers. Those who drafted the regulations knew very well why an enduring relationship, for the same reasons as kissing or other amorous engagement, was forbidden. Only intercourse was permitted.

Was it not dangerous enough for Estelle to have such raven hair and even the hint of a moustache under the nose? Were her father and mother ravens? Who knows who her father and mother are, Maria-from-Poznan said to Ginger in the latrine. They were with Smartie and Long-Legs, so she quickly shut up. It could get to the Oberführer's ears.

Estelle interrupted Skinny's thoughts.

"That Obersoldat who told me I had eyes like black coffee has had his number come up."

She didn't say "And a good thing, too", but her voice implied it. There was something in Estelle that Skinny couldn't understand. Everything was boiling down to a struggle with time.

The water in the tub was dirty now. Blobs of Vaseline were floating on its surface. Uncleanness washed off from their skin, out of their pores, from under their nails. Anything that did not readily dissolve needed vigorous scrubbing.

"I feel swollen," Estelle said.

"I don't see why."

"As though I was made of water instead of flesh and blood."

"You're made of flesh and blood, all right."

"Mucous membranes and glands," Estelle corrected her.

"You seem normal to me."

"Like a lake when it overflows. Maybe they are normal discharges."

She told Skinny that for three nights running she had dreamt that they'd cut her in two with an axe, from her skull through her body to her crotch, and that both parts were alive and in the course of the night came together again and that she returned to her cubicle.

"I can pretend anything now."

"I can't manage that," said Skinny.

"I'm swollen like water," Estelle repeated.

They both climbed out. They dried themselves vigorously, to set the blood flowing through their veins and to get warm again. They dressed in haste.

"Do you ever feel as if your blood is freezing inside you?" Estelle asked.

On Sunday orders came for them to dig a well. Water from the cistern would be for the guards only. They could melt some snow in jugs.

Skinny dreamt about rats. They were scurrying over the snow, down the stone floor of the corridor, between the water tubs. They talked to each other. An old rat said to its young: "What you can't avoid you must endure."

They appeared in her dreams with the bodies of other animals, dogs, foxes, wolves or fish, but always with rat's heads. When she opened her eyes they were gone. When she closed them, there they were again, running in front of her. They were shouting words of advice to her, but she could not remember a single one.

"It's best when you don't even know who you're with," Long-Legs had said. Had she told her this during the night, or was it a dream?

Twelve: Günther Eich, Brentano Wolfenstein, Bern Reding, Viktor Holz, Bertrand Heim, Fritz Barthelms, Gottfried Weinheim, Erhard Wiesentier-Mähring, Erik Unruh, Manfred Reinisch, William Pohl, Suardon Mann.

The Oberführer – so he claimed – had given Tight-Lips her discharge papers in a sealed envelope. She was waiting for her escort to the "Hotel for Foreigners". The Oberführer had been suspiciously silent. He hadn't accused Tight-Lips of anything, nor had he ordered her to be put up against the wall. He'd merely forbidden her to talk to Madam Kulikowa. She thought it a little odd that she hadn't even received a whipping.

The following morning, instead of getting an escort, she went to the wall. They could hear three salvoes, and no vehicle arriving or leaving.

By now they knew what had happened. A corporal in the sappers had been in the cubicle with Tight-Lips rather longer than he was entitled to be. The Madam had been about to ask the Oberführer whether she should point out to the corporal that his time was up, when Tight-Lips emerged, as white as a sheet. She had heard the Madam's bell outside her cubicle. The corporal had had his fun with Tight-Lips – he had shaved her crotch with a razor. Then he had laughed, saying that she looked like a plucked goose. Now and again he had played with the razor, dangerously close to her abdomen. Because she said nothing, he also tried to communicate with her with his eyes and with gestures. Eventually he had stripped naked. His gaze had been wild; he had been like a man on fire. He had pulled out his pistol, slipped back the safety catch and in front of her shot himself through his left eye.

Oberführer Schimmelpfennig established from the Gestapo that suicide ran in the corporal's family. His father, a captain in an infantry regiment, had shot himself through the heart in front of his wife, the corporal's mother.

The Oberführer informed the Madam curtly that neither he nor the Gestapo intended to explore why such elements killed themselves. He considered the chapter closed.

For a few hours the temperature rose. The sun came out and gilded the snow.

"Some places you can swim to, others you can't," Long-Legs said.

Ever since she was eleven she had known that life was not as simple as she would like. It was a mysterious ocean, with shallows and depths, calm and treacherous; with currents and whirlpools, generally indifferent to the fate of girls like her. She recalled how at home she used to look forward to winter, to spring, to waking up in the morning.

"Sometimes they let you choose, but mostly they do the choosing."

"In Japan 'menstruation' is a taboo word," she said.

"We must try," Madam Kulikowa said at breakfast. They had finger-thick chunks of army bread with thin strawberry jam made from potatoes, as well as a frozen jacket potato. They were drinking coffee made from roasted acorns. They had been sweeping the snow in the yard since five in the morning.

"Why?" asked Smartie, swallowing a piece of chewed potato skin.

"That's life," replied the Madam. "You go through doors which are forever being closed."

She had a homily for them every morning. The notion of a door being slammed shut in someone's face if she hadn't put her foot against it and pushed with all her strength was one of these. The girls gulped the hot brownish-black liquid to get warm. Soon they would go to the latrine, into the tub, and to their cubicles. The Madam had other favourite adages: Number one: When a cockerel arrives he wants a hen. Number two: Even a gold ducat passes from hand to hand. Number three: A proper girl can handle a drunkard and a brawler. And: A wise girl does not complain.

The sun was not out for long. The sky clouded over and it began to snow. The wind sprang up.

Later, while they were clearing the snow, the army radio operator found some music – the Peter Kreuder Ensemble. On German forces radio, the war seemed a cheerful business, in dance rhythm.

Twelve: Walhardt Wolf, Stefan Gunther, Alois Merinda, Michael Brunner, Julius Pfeiffer, Franz Kowacz, Herbert Fox, Paul William Wechsler, Juraj Klokocznick, Fred Robert Glas, Franz Gruber, Adalbert von Abele.

That evening, Long-Legs was bleeding from her bottom.

"I'm like a sewer," she said.

She hadn't been able to see her way back from the latrine. The

Oberführer had ordered the fuses to be taken out. There was no light in the dormitory. A single oil lamp was flickering in the corridor, but the wick was low and the flame nearly out. In Long-Leg's eyes there was no pride, only contempt and possibly hatred. Everyone knew she would not see the doctor. Instead of treating her, the Oberführer would send her straight to Festung Breslau. There was lethargy and weariness in her eyes.

"They've turned us into whores."

They could hear the Oberführer outside in the corridor. He was instructing Big Leopolda Kulikowa to save water. The water tanker had not arrived.

"The pure race," Long-Legs grimaced.

She kept her pain to herself. Wouldn't it be better not to live? Was her soul shrivelling like a wilting flower? She was still bleeding.

"I have no soul. It's my bottom that's bleeding."

Skinny was ashamed to look away. She was glad it was dark. She gave Long-Legs her cotton wool, and two sticking plasters. Long-Legs put a sand-filled pillow under her behind, but that was uncomfortable.

Beautiful also gave Long-Legs her cotton wool.

"I hope this won't happen to you," Long-Legs said.

"I hope so too," said Skinny.

"He flung the SS Guidance Brochure Number 17 on my bed, saying it was good reading material."

"What's wrong with you?" she asked Skinny.

"I've got goose-bumps all of a sudden." Skinny said.

"He rolled on the floor with me," Long-Legs said. "He didn't like the smell of the bed."

They heard a noise outside as a truck arrived from the Wehrkreis with two crates labelled *Schutzgummi*, rubber sheaths.

Long-Legs said she was afraid of dogs. While she was in the latrine she'd overheard the handler of thirteen German Shepherds from the Protectorate of Bohemia and Moravia, delivered by a Czech police officer, explain to the Oberführer and commander of the brothel that somewhere near Prague dogs were now being trained to obey

German commands. These dogs were a super-breed – their jawbones had a strength equal to the pressure of 1,000 to 5,000 pounds per square inch. Their bite left a deep wound – a hole where the flesh had been torn out, extremely painful even when a scab had grown over it – and caused damage to the nerves. The dogs could tear an eye from its socket, along with a chunk of face.

"Beauties," the Oberführer had said appreciatively. The new dogs had the strength of wolves. They were to be fed pork and beef, as well as offal.

Long-Legs learned too, that, faced with an enraged animal, she had to stand motionless like a tree on a windless day. An animal should not be annoyed while it was feeding or nursing its pups. The main thing was not to shout, or to stare into the dog's eyes.

Part Two

Chapter Six

Things had happened fast in that part of Poland by the River San. The Germans had been retreating, like a ram lowering its head in resistance while edging backwards on its four legs. They were defending every inch of foreign soil as though it were theirs. The brothel was evacuated and Skinny escaped from the marching column. She was saved by the confusion that swept Poland and soon also Germany, creating a level of disorganization never previously experienced in Europe. She lied, she changed her identity, she stole when she had to. She let herself be hired for work in a laundry with the help of a Polish girl to whom she promised half her wages. Then the Polish girl disappeared, but not before she had obtained papers for Skinny that said in effect that her identity could not be established. She could pretend to be a deportee, and she received a work permit and an identity card. There were about 100 women working at the laundry. Katowice was quite close and she went there several times with the girls, once even for a dance. She also helped out in a kitchen at the railway station. After a long, dreadful time she ate her fill nearly every day.

I had not seen Skinny since September. I found her again in Prague about three months after the end of the war. It was a hot August; the days were close, with sudden brief thunderstorms. She attracted me with something that I probably would not have liked in another girl. I sensed right from our first meeting in Prague that there was in her something she didn't wish to talk about and which I should not even wish to know. But, as is natural, this made me even more curious. And the more curious I was the more reticent she became.

Some people in Prague were told they should not have come back but stayed where they were. One of them jumped out of a window. He had been a machine gunner in the eastern army. Two of his brothers were killed and he had lost his father, his mother and three children. His heavy Maxim gun, so recently effective against the Germans, didn't help him with peacetime. He wrote a farewell note that was published in the Bulletin of the Jewish Communities; they printed it on the last page.

Skinny thought it odd that there could be anti-Semitism when there were so few Jews left. It was rumoured that nine-tenths of them had been killed. Suddenly we realized that one could survive the war and be defeated after it. But that, our mutual friend Ervín Adler argued, was not our affair. Could the echo be stronger than what had produced it?

While in the camps, we had idealized the outside world, not realizing that it didn't give a damn about us. Between us and them were invisible shadows, fences and barriers. Some of the walls were high and thick; getting over was not easy. For a while we each remained behind our walls, peeping at one another over the top. Adler had met an elderly gentleman in the park who, after gazing at him for a long time, eventually summoned the courage to ask him whether, by any chance, he had also come back from a concentration camp. Before Adler could even reply the man said, "I do apologize."

It seemed laughable to Adler, but it was the first thing he told us that day.

"It's an unfinished story," he said.

Fortunately we were at an age when you didn't feel sad for 24 hours a day, even though it was just as impossible to feel happy for 24 hours a day. We endeavoured to raise our spirits with free meals in one of Prague's soup kitchens, where the three of us were frequent visitors. Once Adler said that he wouldn't like to be a widow dining there, being reminded by the blobs of fat floating on the soup of the eyes of her dead husband. Skinny did not find this remark funny. Where did Adler get his ideas from?

"Who did they kill in your family?" he asked her.

"All of them," Skinny said.

"Same here," Adler said.

They fell silent. It was the same for practically everybody. Adler had found it rather ridiculous when his concierge asked him how the world could have permitted it. Now it seemed just as ridiculous to Skinny. I was glad no-one asked me the same question. I had been in an orphanage even before the war. I imagined my grandmother Olga's fate without having to ask. People over 35 had a slim chance, those over 60 none whatever.

"What will you inherit?" Adler asked her.

She didn't answer him.

Because Skinny had so often lost all she had, after the war she clung to everything she could get hold of. She had three pairs of boots. She called them "my dear little boots", even though she just looked at them and wore other shoes. Or she would play with a new skirt (or rather an old-new one she'd been given by Mrs Jäger of the Jewish Community's social welfare department) and address it by name, as "my dear little red skirt". That one kept its name: the Red One. She also had a green one, a check one and a striped one which was pleated. She had to feel things, to touch them. She would reassure herself during the night – getting out of bed – that they were hers. She reconciled herself from the outset to the fact that she could lose her things and she was surprised if she kept anything. To have and not to have, to receive and to lose: inversely proportional dimensions. Loving her new things as she did, she was unaware that some of it looked like stuff from a second-hand clothes shop. But while her wardrobe became more and more colourful, she felt naked and impoverished – probably because she wanted to be ready in case misfortune once more befell her.

She spoke about her family.

"My father saw Germany as a locomotive at full speed. Us he saw as tied to the rails. The train was rushing towards us. Nothing could stop it."

She did not say then that her father had thrown himself at the high-voltage fence at Auschwitz-Birkenau. Nor did she say anything about Rottenführer Erich Schratz. Schratz had beaten her father's face, his head, his private parts for six days running. The seventh day was a Sunday and the Rottenführer was not on duty. But he had given instructions to the block leader. This man did not beat her father so hard, but he could not ignore his orders. That was the day her father took his life.

Her mother had met her fate on a bridge, just a few steps from her native land. And Ramon was dead too. He was almost 14. Would he have gone on with school? Her father had believed that a trade would be preferable.

I could guess what she was thinking of, because she added: "Good and evil. Perhaps Hitler didn't think he was a devil."

I shall not forget the way Adler – with whom we became a threesome with all the advantages and disadvantages of such an arrangement – inspected Skinny one day. It was in Wenceslas Square in front of the Hotel Europa, where we used to meet. For an instant his eyes rested on the centre of her skirt, then he raised them. She was standing before him in a thin blouse, a rather long skirt, high boots as for mountain walking, and floral-patterned socks – a very pretty girl. He appreciated her reticence. Adler was apt to seek in others what he was afraid of in himself. Probably the thing that bound us together was that we didn't have a lot to share, since none of us had very much – a subsidy from the Repatriation Office, a few clothes supplied by the social welfare department, and in Skinny's case, a green US Army blanket from which she had fashioned a single-breasted winter coat with green buttons made by an acquaintance of her mother's. It matched her eyes. We spoke about her, Adler and I. I didn't want to wind up like Adler – he loved her one day and spoke ill of her the next.

I watched her closely when she was unaware of it. There was something of the expression of a frightened deer, as well as its charm, in her green eyes with their gingery lashes and paler eyebrows. Her face seemed to me every bit as pretty as Greta Garbo's, whom the three of us had seen in *Ninotchka*, *La Dame aux Camélias* and *Queen Christina*. She had a kind of dignity, that of the humiliated, in her face, her features, her head and her movements, in the way she behaved and expressed herself.

After all she'd been through she still believed in that empty place between her crotch and her abdomen, which no-one would fill or dishonour or violate unless she invited him in. It was not, of course, the only empty place in her. I tried to imagine her belly as a hidden secret box. And she still believed in her father's love for her mother when she was conceived.

She viewed the world as a huge camp that contained a variety of divisions and reservations. If she was lucky she might stay in one of them for a long time, perhaps all her life, in transit. But to ever escape, to ever be truly free, seemed out of the question to her.

I met Skinny every day because I came to feel as though every hour, minute or second I was not with her was lost time. I talked to her of everything possible. I didn't search for details, even though I nearly knew. It was several weeks before I saw her *Feldhure* tattoo. She didn't show me her belly for the reasons I would have preferred. She wanted me to know where I stood with her. And perhaps also where she stood with me, or with herself.

On Petrín Hill I spoke of love for the first time in my life. I was sending a message to Skinny, Hanka Kaudersová, that the waters were receding – as with Noah's ark. I loved her blindly – if love is blind. This I did not say, I only thought it. I was starting out on a new life, like her, willing to squeeze a whole ocean out of every puddle. I loved her with that invisible urge which has to overcome the boundary between the courage and fear to say that we are in love, because the fact that it's not a lie is not nearly enough.

I loved her with that wonderful and vertiginous balancing act between what we have and what we dream of. The moment when no disease is infectious, no sin unforgivable, no obstacle insurmountable.

And, ultimately, no past forbidding and no bad experience decisive. It was not only uncertain, tormenting and wonderful at the same time; there was also an element of ambition, a wish to climb a steep hill regardless of what we might see from the top.

In her mind she returned to Poland. The worst day had not been the first day at No. 232 Ost, but the second when she told herself, "Oh Lord, now it's starting all over again."

Twelve: Gustav Habenicht, Sepp Bartels, Rolf Baltruss, Fritz Puscha, Heinrich Rinsfeld, Otto Scholtz, Heine Baumgarten, Friedrich Heindl, Wilhelm Kube, Johann Kurfürst, Hans Bergel, Rudolf Weinmann.

The Oberführer appeared at the end of the corridor in fur-lined boots and a fur coat that reached to his ankles. The girls fell silent. He looked at them as if they were not naked, or else it made no difference to him. He regarded them as inferior beings.

A huge gale had uprooted the remaining trees by the river. It had swept through at 90 miles an hour. The torn-up trees were lying in the direction of the wind, their roots uncovered and their branches snapped. The Madam had ordered the girls to drag the branches into the yard. The guard who accompanied them had lost his faith in army meteorologists.

Madam Kulikowa had to chase the girls away from the window. Bumping over the frozen snow, one wing almost dragging on the ground, was a Heinkel. It came to a halt by the gate, its fuselage full of holes. The guards ran up to it and released the pilot from his harness. His temples were crushed, he was bruised and blood was oozing from a shoulder wound. His knees gave way and he sank down and crouched on the ground, letting out his breath as if it were his last. The weak sun was reflected from the gilt tin eagle over the entrance and cast flickering patches on the pilot. He looked like a caricature of an airman from the film *Quax, the Pilot without Fear or Blemish* that the Madam had seen. The guards picked him up carefully.

"Where am I? *Mein Gott . . .*"

"Feldbordell No. 232, Herr Hauptmann," a guard with a scar stretching from one ear to the other reported smartly.

Oberführer Schimmelpfennig came running out to the sentry box by the gate. He introduced himself, giving his rank and title.

"Into my surgery," he commanded.

The airman's blood had stained his flying helmet. He was on the brink of fainting. In his half-closed eyes there was guilt, lethargy and exhaustion. He was shivering now, all but unconscious. Life was draining from him.

"You'll be all right," the Oberführer assured him. His voice was serious but not compassionate. His eyes swept over the aircraft. *Pride not pity. We were born to perish*, the Oberführer thought.

The guards carried the dead airman away. His blood was on their gloves and on their white snowsuits.

The truck from the Wehrkreis that arrived to remove the plane delivered some cases with winter wear. It included three pairs of felt boots with thick soles.

That evening, in her room with the vaulted ceiling, the Madam was massaging Major von Kalckreuth's back. A sebaceous cyst had formed on his right side. He hoped it was nothing worse. The Madam told him that she had dreamed, of all things, of Auschwitz-Birkenau. Each time she mentioned the camp she emphasized that she had been in the Aryan section.

The massage made him feel good.

"Know what I heard?" he asked. "That a baby in his mother's womb will turn into the correct position, head down, if they prick her thumb with a needle and at the same time light a candle with a special Chinese herb."

The major was interested in alternative medicine. The Oberführer did not hold with it.

"The Chinese practise acupuncture on most parts of the body, something our doctors don't even dream of."

He heaved a sigh. He recalled what he knew about the Japanese attack on Nanking, when the soldiers had practised bayonet drill on their Chinese prisoners of war and the civilian population. He had also read in a brochure that the Chinese police in Shanghai were the first, as early as 1920, to equip their men with pistols with six-round magazines. History was racing ahead, that was a fact.

"All our watches are showing five minutes to midnight," he said. "How come you don't have a portrait of Adolf Hitler in here?"

He heaved another sigh.

"Some people still confuse freedom with impertinence."

Twelve: Horst Hoffe, Jünger Strasser, Hermann Bock, Franz Klang, Hans Rössel, Manfred Kaas, Ernst Tippelkirsch, Gregor Schleichner, Uwe Hugenberg, Boris Fricke, Hans Besitz, Harry Höppner.

Estelle had narrowly escaped a flogging.

"I'm marking off the days," she said. "So far I've got away with it. I'm being careful."

Something familiar made them compare their fates. Skinny examined every remark, every hint of Estelle's. In Germany and the occupied territories there were masses of such girls, driven into brothels by the authorities. And thousands who had volunteered.

They were waiting in the corridor for a tub to become vacant. On the thick wooden floor slats, which could be lifted and stacked up, Estelle looked slight, almost frail, with long black hair whose ends she singed and mother-of-pearl earrings in delicate lobes. She burped, but she didn't have sour breath.

"I'm waiting all the time," she said, undoing her buttons. Had she crossed the boundary beyond which girls were no longer forgiven?

"I get cramps – herpes. I'm terrified I might get a rash. When I bleed I'm afraid I might be dying. I feel like when you crack a hazelnut, or when someone steps on your belly."

They stood facing each other. White steam came from their mouths.

"You're warming me," said Estelle.

"The Oberführer went to Festung Breslau this morning."

"To recruit girls?"

"I don't know."

"The first three hours are the worst for me."

It was with them all the time, even if they appeared hardened: Virginity, the first experience, the worst and the better ones, anything that was the first time and began to repeat itself, like menstruation.

Estelle was naked now, and climbed into the tub. Skinny joined her. "Yes," Skinny said.

Madam Kulikowa taught Skinny to sing "The Cocotte". There would be an evening entertainment. Did she know "Deeper than the Sea, Hotter than the Sahara"? They might rehearse a cabaret number about Lucifer meeting Beelzebub.

When the full moon wasn't hidden by clouds and as long as the stars were shining, the wolves seemed white, with huge silver eyes. They emerged from the darkness, phantoms of the night, enfolded in a kind of unknowing. They moved about the snow-covered wasteland wrapped in a cloak of darkness, illuminated by the moon. They made her aware of what humans lacked: fierceness, the dark rays of night. She admired them and she was afraid of them. Now and then the guards caught them in their searchlights. It was a different light from the one the wolves were born into. Day and night made no difference to them. They came from lairs in the quarry and among the rocks. They did not recognize frontiers, any more than the Germans did.

Crows were flying across the same night sky. They could not be seen, like the rats and the wolves, only heard. Croaking, howling and whistling pierced the night. Like unintelligible messages, vague prophecies. Something more ancient than man.

In the morning the guards exercised in the snow without shirts, just in trousers. The SS maintenance staff were extending the gym by breaking down the wall between what had been the cowshed and the stables. The buildings were made mainly of stone, partly from wood. Commandant Trillhase had had the yard paved wall to wall. When the girls had swept the snow away, the stones shone like ancient hieroglyphs. Oberführer Brandenburg-Luttich said once that the stones looked as if they had been inscribed by the Jews who had worked in the quarry. The inscriptions seemed to him like Hebrew letters, or like ancient Germanic runes.

The Oberführer thought that No. 232 Ost was an ideal spot linking them to the front, the hinterland and the Wehrkreis, as if made for defence and attack. He agreed with Oberführer Schimmelpfennig, The Frog, that the substance of which the German soul was made was hardness not compassion. Those who would read the stones would read German.

Twelve: Kurt Wegener, Gerd Wolf, Alexander Penske, Albert Heller-Kaiser, Max Gunther Friedenthal, Martin Schwitzer, Hans-Peter Krume, Kleo Hahn, Fritz Mani, Hans Lage-Hegern, Helmut Binder, Hans Anglia Jürgensohn.

When they had let the water out of their tubs they were to report to Oberführer Schimmelpfennig's surgery to get an injection against Ebola or Marburg disease, something spread by rats and bats and their excrement. Their temperature would go up temporarily. No cause for alarm. As a special concession reveille the following day would not be until 5.30 a.m.

Big Leopolda Kulikowa got the Pole who came over to tattoo the girls to pull out a painful back tooth for her. She didn't want to ask the Oberführer, but she needed a painkiller from him. She hated asking for anything. Out in the corridor she spat out some blood.

"You don't get out of anything on your own – only exceptionally. It's better with some help. You don't have to love them," she said to Skinny, almost apologetically.

Long-Legs called them to the window. For about five minutes a wolf had been dancing, twisting about its own axis as if trying to catch its tail. Abruptly it ran off.

"You can want, but you don't necessarily get," Skinny heard the Madam say to Fatty.

Twelve: Reiner Dressler, Rafael Habe, Paul Hoffmann, Klaus Ruhe, Christian Schulte, Fritz Adler, Seigfried Knappe, Uwe Welt, Demian Schuhmacher, Volker Werner Blind, Willi Lump, Heinrich Burke.

Before lights-out the rats gathered between the latrines. Motionless, they resembled piles of wolf's hair. Suddenly they would scatter, leaving raven's feathers behind on the snow.

During the evening a truck from the Wehrkreis delivered three barrels of salted beef.

Over the radio came the voices of three German singers, one of them Lile Anderson. In a direct relay from Paris, Maurice Chevalier was appearing for the benefit of frontline soldiers, war widows and the victims of the air raids on Germany. He sang "Give me Your Hand, Mam'zelle". The commentator mentioned the soul of Europe and its full stomach. The audience applauded. One mother, he said, gave birth to her baby during an air raid. Her husband, a doctor, had handed the child out through the window to some air defence personnel, so they could take it to a shelter. The child was named Adolf. In honour of the child, Monsieur Chevalier would sing . . .

The station's signal faded.

They were all examined during the week by an army psychologist, Oberführer Michael Blatter-Spirit. His dissertation had been about

Oswald Spengler; on the extinction of life, on the duty to die. The Frog had his own opinion of Blatter-Spirit. The body knew four million kinds of pain? Could one agree with Arthur Schopenhauer that man's most essential longing was to be free from pain? Blatter-Spirit could look back on his respectable series of researches. He had studied the psychological features of blond and blue-eyed people over five and a half feet tall. He'd probed into the Viking and Nordland Divisions of the SS that had levelled the miners' village of Lidice in Bohemia and razed Oradour near Limoges in France. He had examined those who participated in the massacre of Malmédy. One SS man had recalled the end of Oradour. This man had described how it had occurred on a sunny Saturday in the peaceful quiet of a German village. He had exhibited all the qualities of Waffen-SS members – the sons of middle and upper class parents. In Oradour he had killed more women and children than men: 190 men, 207 children, 245 women. Blatter-Spirit had also studied the Germanization of foreigners, that which made the Waffen-SS so attractive to them, a magnet for Estonian, Latvian, Lithuanian, Ukrainian, Slovak, Romanian and French SS. The psychologist wore small round spectacles, his eyes behind them shone like opal glass. His face was pockmarked with childhood acne and duelling scars from his days at the German University in Prague.

He took his subject seriously. The army prostitutes must be made to smile.

"Smile at me," he ordered Skinny.

She smiled at him.

"That's lifeless," he said. "Again."

She had to grin at him 20 times. He promised her chocolate, two hard-boiled eggs and bread with ham.

From smiling lips, he explained, signals went to the brain and triggered energy which – even if the smile wasn't spontaneous – produced positive effects. He based this on discoveries of the French neurologist Duchenne de Bologne, according to whom a hearty smile (not just a half smile) gave rise to a "play of sweet feelings in the soul".

He was trying to get results that could lead to a general instruction. He glanced at her file, at the questionnaire she had answered.

"What do you know? Rat – rabbit? Ox – cockerel?"

Oberführer Schimmelpfennig remained doubtful about these theories. Either Dr Blatter-Spirit was right, or he was an idiot – and he'd decided which. The Oberführer himself recognized health only, and the opposite of health. Nothing in between.

Over tea Blatter-Spirit expressed the view that Columbus was a Jew. He had brought syphilis back to Europe. And weren't the Jews everywhere? The two men talked about experiments carried out by Japanese doctors using horse blood for human transfusions. Then they discussed pressure chambers and the point at which a person's eyeballs popped out.

At daybreak on Sunday repair gangs and teams of camp inmates from Auschwitz-Birkenau and Blechhammer, Monowitz and Gleiwitz, where the rolling stock repair shops were located, arrived at the steel bridge. Under the guidance of railway engineers they reinforced the piers and replaced the rails. In the fierce wind they broke the ice on the river with hand grenades. They encased the piers in heavy timber. There was a sound of gunfire, shouting and the clash of metal against metal. The guards were warming themselves at iron braziers with red-hot coke. A few camp inmates drowned in the ice-cold water.

Throughout the night, troop trains and trains carrying war material roared east. And in the opposite direction came long trains carrying wounded men, bits of booty and damaged heavy weapons. They fought their way through snow, blizzards and artillery fire. The rails were bending. Ruby sparks swished through the darkness and the snow.

On Tuesday a Mercedes with its escort arrived with a new girl from Festung Breslau.

The girl addressed the guard at the gate in passable German.

"My name is Debilia. I fuck like a tigress."

The guard liked her guttural "r". She had been in an institution from the age of eleven to fourteen and believed herself to be a cat. After her discharge, no school or training college would accept her. When the first soldier entered the cubicle she had inherited from Tight-Lips, she sat on his lap, spat, miaowed and purred, and then licked his nose. At dinner she said that she liked everything and then proceeded loudly to list all the things she didn't eat. At roll-call she got her first three strokes with a cane.

"In China," the Oberführer said, "the mandarins used to dish out 30 strokes and nobody thought it out of place."

Debilia squealed, so he ordered more strokes. After five he ordered that she be given 25. At the eighth fall of the cane she stopped yelling. After the twenty-first they carried her away. The Oberführer ordered the other prostitutes to sing. He was going to demand a replacement for her from the Wehrkreis, he said. It would be no bad thing if they started to send German girls.

"It's up to you to make sure the word 'woman' has no bad flavour. Remember, there are two kinds of girl. The first kind were born into the right bed, the second climbed into it. Don't think that what's bad for the Germans is good for you," Madam Kulikowa told them later.

They should not behave like a bad innkeeper who drove her guests away instead of welcoming them. Or who simply waited for a guest to put his money on the table and leave. They had something to display – youth, hair, breasts, a feast for the troops. They saw the men at their most vulnerable moment. A girl was like a doctor in some respects. She had to discover the best in everyone.

Was Skinny Jewish? Or Estelle? The Madam sometimes wondered. If the cards had been dealt the other way round, would the Jews behave like the Germans and the Germans like the Jews? You couldn't tell anything from a girl's crotch. What could she have in common with the troops who came here for an advance on their home life? The cemetery was nearer for her.

After supper a messenger on a motorbike with a sidecar brought a parcel for Skinny. A couple of pounds each of sugar and lentils, a chunk of salted beef and some pork crackling in a jam jar. A two-pound bag of millet. And a visiting card from Captain Daniel August Hentschel.

"The Germans are still gentlemen," observed Madam Kulikowa. "Knights without fear and blemish. They know how to share even what they steal."

Skinny shared her parcel with the rest of the girls. The Madam took the salted beef.

Twelve: Karl Meissner, Hans Bellow, Anton Bruckner, Frank Epp, Hermann Fegelein, Fritz Albert Klausen, Gustav Kriebel, Rainer Maria Hilger, Donar Hörbiger, Alex Neurath, Uwe Schmidt, Kurt Witzig.

Estelle held Skinny by her hand.

"I'd never been with anyone before. I didn't have it off with him; he had it off with me. He told me I was nice and if I weren't a whore he'd marry me. He waited for me to moan. So I moaned. He wanted me to open my legs; to put them on his shoulders. I heard myself croaking. I was gasping for air. He said it was so good. It hurt me, and I was covered in cold sweat. He slapped my bottom – as a reward. Out of sheer fear I smiled at him. Then he fell asleep. He was no longer interested in me. No-one was ever interested in me afterwards."

She didn't mention those two soldiers, brothers perhaps or cousins, who it was rumoured she was interested in.

The sky, frosty, deep blue and clear, was filling with stars. The Madam announced that it was Christmas Day.

"Do you also imagine God as a shiny fish?" Estelle asked. She looked at Skinny.

"Were you really in a camp? Like the Madam? She was in the Aryan section."

The wolves were howling outside the windows.

Behind their words self-denial was hiding; that secret life no-one knows about, that life which had deformed them, but in which there was still a grain of hope.

"When I lie next to you, things come back to me," Estelle said. "I'm walking in the park with my mother. She was raven-haired, like I am. I run ahead, stop in front of her and face her, so she has to stop too. And I say to her 'Mummy, you're walking too fast'. And then I do it again and say 'Mummy, your breasts are wobbling too much'. My mother stares ahead, as if she's lost in thought. Am I really there? I say 'Mummy, why are you looking so odd?'"

Skinny did not tell Estelle that they were killing people at Auschwitz-Birkenau from morning to night and from night to morning, killing on a conveyor belt. She said nothing about the prisoners who were grinding the bones of the dead into fertilizer that was taken away by rail in open wagons. About the mass murders which had become commonplace. About the women waiting their turn in snow and ice and rain, powerless and emaciated. They were no longer being moved by trucks; fuel had to be saved. They had to trudge along, step after step. She remained silent about the things the Germans had thought up in order to cleanse the planet of the inferior race. About the sick bay where experiments were carried out on human beings.

About the killing of children and the sick, as well as the healthy for punishment, simply to make room for the next transportees. About what seemed normal to the SS men in their service to Germany; about what, after a few weeks, no longer seemed insane to her because it was being repeated every day. That was what she had escaped to save herself.

It occurred to her, as it had before, that Estelle might not believe her. She would not have believed it herself if she hadn't been there. And she only knew a fraction of it, the general picture, the taste of damp ash, the choking smell of charred bones like the smell of boiled glue.

"I ran away so I didn't have to go to a camp as you did," Estelle said.

Skinny remained silent. Estelle turned over in bed and caught hold of her with both hands. She was not the only one to have run away and ended up here. Perhaps she'd just had a different reason. That unknown reason was a bond between them.

"I don't have to see killing first-hand. What's here is quite enough for me – what they did to Big Belly and Krikri, and maybe Maria-Giselle."

"They don't give you a choice," Skinny said.

"Is it the same there as here?"

"No, it's not. Except that neither there nor here can you get out."

Skinny wondered why the camp had such a fascination for Estelle. Why was she thinking about it so much?

"What did you do there?"

"I assisted the doctor."

"Would they have sterilized me?"

"They sterilized all the girls."

"Did you have any of your family there?"

"Did you?"

"My grandfather." She let go of Skinny's hands.

For a while they were both silent.

"Is it a sin to want to die?"

"Why do you ask me?" Skinny said.

"Is it a sin not to want to die?" Estelle asked.

"Some decide to die with honour if they can't live with honour. That's why my father killed himself."

"I know why you're saying this to me. You probably know why I'm asking."

"You too?" Skinny breathed.

It was out now. They had both betrayed themselves, simultaneously. Estelle bit her lips. A little drop of blood appeared, which she licked off in the dark. What would they do with this knowledge, now or tomorrow? What would it do to them?

The moon had risen to its highest point. In a while it would begin to go down. From the field kitchen, wafted by the wind, came smoke and the smell of pea soup with bacon and lard.

*

In the morning Long-Legs gave Skinny ten marks. "An interest-free loan from an Obersoldat."

"If they caught you!"

"That takes two. It doesn't matter whether you steal or not, just don't get caught."

While peeling potatoes in the kitchen Skinny had stolen a tin of Slovak chicken. She would share it with Beautiful. It was already cooked, all she had to do was let it thaw out. Had Beautiful heard her and Estelle talking during the night? She slept right next to them.

Twelve: Jürgen Henning, Werner Schlossberg, Erhardt Kassel-Mahdun, Heinz Fesl, Noel Schulte, Gerd Siemens, Franz Otto Schröder, Oskar Herder-Altmann, Helmuth Krantz, Otmar Bartelsmann, Kurt Biedenkopf, Reinhardt Eich-Ochmanek.

Chapter Seven

It was Saturday. Snow was falling. The yard was noisy with truck engines, German shouts and laughter. Piled on the rubbish heap in the corner were broken mugs, pieces of rusty metal and swept-up spent cartridges. All that would be tidied up and removed before the inspectors arrived from the Wehrkreis. Some infantrymen outside the brothel were whistling and calling to one another. Here the German army was not retreating but advancing towards its goals. The guards on the towers heard the same dirty jokes for the hundredth time.

"A little debauchery does no harm, no debauchery does a lot," a lanky youngster shouted across the yard. A lock of pale hair showed under his cap. He could not be more than eighteen; this was his first visit to the brothel. He had already had his baptism of fire in battle. There was a new medal on his tunic.

"Everything in moderation," muttered Oberführer Schimmel-pfennig. Steam was rising from his mouth. He had no wish to act as a father figure. There was no point in cursing the frost. They would all get their full measure of winter.

The brothel was a long low building. The men leaving it were almost creeping along, some of them let their knees give way. They were greeted with jeers in the yard.

"I've been here before. You'll read about it in the book on the descendants of the SS," one SS man shouted.

The soldiers by the vehicles stood with their hands in their pockets. The Oberführer noted with chagrin that the sight of the army from here was grotesque. That morning he had received a report of a tactical withdrawal. If this batch of troops were thinking that No. 232 Ost was some Lusthaus in France they were mistaken. All they had to do was listen to the approaching artillery fire. The Oberführer would be glad if he was transferred. He was not sure where he would prefer to serve – one's head was on the block wherever one went. But it was disagreeable to have the Russians at one's heels. He had a vision of the devil, tongue sticking out and genitals exposed, approaching with giant strides. He had more than once considered applying for a transfer to the front. Here it was not as comfortable as they might think in Berlin.

It was as though from morning to evening he was fed on something distasteful. He was disgusted by his surroundings, by the animality of the soldiers who came here with an eagerness worthy of a better purpose. He was disgusted by the company of the prostitutes, by his collaboration with Madam Kulikowa. He looked down his nose at the guards, even though they belonged to the same élite unit as himself, the Waffen-SS. He watched them as he used to watch the birds, the wolves, and the rats. He found the Madam distasteful, even if she performed like a virtuoso. He did not care for her solos or recitals. He had not been to a concert for two and a half years, not even on his home leave in Berlin. Was finding himself among tarts really the pinnacle of his career as a medical officer? They were sending him suspect and unscreened girls. If it did not mean such a lot of administrative trouble he would have found out from the Gestapo at Auschwitz-Birkenau about the youngest whore. Was Kauders a German name or a Jewish one? His vigilance and concern were tearing his nerves but he had lost his zeal. He had made it a condition that he did not want anyone below 14 or over 20, and the Wehrkreis was complying. So why was he anxious? He liked to think that the machine was still functioning properly.

He had a feeling that he was not living well, but wouldn't admit to himself that things were slipping through his fingers. He proceeded with an unshakeable conviction that man was basically evil just as animals were evil, and anyone good behaved calculatingly and was therefore suspect.

He glanced at the gilded tin eagle on the gate, its head and beak thrusting from a white collar, its thick rough neck and huge wings.

He would have to replace the mouldy mattresses in the cubicles. They squeaked. But he couldn't really complain. No. 232 Ost ran like clockwork. Yet, as far as his military and medical career was concerned, he was treading water. Gone were yesterday's dreams of advance, by the army and by himself, collectively and individually. He had every right, when the inspectors from the Wehrkreis came, to liken No. 232 Ost to a railway station with sixteen tracks and a punctual timetable. That was something at least, if not everything.

On the walls, which were topped with concertinas of barbed wire, the ravens were perching. They seemed to him like vultures.

The guards standing behind their machine guns were watching the green Daimler of an Einsatzgruppen officer through their field glasses. It was moving cautiously, skidding in places. Obersturmführer Stefan Sarazin of the Einsatzkommando der Einsatzgruppen parked by the wall, in the same spot at which he had tied up his horse the last time that he had been here. With the assistance of two guards he covered his windscreen and rear window with tarpaulins to stop them from icing over. It was obvious that he knew his way around. He moved confidently, as if he had come to have breakfast here.

He'd been on an operation. Just as he was a passionate football player and driver, so he was a useful member of a Jagdkommando. Wherever he served, he did so without fear and with total enthusiasm. He felt that he was getting better with time. It was alchemy of age and experience, the two going hand in hand. And there was a growing sense of belonging. He was becoming part of the Einsatzgruppen just as the Einsatzgruppen were becoming part of him. It was something elemental, it inspired him and became the foundation of his self-assurance. He felt himself straightening and growing, secure in the knowledge that there was no blemish on his military character. As to his army profile, name and reputation, he had no doubts. It would be ideal if he were just a soldier. Nothing but the Einsatzgruppen.

Something provoked his irritation. Somebody had torn out the wall

93

hook and ring to which he tethered his horse. Had they donated the metal to help make guns? Or had it been done to annoy him? He had his reservations about the administrative efficiency of No. 232 Ost. The army was getting too bureaucratic. Not so the Einsatzgruppen. For many Germans the organization was no longer what it should be. The era of comradeship between Wehrmacht and Waffen-SS was over. Somebody only had to tear a hook out of the wall and his good humour was extinguished. That was not what he had come here for. He had his own ideas about running things. What would he tether his horse to next time? He despised organizations and individuals who had a logical reason for everything, even the most trivial decisions. He would punish excuses by shooting. The army was full of pen pushers. He was glad to have joined the Einsatzgruppen, on whom no army regulations or laws were binding. He would not like to see the Herrenwaffe change from a company of the brave into a bureaucracy.

As the snowflakes sailed down, he quoted from Adelbert von Chamisso, one of his teachers:

> Die Sonne bringt es an den Tag.
> Du weisst nun meine Heimlichkeit,
> So halt den Mund und sei gescheit . . .

He wished that he had written such a jewel himself.

With his right arm raised he saluted the Oberführer, who was watching some men unloading boxes of books, covered in snow. It was enough to make him sick. The army were retreating, and Berlin was sending them literature via Cracow.

Obersturmführer Sarazin disappeared into the building.

The Lebensborn and the field brothel – two related institutions, the former giving way to the latter as the requirements of the Herrenvolk and its army changed. For the Party and the army high command,

Sarazin had the gratitude of a son, a closer filial relationship than he had enjoyed with his own father. He was filled with warm recollections of the Lebensborn. His seven days there had given him, day by day and night by night, the self-assurance a man has when he has impregnated a woman. That deep, irrepressible primitive feeling. The triumphal attitude of a man who has conquered a woman or to whom a woman has submitted, a woman he has helped to have a child, his child. The sense of immortality a man has when he looks up at the stars. He remembered a few of the women's names, mostly just their first names. He was never quite sure he remembered those names correctly, but that was unimportant. It was part of the rules of the game not to ask to whom he was giving a child, just as the women did not ask who he was. All that was needed was mutual attraction and orders from above. The authorities would deal with everything else. The future of the Reich was being laid down, and from the best material. As the German children would be, so would the nation. As the children were brought up, from swaddling clothes and dummy, to kindergarten to elementary school, and from there to secondary school and university, then to the army – so would the country be in the years to come. This knowledge was enough for inspiration and arousal, for a sense of satisfaction. Added to this was the secrecy, like the secrecy of the night, the lure of a woman's body in the cubicle with its curtains drawn to ensure that the combination of darkness and light stimulated the participants. It was wonderful not to know who that woman was. The Lebensborn, the Spring of Life, was an island in a white snowy sea, a silver moon with its invisible side in a deep-blue cradle.

He listened to the sound of his boots on the floor, the impact of 38 steel nails in each sole and the metal edge around the heel. For a moment his memories of the Lebensborn – the first steps towards a Germany without frontiers, towards a vast territory running from the Rhine to the Ural – merged with the prospect of having an unknown young whore, one he had ordered for himself. The Madam had told him her name, but he had forgotten it.

Obersturmführer Stefan Sarazin didn't like Big Leopolda Kulikowa. Stout women always reminded him of cows. He had reconciled himself to the fact that he couldn't eliminate all the people he did not like. He had his vision of an ideal world. A slightly arrogant one, perhaps, but wasn't arrogance beautiful? If it were up to him, the world would already look different – something like an overpopulated paradise.

He sniffed the air to see whether Madam Kulikowa, in her eagerness to please him, had sprayed too much perfume. He didn't care for it, and he had warned the Madam in advance. Perfume gave him migraine. He found it repulsive, as he did mushrooms in potato soup. But what he smelled, more than perfume, was the stench of rats. Hideous creatures. The stench of rat poison and of rats – how could he forget that smell? He could not even stand the perfume they used for spraying the gas chambers at Auschwitz-Birkenau, at Treblinka, Majdanek and Sobibor, so the new arrivals didn't panic but let themselves be gassed without struggle. It was a pity to waste a single bullet. He reminded himself that he was the bearer of a Reich secret, one of the initiates.

Unconsciously he straightened his back. He wouldn't have minded being three or four inches taller, but he had a reputation he could be proud of. Women never had him totally in their power, even if he needed them. His steps were guided not by Venus but by Mars. His military assessments noted his hardness, toughness and fighting spirit, by which he compensated for what he had lost after suffering a severe head wound. Few people knew that a grenade had struck his head like lava hurled from a volcano, turning him into a living torch, and that his comrades had saved him by dousing the flames. There were consequences, of course, both internal and external. His scalp had not escaped damage. *Die Sonne bringt es an den Tag.* He didn't need to remind himself of it, the scar reminded him constantly. As for that other weakness, the army doctor had assured him that it was not life-threatening.

He was filled with a sense of superiority which would have been appropriate in someone twice his age. This did not exclude, but on the contrary confirmed, a craving for brutality without which he probably would not be in the Einsatzkommando. As for proving himself, there was no stiffer test than the Einsatzkommando. At Treblinka he had forced a professor of mathematics to thank him in advance for sending him to the next world. After terrifying him by putting a pistol against to his head he gave the man the option of running along to join his own people. For his age he ran quite well. At the last moment he joined a column destined for the gas chamber. He did not enjoy his escape for long. There had been irony and drama in it; a piece of theatre with its dénouement. That Jew was said to have been an expert on differential calculus. He spoke German, English and French fluently and could make himself understood in Spanish, Italian and Portuguese. He played Bach on the piano from memory. He had been married twice. He had come with two sisters and three grandchildren. He was even able to bring his first wife with him. The impertinent Jew! To cap it all, he was called Faust and had studied in Heidelberg. Chutzpah, as the Jews say. What did a Yid know about blood, about Germandom, about pride or about soil?

Obersturmführer Sarazin knew that there were many people in the Einsatzgruppen who thought the same as he did. Life was a string of pearls of varying sizes. Everybody born of a good race was entitled to reach the highest level. Apart from the prostitute Ginger and that acrobat, Long-Legs, he knew in advance that even if he left having achieved what he wanted he would be unsatisfied. Sometimes a prostitute had a good body – the Madam, say – and a lousy nature. Or she might be good at her job but be unwilling to let herself go completely. He was looking for a girl who, without being told, could read from his eyes what he wanted. He did not believe that anything should be denied him. It was he who held all the cards – well, nearly all.

He had read somewhere that everyone carried their own invisible baggage with them. He was not prepared to stop judging people by his own yardsticks.

As he walked towards the cubicles he thought he saw a rat rising to its hind legs under a dangling lightbulb at the far end of the corridor.

He did not change his pace. If he drew his pistol and fired at it he would rouse the soldiers from their mattresses and frighten the girls. Why shouldn't they have a bit of fun? He was only a few steps from Cubicle 16. He had passed Number 13 on his left. Number 16 would be on the right, as in a bad hotel. His hands and forehead were perspiring, probably because he'd come indoors to the warmth from the biting cold outside. Sometimes a thought would make him sweat, no matter whether it was a decision, or a verse, or an even target in the sight of his gun. Barrel, sight, trigger. Load, fire, a Jew. He enjoyed the idea, if only for the fraction of a second, when – thanks to him – his enemies were meeting the mother of everything on that other side of existence. That most faithful mistress of existence. A gift only he appreciated. Palm, butt, barrel, sight, a Jew. In his mind he heard the echo of nearly all the shots he had fired, had indulged in. He perceived it all as a huge detailed picture. That was how poets saw things.

Obersturmführer Sarazin had been preoccupied by numbers lately. Especially with two and three. He sought and found all kinds of connections. For the fifth day running (two plus three) he'd had a dream he'd first had at Treblinka. He had residential rights there; he had been a member and later the commanding officer of the guard detachment. The newly-raised Einsatzgruppen would be sent there to be tested, toughened up and tempered like steel.

He could have chosen between Treblinka, Auschwitz-Birkenau and Majdanek. That was the number three. There remained Mauthausen and Sobibor – two and three made five.

It would be silly if he had not dreamt it so often. He did not know whether it was a prophecy of the future or something that had happened to him in a previous life. It was about three Jewish women and a train with two engines. The engines uncoupled themselves and came to a halt in front of him. He tied the Jewish women to the near tender by their pigtails. Then he signalled the engineers to go full steam ahead. The two engine drivers sounded their whistles in unison. Three long blasts cut through the air, like horns playing some unknown music. Two engines, three blasts. Two engines, three women with pigtails. Then his numbers got confused.

The advantage of the dream was that he could dream about Jews even if there were none left in the area. He saw this as a personal achievement. He felt himself growing, felt the invisible magnetic force contained in killing, as if he were cutting down tall grain with a scythe, the black earth under his feet and white, wind-tattered clouds against a translucent deep blue when he raised his arm towards the sky. He had killed in many landscapes, now along the banks of the River San, where cattle would one day feed on grass fertilized by countless dead Jews, Gypsies and Poles. Every lizard would be fat with Jewish blood, fish would grow from the nutrients he had provided for them. Blood to him suggested crimson and all kinds of aniline red. He had seen a river turn red. It was to his credit that on historic maps Europe would be marked judenrein, cleansed of Jews. He knew that the Jews were his obsession. He didn't ask himself why. Poets were guided by their unshakeable intuition, that was how it was. He had one advantage over the circumcised: he saw what they could no longer see.

He stepped into Cubicle 16. He looked about him in the dim light, then shut the door. The ceiling seemed low to him. The prostitute he had chosen and booked for the whole shift was standing by the window, facing the door. Snowflakes were swirling outside. He had no doubt that she had been waiting for him. He could tell at once, washed, with oil handy. She'd be all the more willing to do what he wanted after his self-assured entry. And, of course, because of his rank and unit. Was she taller than him? Perhaps he should will her to stoop a little. She had light, gingery hair. Good. She was better dressed than he had expected. That was probably due to the obliging nature of that cloying, ageing Madam. He noted the lit candle and the shadow that the prostitute's head cast on the wall, like the shadow of a wounded bird whose head was drooping.

"Here I am."

Skinny did not reply. She could see he was there.

"I like being pampered," he said. "Future German children will be born as giants."

She did not know why he said that.

"I don't like ducking," he said. It was obvious that he had come in from the cold.

He straightened up. He had come in as if expecting a servant to follow him. He had walked across the yard and down the corridor with his hands in his pockets, but now he took them out and let them hang down. He still wore the air of superiority he had displayed when the guards helped him with the tarpaulins for his car.

He was her second officer.

"Stefan Sarazin, SS Obersturmführer, Einsatzkommando der Einsatzgruppen," he said by way of greeting.

He enjoyed the fact that the first six letters of his rank, *Oberst* or colonel, suggested what he might still rise to during the war.

Was he waiting for her to introduce herself by her name or only her nickname? For a week now, since Captain Hentschel's visit, she had been called Lovely Green Eyes. He glanced about the cubicle, noting what she had done to it. She was young and healthy, just as he had been told, but it was hard to judge her experience. Perhaps she did not have a lot, he would see. He decided to put his cards on the table. He had not been able to manage a lot with her ginger colleague on his last visit, nor with the whore with the high ankles who reminded him of a foal. It didn't occur to him that the fault might be his. The rôles were clearly defined. One knew from the start who the prostitute was and who the client. The military character of the brothel made no difference; on the contrary. And it was not a matter of merit in serving the troops, the army, the Einsatzgruppen; it was a privilege. In the meantime, a lot had happened on other battlefields. He could not guarantee that the girls wouldn't all be shot in the end. He could tell himself that he wouldn't only have sex here, but have it with a living corpse. Ginger had disgusted him by talking of her vaginal blood. Later he had, out of that disgust, written a poem about it.

He knew very well in what aspect he was sensitive and why he could not overcome his revulsion at certain things. He felt driven by an impulse not to beat about the bush, but to come straight to the point.

"I've never slept with a Jewess," he said. "I'm fussy. I don't mate with dark-haired, dark-eyed or inferior women, or with those who are shorter than myself. I'd appreciate it if you could tell me that you have never slept with a circumcised one either."

His smile did nothing to lessen the tight feeling that enclosed her like a hoop around a beer barrel.

"You aren't going to answer me?" Obersturmführer Sarazin asked.

She had got used to the way the soldiers eyed her all over. She knew the path of their gaze, the way it mapped out what more or less made up a girl, at least from the outside – hair, chin, eyes, breasts, hips, buttocks, legs and crotch – assessing her in a hundredth of a second usually, though sometimes lingeringly. She had grown used to the fact that the men regarded her as a piece of colourfully decked-out flesh. Sometimes, when their glance intensified or became detached, she saw a moment of recognition in their eyes, as though she had reminded them of someone, or they had failed to find in her something that they were looking for. Then she would know that they were comparing her to someone in their memory, or in their imagination, and she had no wish to know who it was – a wife, a mistress, a sister, a whore. At times she felt that a soldier's glance was casting a shadow, or a different light, over the cubicle. On one occasion, with a corporal engineer, it occurred to her – with a terrible shock – that he might recognize her because he came from Prague and might have seen her in the rolling stock workshop or by the Harmanze lake. She was glad that he was a corporal in the Wehrmacht and not in the SS. It had only been a moment, but it produced a greater fear than she had so far experienced. Under the gaze of the Obersturmführer she felt like a false coin that he was examining before tossing it so that it would flip over and reveal its reverse.

To the Obersturmführer she was a new girl. A novice, as he had said to the Madam.

"No," Skinny answered absentmindedly. "Yes," she corrected herself, "I am answering you."

"Wake up!"

"I'm here . . ."

"You can sleep when I'm gone. There's a time for everything."

"Jawohl."

"Suppose I made you swear?"

"Swear what?"

"On your race."

"I'd swear."

"I'm glad to hear it," the Obersturmführer said.

She must pull herself together.

Last time he had played games like this with Ginger and with that tall prostitute. She had got on his nerves with her height, her big breasts and her moistness. But he had liked her nose – a large, straight Aryan nose. Should not prostitutes also be informed of the importance of race? Of what it meant? What far-reaching consequences it implied, here and now, for everybody? He swept his eyes over her as he spoke. He'd see. Soldiers like him should be offered if not princesses then at least virgins. Or perhaps not? Virgins with fairly extensive experience. Or girls with a quick grasp, quick learners, those who anticipated what was expected of them. There was more to it than just simply lying down and opening their legs. Better still, girls who understood even the unusual.

He had already summed the girl up. He was startled by her childish appearance. He wondered what she knew about him. He looked around the cubicle, hoping there wouldn't be rats here. In the corner he caught sight of a cobweb, but the spider and the flies had gone. He realized that he was cold, and glanced at the stove. She had built a good fire. A good mark. He wanted her to understand that she was not irreplaceable, even before he convinced himself of it. He warmed himself by the fire, ignoring her. He scowled at his watch, as if planning his time. He tried to visualize what was happening at his unit, who was doing what while he was here.

The fact that he was an officer made her nervous. Not that she would have preferred NCOs, but his being an officer increased her fear. She did not worry too much about having to lie; but she was afraid of committing the sin of carelessness or of anything happening which was beyond her control. At least she could see that he was pleased with the fire in the stove.

He listened to the howling of the gale, separating it from the roar in the stove. The elbow of the flue radiated heat. He liked its red-hot colour. At moments it would turn white, blue and red again, sometimes all colours together. I have a taste for unusual beauty, he told himself. I am able to find it in the most unexpected places. This prostitute was probably still in training. Probably not a mistress of her profession yet, but he could handle that. Did not everybody have to learn all the time?

"I hope you're not like my former neighbour's cat," he said when he had warmed himself. "The more friendly I was to her the more she withdrew."

"I'm not withdrawing," she said.

He was accustomed to people being afraid of him. Nothing to be said against that. It was better to count on the fear of the people one was dealing with than to rely on their meekness or humility, which might, at an unguarded moment, undergo an incredible change. He had seen what became of escaped prisoners in the forests and among the rocks – frenzy was too weak a word. It had happened countless times. He wished to prove to himself that he was strong not only in being part of the group, but also by himself. Sometimes he thought of himself as one of the wolves in the wasteland. Be oneself towards oneself and also towards others, he thought.

"A girl like you is like a heavenly body," he joked. "They only show one side. I'd like to understand you. But first you have to understand me."

He was treating her like a servant. And she felt like one. She would imagine that she was tidying up a room. She would accept that all employers had their whims. That brought her closer to the Obersturmführer without her realizing it. She could not know that he had just judged her young, healthy and generally fit – maybe not the best material, but in the circumstances and considering where they were, better than nothing.

"As a rule I get on well with a girl like you."

He was filled with a sense of superiority. He knew there was no harm in working on a girl, especially one as young as this one, with words first, before it came to hands and body. He could afford to take his time. He blamed himself for not feeling at ease with himself, as he would have liked. Why was he sweating? Was he too close to the stove?

With no-one else had she been so aware, right from the first moment, that she was Jewish. She wrapped herself in caution. She could not compare him to Captain Hentschel. She would have to remain careful.

He searched her face. Surely she must realize that his eyes were boring into her? Perhaps she was telling the truth. She was not that old and all Jews, with rare exceptions, had vanished from the region. Was she blushing? Perhaps he was imagining it. He was convinced that Jews did not blush. It was a matter of the quality of blood. He could not recall now where he had heard that. To be on the safe side, crossing with dark-haired, dark-eyed partners would be forbidden in his family. That would be his legacy to future generations. Nor anyone below army regulation height, or with doubtful background. That was if he ever had a real family. So far his immediate and wider family were the Einsatzgruppen. Rankers, NCOs and commanders, including the supreme Führer. The Nazi Party. The élite, the only ones with whom he felt an equal among equals.

He regarded it as a lucky accident that the initials of his name were S.S. Stefan Sarazin. He always introduced himself as "Stefan Sarazin, Obersturmführer in the Waffen-SS," stressing the sibilants.

"You were blushing?" he asked.

"I'm not blushing."

"I should hope not. Do you know how to recognize a non-Aryan reliably? He hasn't enough blood in him to blush."

She was unable to guess the colour of his eyes. They were like the openings of two empty beer bottles. Poorly-blown glass. He reminded her of a girl she'd known with cataracts.

"The Lebensborn organization used this place," he said. "I was invited here for a week. Together with my colleagues I impregnated my quota. We were a dozen chosen men under 25 from the Waffen-SS, without an iota of Jewish blood. The master race. Vigorous individuals who could trace their family tree as far back as 1775. Thirty-year-old German women who haven't found a husband are reporting for the Lebensborn. The state takes care of them and ensures that they become mothers."

He was drawing her into his world. She tried to guess his age. Not more than 25 or 26. She was afraid he might show her photographs. He was shorter than she was. It was a good thing that Captain Hentschel had not come again. Still, the previous night she had slept in his green pullover.

He fixed his milky eyes on her mouth, then they slid down, but not all the way to her boots.

"You have small breasts. We'll see more when you take your clothes off."

"I don't know. Yes, I have small breasts."

"And a small bottom."

"I can't see my back."

"Is everything you have small?"

"I don't know."

"You should know. You're new, aren't you?"

"I've been here a fortnight."

"Do you get enough to eat?"

"Yes," she said quickly.

"You're keen on food?"

"No, I'm not."

"Perhaps you should be," said the Obersturmführer.

"I only give the best, the very best, if you know what I mean."

She didn't say that she did not know.

"I'd know if you lied to me." He gave a brief smile. "We'll see."

She was afraid of the ambiguity of his remarks. She looked for something in what he left unsaid.

He decided to play with her a while longer. She had a nice little oblong face. He felt the heat coming from the flue and from the cast-iron barrel of the stove. A few red-hot cinders were dropping through the grate. He found it agreeable to stand in the warmth and look out of the window at the blizzard. So far it had not abated. He hoped it wouldn't bury his car. He looked again at his prostitute. Her colour had come back, but the general impression was still one of pallor. Was she perspiring too, or did it merely seem so to him? And was she half-closing her eyes, perhaps looking at his pistol?

"Are you afraid to die?"

"Why?"

"Are you questioning me or am I questioning you?"

"I don't know," she said.

"In a while I shall know more about you than you do yourself."

He didn't know yet if he would reward or punish her. Was she undernourished? Compared to her, his own features were bursting with health. He thought of Pomeranian Jewesses. They were dark-haired, though some of them had ginger hair like the girl before him. The Einsatzgruppen had used them as targets for their machine gunners.

"You might think I'm obsessed with the Jews," he said. "But it's handed down from generation to generation. It gives me self-confidence, as if I were drinking life-giving water."

After a pause the Obersturmführer said, "We don't have anything to regret, wasn't it the Jews who claimed that a good lawyer was better than the truth?"

"I don't know," she said.

She tried to answer politely, with humility rather than rebellious-ness.

"How come you speak German?"

"I learnt it."

"I'm glad to hear it. Did they tell you I liked redheads?"

"No."

"Girls with long legs and your complexion? What did they tell you about me?"

"Only that you would come."

His eyes seemed to her like a well without water. Or a puddle which had dried up after a shower. She thought of the muddy bank of the Harmanze lake. She resisted speculating who the Oberführer was; it was enough to know what he had come for. What he would want. There was brutality in his eyes, and a moment later also sickness and fastidiousness. At once determination and confusion, a kind of uncertainty which was confirmed by his words. Why had he asked her if she was afraid of death?

He had chosen Skinny because Ginger had failed him the last time. *So ein Luder!* She had been given a flogging. For a third complaint she would go to Festung Breslau. He had stayed to watch the Madam flog her. After the third lash on her bare bottom she had kissed his boots. And Long-Legs was too big for him. How much did a girl like that eat? And how much, it occurred to him, did a thin girl like this one, get into her stomach? Maybe she had threadworm, like he had had as a child. It amazed him, the number of superfluous and useless stomachs Germany was nourishing. Weren't the simple soldiers, the workers and the peasants and the teachers, right when they said that he who does not work, neither shall he eat? The Nazis had widened this to include the unhealthy, the incurably sick, the feeble-minded, the ailing. One had to have the courage to cut into one's own flesh. Cut out all tumours, large and small. Perhaps he should tell this little whore how they brought up their children in ancient Sparta, how the king erected a small rail over an abyss and if an infant lost its grip and fell into the abyss he would congratulate its mother for having spared Sparta a weakling. The Nazis would transform Germany into a modern Sparta.

"I distinguish between a well-intentioned inferior race and an ill-intentioned superior race, which includes also Germans. You're not one of them."

"No," Skinny said.

"Not even partially? Some of your tribe got as far as Berlin."

She heard familiar voices from the neighbouring cubicles. The girls were hard at work. Sometimes a soldier cried out, sometimes a girl. They were ridiculous, animal sounds, and she tried to shut them out. Maria-from-Poznan had learnt to fake a whole scale of cries and moans, from ecstasy to gradually abating satisfaction. Some soldiers gave free rein to what they could not permit themselves elsewhere, either because they weren't allowed to or because they felt ashamed. Sometimes the soldier and girl would laugh together. Skinny could imagine what seemed laughable. In addition to the brutal and wild element, something childlike would come back to them – something that was receding from her.

She would not have to be with anyone else today. The Frog had let them sleep last night from 8.30 p.m. to almost 4 a.m. They had been cold, wearing their pullovers under their blankets and coats. Madam Kulikowa kept reminding them that they were a lot better off at No. 232 Ost than in prison, where she had been prior to a concentration camp. The prostitute with whom she had shared a cell had given birth to a boy. They had beheaded the woman for high treason against the Greater German Reich.

"You haven't told me much about yourself," he said.

"I don't know what you want to hear."

She was being careful, but in a different way to when she had been with Captain Hentschel. Since then she had six days' more experience. Yesterday one of her soldiers had wanted her to sing. They all wanted something she couldn't provide. The soldier had wanted her to dance for him. He wanted to feel as if he was in Morocco, he'd said.

The Obersturmführer stamped his hobnailed boots to shake off the remnants of the snow. He took off his cap. For the first time she saw the scar on his forehead, just under his hairline.

Stefan Sarazin had joined the Hitlerjugend at sixteen. His first service had been with the Verfügungsgruppen from which later developed the special units for the extermination of the racially inferior east of the Oder. They included the Sipo and the SD, the Sicherheitspolizei and the Sicherheitsdienst, the security service of the SS. Now he was serving in a disciplinary unit made up of six Waffen-SS members under punishment. It was their chance to atone for their offences and to win new spurs.

After the Anschluss he had been present when the Verfügungs-gruppen destroyed the synagogue Hitler hated, just as he hated all Vienna, that nest of Jewish, Czech, Hungarian and Balkan rabble. Before they set fire to the synagogue they attached three bundles of hand grenades under the huge olive-wood crown, as large as a horse's behind. They celebrated with a march, complete with music – fifes, flutes, drums and bells. The pavement had echoed with their steps and every third man in each rank carried a burning torch.

"Have you had a good sleep?"

"I slept."

"Good. I gave orders that they should let you rest. You have me to thank for that."

"Thank you."

"That's right. *Richtig*. Very good."

This whore was a little ashamed. Shame and fear were all right in a prostitute. It was merely a case of mixing the correct dose, as the old German alchemists knew! He stood with his back to the stove and gave her a lecture, to make sure she knew in advance that it was an honour to be with him. His Einsatzgruppen were uprooting the world where people were living in luxury at the expense of others. She could be sure of one thing: the key word was Endlösung, the Final Solution. It was a breathtaking concept. The end. Ruination. After this end nothing would follow. He had more pity for a worm than for a child that would grow into a Jewish vampire.

"The end is the beginning and the beginning is the end. It's like a poem. Or like a mathematical equation. The interplay of numbers. Do you understand?"

Should she say she understood? She didn't understand at all.

"With a few exceptions there won't be any circumcised in this neighbourhood any longer." He could take the credit for that.

"I know that," she said.

"They're breathing their last. We no longer send them to camps. Their Endlösung is my Jagdkommando. Even if only every sixth man kills one Jew, we'll exterminate them. If you calculate how many there are of us and how many of them, you get the result. The numbers speak for us. We rely on ourselves, and we don't betray collaborators. We are the guarantee of success. The fewer there are of them, the more marked are the traces they leave behind. The locals are protecting them. The fact that Jewish women can't read doesn't mean they're not cunning. There's treason all round. Nothing is innocent. A well. A room. A cellar. We've searched Russia, the Ukraine and Poland with a fine-tooth comb, like the lice-infested head of a giant. Their world has collapsed like a house of cards. The more they deny themselves the more they unveil themselves. I couldn't tell you why. It's in their eyes. Inferiority against our superiority. Fear against our courage. It's in their features, in their eyes."

Why was he saying all this to her? What did he want her to say to him?

"The more you deny yourself the more you reveal yourself," the Obersturmführer continued. "You speak just by moving your eyes."

"That other redhead you have here does not give what she should give. That's why she got a flogging. I broke her in. For someone else, not for myself. I hardly ever have a woman twice. For that she'd have to be quite something. But I don't rule out the possibility of exceptions."

Skinny repeated what she had told herself on the very first day. You've become a whore. So do what whores do. In return you'll take what you need. Just do what Estelle kept telling her to do: make it possible for them to get what they wanted.

She reflected on what he was right about. People were not born equal, they were born different, but to her this did not suggest lice, although she could see herself as a louse. Some people were born with hard-working hands, others with a hard-working head. Some, like her uncles, with both. Some were good by nature, others less so – like her uncles again. She knew of distinctions of which The Frog would not want to hear. Of the line between justice and injustice. If people were born equal she would not be here with Obersturmführer Stefan Sarazin, or earlier with Captain Hentschel, or with so many soldiers that she was ashamed to count them. It was enough that they were counted and recorded by Madam Kulikowa.

"I do what I have to do. That is my unshakeable principle," he said.

It was obvious that he enjoyed the sound of his own voice. He enjoyed the warmth, his words – she had not encountered this before. His world was incomprehensible to her, a place that she could never share, nor would wish to. He had seen things she had not seen.

The puddle of melted snow around his jackboots had spread as far as the fuel box. She would have to mop it up. Should she ask him to move? She didn't want to interrupt him.

"The east is almost cleansed of Jews. Not brutality at all. Absolute necessity."

He was dreaming. He bent his head, proud at his greatness.

"The Jews are like cats, they have nine lives. Either we crush them or they'll crush us. A pity we aren't allowed to keep diaries, in which a person could feel free to reveal more than he would otherwise. In summer we hang them in cherry orchards. In winter we let them freeze to death. Of course they scream. Especially the women when it is the turn of their brats." He laughed.

"They hang from the trees like dirty stockings."

They could hear a train. The Ostbahn, the eastern railway. He knew all the main stations and railheads. She'd not believe how many camps he'd served in, how many he'd visited in an official capacity. He was warmed through now. He started whistling. Sweat appeared on his rather low forehead, or was it melted snow? His scar glistened on his forehead. It reminded her of what a corporal had told her about the Maginot Line winding along the frontier until the Germans passed through it like a knife through butter.

"Hatred changes to joy in me, to a special kind of joy, perhaps to Schadenfreude," he said. "I couldn't live without hatred any more. To deprive me of hatred would be like depriving me of oxygen. Like pulling the ground away under my feet. Like walking on one leg, like fighting with one arm. While I hate, I am. While you hate, you are."

He wanted to know what she hated.

"I don't know," she said. "I'm afraid to hate."

"You're making a mistake. Once you've learned to hate you'll realize what you've missed."

"Perhaps," she said, avoiding his gaze.

"You should look at me."

He waited for her to ask why, so he could tell her she would find out, but she didn't ask. People who could not hate were like a rag for wiping the floor.

The Obersturmführer unbuckled his belt, took his pistol from its holster. He stepped over to the window. He had quite a job opening it; it was frozen to the frame by snow and ice. No-one had opened it since the autumn. The storm swept into the cubicle. The Obersturmführer drew the chair up to the window and climbed onto it. He looked out into the twilight. In the blizzard, as though behind a curtain of mist, wolves were moving. He released the safety catch, aimed and waited before firing.

"Not too bad for the first shot!" He was pleased.

"Last time I got a she-wolf. I stepped on her lower jaw and tore her mouth apart till she bled to death. You should know what that means."

He realized that she wouldn't understand if she hadn't been taught the Teutonic legends.

"Victory goes to the strongest, the fastest, the best prepared," he said.

He took a deep breath and continued.

"The best thing you can do is what you do just like that, without reason. That's what amazes those we overcome. They don't under-stand."

Two minutes later he fired again. Sharp, frosty air filled the cubicle. She was standing by the bed, in the draught, feeling cold. She wasn't sure whether she dared put on her coat. He emptied his magazine.

"I shouldn't have done that – fired my last round. A soldier should save that for himself. What do you think?"

She remained silent. Only later did she understand why he'd said that. He was not as simple as he pretended, even though some of his sentences were assembled as though from a child's building set.

Just as laboriously as he had opened it, he shut the window. She was glad the glass didn't fall out.

"Practice kills boredom," he said. "It passes the time."

He saw that she was cold. Closing the window did not immediately warm up the room. "Put some more fuel on the fire," he commanded.

He carried the chair to the stove and returned his pistol to its holster.

"I'm a good shot," he said.

She went to stoke up the fire, relieved to get to the stove. She put three shovelfuls of coal on top of a birch log. It was damp. She warned the Obersturmführer that it would smoke for a while. She shut the stove door, taking care not to soil her new clothes, then waited for his instructions.

"They ought to supply you with anthracite," he said.

"I take the coal from the pile by the kitchen." ·

"It's Scheisse from the mines further up the river. I hope they ship the better coal to the Reich."

"It doesn't draw well."

"You should have put it on earlier."

"I put on two shovelfuls."

She picked up a rag and mopped up the little puddles that had formed when the Obersturmführer opened the window. It was almost dark. Sarazin hung his belt over the back of the chair. She washed her hands and lit a candle. The candlelight gave the evening outside a purple hue.

Again she saw the scar on his head. It went from the roots of his hair along his forehead and circled his skull.

"I prefer wolves to people. At night they pursue the moon. It's a world we don't know yet."

He spoke in a different tone from when he spoke of the Jews. Snow and blood, he told her, were pure colours for him. They marked the purity of the territory, the purity of the thought that inspired him: Germany from the Rhine to the Urals; with its allies from the Bay of Biscay to Latvia. Conquered territory on which – one day – vast numbers of Germans would live. A Nazi structure similar to a system of dykes. Rivers flowing into a German sea. A wonderful ocean not yet on any map. Compensation for centuries, or millennia, when they'd had to crowd into territory smaller than their worth. Just as Germany was once almost lost on the map of Europe, so the subjugated countries would now be lost within Greater Germany.

"No more rotten wooden synagogues, which burnt more quickly than showy Viennese stoves of marble and granite with false oriental decorations, as if they stood in Jerusalem. If the circumcised were given a free hand, there'd be Jerusalem everywhere. Do you hear me?"

"I hear you."

"You aren't saying either yes or no."

"I'm saying yes."

"Jawohl. That's what I like to hear. Schon gut . . ."

He thought of what he'd had to give up in order to purify himself, to liberate himself.

She was looking at his holster. How many bullets had he left? Surely he would have more than one magazine and changing magazines was easy? Perhaps he wouldn't wish to shoot again and make her freeze in the cold draught.

"Stoke up as much as you can," he said.

"As you wish."

She piled more coal on and raked the grate from underneath. The heat breathed into her face, her hands, her chest. Whatever she did, the damp brown coal would burn slowly. Again the place would be full of smoke.

"It's smoking," she said cautiously.

She could not be sure of the meaning of anything he said.

"You like mucking about on the floor?"

"I don't know what you mean."

"Isn't it more comfortable in bed?"

She didn't know what to say.

No-one had come yet without wanting what they all wanted. It might be the last thing they ever enjoyed. She shouldn't expect more from his babbling than simply a preface to the usual. She did not wish to think of her back, her belly, her joints. She would have to rely on being young and in good health. Nor was there any point in tormenting herself with thoughts of sin. Whenever she undressed she persuaded herself that she was slipping on a protective ring. Or that she was hanging on to a weir or to rocks in a river in flood.

She felt beads of perspiration on her forehead, and wiped them off. She concentrated on the stove, on the coal box and what was left of the firewood. She stretched her fingers which had been gripping the coal shovel. The mist in the Obersturmführer's eyes was fixed on her. She knew what this meant.

There was silence in the cubicle. Only the wick with the little flame spluttered.

"I'll mix you with a drop of my blood," he said.

On his uniform there were ribbons – the Iron Cross, the Blutorden, the Nazi Party's Blood Order. From the pocket of his tunic with its silver buttons he produced some cords.

"Don't be afraid, I'm not going to hang you. Are you afraid?"

"No," she lied.

"If you had a sister I'd need both of you."

"I haven't got one," she said.

He lay down, still dressed. He spread his arms and legs. Was he going to order her to undress him?

"We'll have a little excursion. Somewhere you haven't been before," he said.

He ordered her to tie him to the head and foot posts of the bed; by his wrists and ankles, as tight as she could, each hand and leg separately. The ropes had buckles. He hoped she would express no astonishment.

"We'll make time stand still," he added.

That was it, round the wrist. First one ankle and then the other. Pull hard. Or wasn't she strong enough? That might be bad for her. He wouldn't like to have to complain. Three floggings meant the wall or the "Hotel for Foreigners" at Festung Breslau. He did not wish her to protest or to have to command her. On the other hand, she would not be sorry if she did what he wanted. His voice was hoarse. Surely she realized that not all men were alike?

"Haven't you tied anyone up before? Well, you can learn from me how it's done. I'm glad I am the first. You too will be the first – after a long time."

She was confused by the way he was acting. He was speaking in a jerky sort of way, no longer so haughty. Creases had appeared on his forehead, running across his scar. Why did he want this from her? There was impatience in him, almost anxiety that she might not do what he wanted of her properly. There was no longer the aggression or the self-assurance there had been when he had spoken of the inferior race or when he was shooting at the wolves. He had changed as though at the waving of a wand.

She tied him up the way he wanted. She avoided his eyes, concentrating on what she had to do and at the same time trying to detach herself from it.

"Freedom," whispered the bound Obersturmführer. "Do you hear me?"

In the corners of his mouth there was a trace of arousal as well as anxiety or uncertainty. Tied up on the bed, the Obersturmführer looked like a captured animal. Or like someone who had voluntarily surrendered. She had never seen an SS man like this.

"I appreciate military qualities in a girl," he whispered. "Keenness and obedience."

He cleared his throat and swallowed. He was seeking a more comfortable position. The bed shook. He didn't seek love or proximity as others did. He didn't admit to himself that this was so because he himself was incapable of such things. He refused to regret what he was missing. What were prostitutes for? This, too, was free and he did not have to share any feelings of exclusion or inferiority. Here, no-one had vanquished him.

She was waiting for his next instruction. He told her to undress.

"I know how to tie and untie eight different kinds of knots. A friend from the navy taught me. He'd been three times in the brig on the cruiser Tirpitz. He'd slept with negresses"

She folded her dress and underwear and placed them on the chair by the stove. She took off her boots and pulled off her socks and stockings. It was warm in the cubicle now, but the floor was cold. For a moment she thought of Long-Legs who complained of cold feet.

Skinny felt alarm bells ringing inside her. She saw what at first glance was invisible. All the colours and shapes, all the outlines of mouths, jaws, noses, lips and irises suddenly turned into mist. She could not afford to make a mistake. She would always be on the losing side. She was very different from Ginger, who would get closer to men the worse they treated her. She couldn't show gratitude as Maria-from-Poznan did to someone who treated her body as a butcher's dog would a bone.

"You're too far away. Come here, to the bed." She obeyed.

"Unbutton me."

She knew that what he wanted her to unbutton was not his shirt. She half-closed her eyes, and tried to stop her hands from trembling. He mustn't sense how unwilling she was. It took her longer than it should have done. She heard his squeaky voice. His head was tilted back and it was hard to understand him. Maybe Madam Kulikowa was right – there were worse things. She let her hands do what they had to. He couldn't see, he only gave her instructions as if he were telling her how to lead a horse to stables or lean a bicycle against a wall, or thread a needle. Then his voice grew weak.

"Are you looking at me?"

She raised her eyelids. "I see you," she said.

"You're no good."

She felt like an actress who had forgotten her lines or who had not studied her part.

He was irritated. Again she had witnessed something that should not be seen. She could feel the anger rising in him. She would have preferred the candle to go out, even though the Obersturmführer could not see it. He was gazing at the shadowy ceiling behind his head, at the beams and the wall. She did not know what to do. She was bending over him like a nurse over a strapped-down patient. She thought of Stefan Sarazin's injury, of his name, of the origin and the consequences of his scar. She had no idea that he was getting aroused by the memory of how, long ago, he had asked his mother to feel the hardness of his penis. It had taken a while before she did. In her caring and good-natured way, she had expressed admiration, but then made him feel foolish by reminding him "My boy, I've seen you like that a thousand times." He hated the bitter-sweet tone his mother had used.

Skinny noted his ecstasy, in which she played a lesser role than she realized. She closed her eyes.

"Yes," he whispered as he taught her how to touch him. He sounded sick, pitiful, helpless and angry.

"Yes, Yes."

The small flame of the candle was now elongated, but flickered continually.

"You've got stupid hands," the Obersturmführer croaked. "Utterly useless."

His eyes misted over. Outside an engine was revving up. One of the buses waiting until its complement of 52 men was ready.

"Am I as white as ash wood?"

The Obersturmführer's face turned rigid with a spasm. He began to convulse. The bed beneath him creaked and groaned, the straw emitted whistling sounds which accompanied his panting. Slowly he became quiet.

Outside a column of trucks was leaving. There was a lot of tooting. A detachment of SS volunteers were arriving. They exchanged Waffen-SS horn signals. Hungarians were singing an incomprehensible song. It seemed to her that she caught some Slovak words, but she wasn't sure.

He freed himself from his bonds, even though she had tied him up so carefully. This small victory restored a little of his self-assurance.

"I'd thought you'd be more skilful," he said. His face seemed to have shrunk a little after his struggle with the ropes. "Perhaps I am somewhat unusual. But that's what I want. No-one is ever bored with me."

What else did he expect, apart from what she had already done?

"If you want to be an actress," he said, "you must act in the play that I am writing for you."

She did not know how to answer. She was waiting to see what the Obersturmführer would say next.

"I can tell you're new here," he said. "To judge by your skill I'd say this is your first day. Perhaps the second."

"You know how long I've been here."

She was used to that kind of complaint. They didn't want her to be passive, but she couldn't imagine an alternative. She wished she could be dulled to an extent that would relieve her of thought but not the capacity to do what she had to do in order to survive.

When he told Skinny to lie down on the bed with him "like a married couple" it didn't seem ridiculous. It was better than if he had beaten her.

She wished she were more mature than she was. She could pretend to be, just as she was pretending that she had been born into an Aryan family. She was surprised at how quickly she had adjusted; she didn't have to feel that she was lagging behind. She couldn't afford to. In some respects she had already caught up with Ginger, Maria-from-Poznan, and Estelle. Maybe even with Long-Legs.

Skinny tried to take her mind off the Obersturmführer's body and her own. She thought of Maria-from-Poznan, who rolled her eyes when she heard something that she didn't like. According to Ginger, Maria rolled her eyes about like a merry-go-round, so that one of her soldiers mistakenly took it for an expression of ecstasy.

"Better to be blown up by a shell than sleep with a Jewess," he said. "We can proclaim with pride that the Einsatzgruppen are the war. It is through us that Germany will become great, just as without us it would go under. Let me tell you, I would kill my own father and mother if they stood against the Reich. Or a brother, if I had one."

Chapter Eight

Obersturmführer Sarazin vividly remembered a punitive action in Pomerania, an action he was ordered to carry out by Karl Jäger, the commander of the Einsatzgruppen battalion. It took the rounded-up men, women, children and old people well into the night before they had dug a pit big enough for 5,000 people in the clearing of a pine forest. The soldiers ordered them to strip naked. There was a fresh breeze, a full moon and a cloudless sky. He would never forget that night, the scent of resin, the silence of those they shot one by one or in groups. He remembered clearly the way they fell or slipped into the pits, leaning forwards or kneeling, as the firing squad ordered them to make sure they dropped inside.

They advanced from the edge of the forest, one line after another, in groups of about 50 or 100. The firing stopped at about 20 minutes after midnight. The soldiers were anxious not to let those merely wounded at the bottom of the pit scramble out through the mass of cooling corpses and escape under cover of darkness. To make quite sure all were dead Sarazin gave orders for salvoes to be fired into the pit. He set his men an example by emptying several magazines himself. Then there was no need to post more than two men as sentries on each side of the mass grave.

He ordered tents to be pitched, so they wouldn't have to sleep in the open, and gave instructions for reveille at 4 a.m. He arranged for the clothes of the dead to be packed in crates. He had a special tent put up for the representatives of the local administration, including the mayor, to ensure that the men, both volunteers and those hired as casual labourers, could begin to fill in the pit with clay at first light.

He was not afraid for himself. Only once had he had three sentries guard a spot where he spent the night – in an abandoned quarry – because he could not be absolutely certain that some Polish or Jewish bandits were not still hiding out nearby. He valued his life higher than the lives of bandits, and hadn't blinked an eyelid when the Gestapo chief at Auschwitz-Birkenau informed him of the number of transports they processed there every day and night, or of the burning of the bodies in their own fat, even though that required using precious petrol.

He was quite used to the sight of a yellowish mass of corpses interlaced with each other like plaited rolls or Christmas loaves, piled from one side of the pit to the other, a mass of arms, legs, stretched necks and lifeless heads. Before falling asleep he relived the operation, the shots ringing in his ears – volleys, single shots – the orchestra of machine guns. But what he saw the following morning was beyond anything he had seen before – and he had seen plenty. It was an image worthy of a great poet, horrible and beautiful, because exceptional. He knew that this was something hardly anyone, and certainly none of his friends in the hinterland, had ever seen. For a moment it took his breath away. The dead, piled together in wild confusion so tightly there was practically no space between them, all of them the colour of a yellowish candle, had begun to move. None of the bodies remained still. They moved in waves, they shifted like branches rocked by the wind. He knew that they were not alive. He had already, by the light of a flashlight in his tent, begun to write his report.

They were dead. Even if some escaped the shootings they would have died of their wounds down in the pit. He had an accurate record of the number of rounds fired. His corporal had completed the account of ammunition, fuel, provisions and the number of trucks employed. The dead mass was moving its arms, legs and heads, hair was being ruffled, their lips and eyebrows were twitching and their eyes were being opened. Not even their genitals remained at rest, male or female, behind their pubic hair. What was going on? He rubbed his eyes. Huge numbers of rats were scurrying among the bodies, gnawing at the dead, creeping into their mouths and other orifices, into their armpits and between their legs. There were probably more rats than bodies. He felt sick. He wanted to vomit. He covered his mouth with his hand and felt a spasm in his guts. Blood rose to his head and into the scar round his scalp. He leant against a tree, but after a few seconds pulled himself together.

The sentries and the locals saw the same sight, but they had probably seen it before and didn't seem surprised. The workers picked up their shovels and began to fill the pits. They were paid by the hour and already had forms in their pockets for the next job, also filling pits.

One day he would write a poem about it, a composition such as the generations before him had not encountered.

He could not resist the temptation of describing the event to this young whore.

"It appeared before me out of the night," he said, "with the first rays of light, and it was disgusting; not only disgusting, it was revolting; it would have made you sick, but it was magnificent at the same time, wonderful, different from anything I had ever experienced. That night I stepped into a new era. I crossed a border which every one of us has inside us. It was the brutality and the inevitability of nature, for which nothing is extraordinary. The dead and the army of rats. I can't forget it. If ever I write a great poem about anything – one that endures, after me, after us – as the greatest thing witnessed by my generation, then it will be about those bullet-ridden corpses looking like slaughtered pigs, and among them the nation of rats. The living feeding on the dead, the eternal cycle of life upon which we imprint our will; what for us began the war which will never end." He paused.

"Those rats signified life. They brought movement to the dead, the way waves rise out of the ocean, the way grain crops wave in the breeze, the way clouds are driven who knows whither by a strong wind. I ordered my men to fire into the pit again, so that nothing, literally nothing, should move, but it didn't seem to frighten the rats. They appeared to be at home among the heaps of corpses, from the bottom up and from the top down. Now, whenever I see a rat, and I saw some here in the corridor and beyond the gates in the snow, I feel as if I had failed to fulfil my intention of burying in the pits anything that still moved."

Skinny remained absolutely still.

"A stench rose up from the corpses. No-one who hasn't experienced this smell can know what it's like. The wind brought the resin fragrance of pinewood and deep within the forest was a silence that suggested eternity. Some things one doesn't forget," he said.

She would never forget his words.

"Are you afraid of me?" the Obersturmführer asked.

"Perhaps."

"Would you kindly decide on yes or no?"

She did not know which way to move.

The Obersturmführer pinned her legs down so that she could not move. The ceiling seemed to her to have dropped lower. You are a whore, so act like a whore, an inner voice told her. Do what he wants. But what did he want? She would understand if he struck her or shot her. Why else had he picked up his pistol?

Her legs turned numb like blocks of wood. The Obersturmführer forced himself, now flaccid, between them, colliding with her protruding pelvic bones. She changed into clay kneaded by strange hands. She tried to receive the Obersturmführer, but he was incapable of achieving what he wanted. The world shrank for her to a pain in her belly, to smells and sounds, to the impacts of abdomen against abdomen. He was holding down both her shoulders with his left arm; in his right hand he still held his pistol. He had more strength in one arm than she had in her whole body. He must surely feel, if he was capable of feeling anything, that giving him what he wanted was not a matter of good will. She was gasping for air. In her mind she was withdrawing from him.

"I'm doing what you want," she said.

"That's what you think. To you it's all *scheissegal*. Are you or are you not a whore? You're useless."

She no longer wanted to consider whether wanting to live was wrong. Nor why she was born. If somebody had asked her, she could now say what a human being was, and what one was not. What it meant to have been born a girl. A spiritual poverty seemed to envelop her like a foul smell. Within her she heard an echo that she could not silence. She did not want to make the excuse, not even in her mind, that her father's God had sent her here when she had been due to die in Auschwitz-Birkenau. She knew she had volunteered.

The Obersturmführer would not let her move so she might lie more comfortably.

"Stomach ache?" he asked.

"No," she lied.

"Why are you gripping your belly then?"

"I only put my hand there. I've nowhere else to put it."

"Do I have to tell you where you should put your hand?"

The question remained hanging in the air. She did not say no, but her lips formed the word.

"Lie closer to me."

"How close?"

"Do I have to tell you?"

She felt as if she was on fire. She thought of Dr Krueger's human guinea pigs, of his daughter Hannelore who had been serving in Alsace. The day the doctor got his promotion he received two telegrams. The first informed him that Hannelore's legs had been torn off by a mine. The second was a congratulatory telegram from the head of the Kraft durch Freude organization.

Oil brought her some relief from his desperate efforts. Above her was the breathless depraved 26-year-old face scarred by sleepless nights, punitive actions, a hundred terrors associated with his massacres. And by the injuries he had sustained, wounds like the one to his head.

He wanted to know how she had come by the frostbite marks on her face.

She had to whisper. Her mouth was close to his.

"On the way from the train, when I was under escort."

"Have you got good boots?"

"I have boots."

"You should have taken better ones from somebody."

"I didn't take mine from anybody."

"I doubt that you're in the right place here."

"This is my place."

"Aren't you a whore?"

"I am a whore," she said.

"No-one goes to bed in the evening as a virgin and wakes up as a whore. Better not ask why I slapped Ginger's face to make her remember me."

He put the pistol down and lit a cigarette, then told her what he wanted her to do next.

She pressed her lips together tightly.

"Why don't you take that plaster on your bottom off?"

"It wouldn't look nice."

"I've seen worse things."

Then he became insistent.

"Don't you think you should do it for me?"

"What you want is forbidden. It's on the notice on the door."

"You expect me to stick to notices?" In his squeaky voice she could hear the knowledge that he could get whatever he wanted.

He ran his fingertip down her nose.

A huge raven was sitting on the window ledge.

"Are you trembling?"

"I don't know."

"Are you afraid?"

"No."

The bird flew off.

Was it possible that he could tell by her nose that she was Jewish?

"Do you think you have an Aryan nose?"

"I hope so."

"Almost," he said.

His forefinger moved down her nose and stopped at the tip.

126

"We all have our secrets," he said.

He had told her some of his secrets. He acknowledged his Aryan god and those who were next to him – Reich Marshals, Sturmmänner, Scharführers and Oberführers. He acknowledged brutality as the supreme virtue, as the call and command of nature. He had no consideration for anybody; he asked no-one for permission, he needed no witnesses. He lied, stole and cheated just as others breathed. He was not constrained by rules and broke them whenever it suited him. He did not allow himself a moment's respite, not an hour, not a minute. He did not burden himself by respect for family, parents or children. He considered it his duty to denounce – just as throughout the Reich children denounced their teachers and teachers their students, parents denounced their children and children their parents. His honour and pride were of a special mould. Ahead of him he saw a victory such as had never been won before, and no price was too high for him to achieve it, even if it cost his life. He believed in his race which would prove its worth to the extent that he prevented its dilution by other races. He made darkness and shadows subject to himself. He saw himself as the light. To him the key to the secret of life was obedience.

"They won't forget us," he said.

"No," she agreed.

Behind them they left a desert, a depopulated scorched earth. And indelible milestones of history. From the *Kristallnacht*, when throughout Germany synagogues and Jewish shops were going up in flames, Jewish business people disappeared in the darkness from the southern border of Bavaria to the North Sea, and the Germans exacted a fine of a billion marks for the damage – the burnt or destroyed property and the danger to human lives – though they themselves had caused it; all the way to their *Blitzkrieg*, their lightning war, which had already gone on for six years.

They appropriated a Czech town, Terezín, and turned it into a transit station. They established camps such as Auschwitz-Birkenau and their crematoria. Skinny did not have time to reflect on this at length. It came to her with him, as it did with every soldier before and after him. She saw the Obersturmführer's world and she felt his finger on the base of her nose for what seemed like an eternity. She wished he would take it away.

"*Würden sind Bürden*," he said softly. Honours are burdens. When he whispered his voice wasn't so squeaky. "*Die Sonne bringt es an den Tag*." The sun reveals all. He would test her, in a while she would see how. They would discover who each other was.

"Don't you confide in one another who each of you is?"

"No."

"Can I believe you?"

"Yes."

"No-one told you, before I got here, what I would want?"

"No."

"You're lying."

"No, I'm not. We are forbidden to lie."

"Do you remind all your visitors of what's forbidden?"

She remained silent. She knew from Long-Legs what to do to prevent herself throwing up. She thought of her taste buds, which were at the tip of her tongue and not at the back of her throat. She had been feeling sick for a while.

He touched his scalp.

"I got this from an ambush, on the far side of the quarry, where you've probably never been."

"No."

"I'll find a doctor in Germany who'll glue me together again," he said. He ran his finger along his scar.

He struggled free from the blankets, pulling them off her too. She had a little lipstick on, her arms and legs were weak, and in her face the kind of fear children have when they have done something wrong and are waiting for punishment. A whore's failure was not exactly high treason, but it was close to it. To stand up, to overcome, were Aryan virtues. She had to meet three fundamental conditions – obedience, devotion and willingness to co-operate.

"You should be glad I chose you. Your turnaround time here must be faster than our fuel convoys."

"I am glad," she lied.

She avoided his eyes.

"I started on a poem entitled "All Rivers Die in the Sea," he confided. "It could even be a song."

"Yes," she agreed.

"Death interests me. It is like a cat that won't come to anyone it doesn't like. Death is also like a dog, a faithful fighting companion. You've got to pay for this realization. In the past it was enough for me to swear allegiance to my commanding officers and to the anthem of the unit; 'May death be our companion in our black column's fight.' Have you ever heard the men of an Einsatzkommando sing? The words, the tune, the sound of hobnailed boots are like a north wind. Our war cry is lively and sad, foreboding and joyful. We are like tempered steel. That is what the east has done to us. I'm not bragging."

"Yes," she agreed softly.

"We were born for death, that great bubble. Every one of us may proudly proclaim, 'I am an oak and an ash'."

He should read to her what Nietzsche had written. Wild beasts with unclouded conscience, monsters filled with jubilation.

"He probably said this about us even before we were born."

She should learn that too. It heralded the revolution which meant blood. An eye for an eye. Yesterday a peasant had cut off the foot together with the boot of the dead Scharführer Meinhofer. She should not be surprised if on a German foot she saw felt boots cut from prisoners of war. The girls were protected here as if they were in the Garden of Eden. They should lick the boots of all officers.

If he told her what their daily service had consisted of since 1941, she would appreciate everything. She would absorb their principle, that nothing that befalls an inferior race is terrible; it is necessary. It would be boring if it was not also exalted. Yes, brutality was exalted. For him it was enough to compare German towns and villages with those in Poland.

"In Russia I saw hovels with trampled earth for a floor. In the middle, tied to the post which supported the roof, was a goat or a calf. Villages without men, with swarms of black flies in the summer and worm-eaten corpses in the winter."

In one village they had ordered wood to be piled up for the bodies to be burnt. Afterwards, women and children scrabbled about in the ashes looking for wedding rings on the charred fingers of corpses.

The Obersturmführer climbed into the tub; ordering her to wash him down with the water that had been heating on the stove. He drew up his knees, leaning his back against the slime-covered rotten wood. He got her to scrub him with a brush and then to rub him dry. Swarthy as his face was, his body was white.

He ordered her to rinse herself in the tub after him, and then get back into bed with him. He picked up his pistol. Now his scar reminded her of a thistle. Under the bed she saw his boots with the several rows of hobnails in their soles.

He got her to bring him his field flask from his tunic pocket. He unscrewed the little beaker, and filled it slowly, carefully, almost to the brim, and drank it quickly. Then he began to speak again.

The history of the Jews was a story of cunning, fraud and deceit. They were all liars. The worst crime of the circumcised was their assertion that all men were equal. There were only two solutions, converging in Entjudung, the liquidation of the Jews, in the Endlösung, the Final Solution.

There had been a lecture for the Einsatzkommando der Einsatzgruppen about their conflict with the Jews. Strength was more than truth, they had been told. Power is the bride of the bold. The clenched fist, ready to strike the enemy, was more convincing than the outpourings of all aesthetes or the books written by the hook-nosed since the beginning of time.

He regarded it as good luck amid misfortune that he was not born to the circumcised. Race was his pillar.

He turned to look at the girl.

"I'm going to test you in a different way from that which you're accustomed to."

He ordered her to sit facing him and to lean against the end of the bed. He leant against the head, the scar throbbing in his forehead.

"I savour each second three times. The poet utters what he hasn't known before. Three times and twice. The dance of my numbers; the principal one is the three – birth, life, death. Intention, action and lesson."

She would be happier if she could believe that the Obersturm-führer had gone round the bend. She followed his strange gaze. Had he had a drink for Dutch courage? Unlike Captain Hentschel, he had not offered her any.

"You should know, before I leave, that I am my own man. Not like the majority, who are dead while still alive."

The fire in the stove was drawing well. The flue roared as the flames leapt up. She could hardly pretend that she had to add more fuel.

"Imagine a mirror spattered with the blood of those I have killed. These three years, every day, every night. Moments of decision. I see myself in that mirror. I can look at myself in a blood-spattered mirror without soiling myself. In the western Ukraine we killed a whore who turned out to be a Jewess. I thrust a hand grenade between her legs."

He paused.

"You haven't answered me yet."

"I don't know what you want to know."

"Are you afraid of death?"

He took his watch off and put it on the chair by his empty beaker and the holster. He pulled the chair nearer. She imagined she heard the watch ticking.

"Do you know how to handle a pistol?"

"No, I don't."

"Why not?"

"No-one's taught me."

"No-one, not anywhere? Shooting is something we learn ourselves.

131

The sooner the better. It's like riding a bike. You get on, you pedal and you're riding. Know what kind of gun this is?"

"No."

"A Steyer? A Bergmann? A Luger?"

"I don't know."

He was weighing the pistol in his palm as if acquainting himself with it, as if it were not his own weapon.

"Are you fond of money?"

She remained silent.

"Are you happy?"

"I don't know."

"You've no money, you don't know how to fire a gun, you don't know if you're happy. You certainly have whims. I'll remember that."

"Why do you want to test me?"

"To discover what I don't know," he said. "What you perhaps don't know yourself. What few people know about themselves, before they see themselves as others see them."

He was still confusing her.

"Do you know how many parts my pistol has? How much it weighs?"

"No."

Could he possibly know about the 30 marks Captain Hentschel had given her and which she had hidden under her mattress?

"What did I do to you?" she asked suddenly.

He looked into her eyes thoughtfully.

"Wrong question. What didn't you do to me?"

"I did what you wanted."

She was unable to read his expression.

"Weren't you in a youth organization before they sent you here?"

"No."

"Always no. No, no, no. Are you concealing your background? It won't get you anywhere."

"I wasn't in an organization."

Every word could have several meanings.

"Do you think they'd accept you into the Bund deutscher Mädel?"

"I don't know. No-one here got an application form."

"You're probably telling the truth now. You're not German after all."

For the fraction of a second she felt relief, then her fear travelled down to her guts. What had he meant by saying that everyone had secrets? She broke into a cold sweat. She thought of her father's sacred books. The Obersturmführer might not realize how close he had come to the truth. Had he come to the end of his "test"?

"Why not tell Uncle Sarazin what's on your mind? Do you think I want to shoot you?"

"That's for you to know."

"You're wrong. Not yet. A pity they didn't enrol you in our youth organization. You'd have learnt to fire a gun, or how to use a hand grenade. These things shouldn't be put off. Were you in some youth association – when you were still at home?"

She could not say that she didn't remember. But she didn't want to trap herself. Surely he had asked her this question already? How was he testing her and what did he hope to discover?

"I used to go on school outings."

From the age of ten she had been in the Jewish Girl Guides. They went on outings along the banks of the Vltava, to the Davle reservoir. For a second she saw the rock face under which they had erected their tents and made their camp fire. They would sing Czech and Zionist songs. None of them had been to the Promised Land. In the evenings they were taught to recognize the stars, during the day they went out into the woods and read signs or learnt to orient themselves with a compass. They had swimming and running races. Once she came first in the 400 metres. They shared anything they had brought along; they called it a commune. Everything was still ahead of them. Life was comprehensible then, the future was far away and good. She remembered every minute of it.

"Our young people know from earliest childhood what a dagger is, or a pistol, or a hand grenade. It's the responsibility of the parents. At eighteen the boys put on a uniform and join the Waffen-SS or the

Volunteer SS. They learn to operate anti-aircraft guns. Some as young as sixteen. They disdain death – that is the test. They do sentry duty at air-raid shelters, they guard factories and sewers to prevent sabo- teurs from damaging them. They disdain death because they love Germany. Killing is part of basic education, of basic morality. You'd better hurry and catch up with what you've missed. I know what I'm talking about."

She remained silent.

"Two things are all you need – fire and a pistol," he added. "The third is loyalty. Suppose you had to defend yourself? Or defend me?"

"We have guards here, watchtowers with machine guns, guard dogs," she said carefully. "We're protected by a wall. We're here on your territory."

He looked into her green eyes.

"I'm just like all the rest," she said weakly.

He looked at his Luger with admiration and gratitude, with what he would call love and loyalty; something she didn't understand and could explain to herself only by the power that the weapon lent him, the superiority it gave him. It frightened her, as did everything in which she could not orientate herself and against which she had no defence. She sensed the danger in her whole being. She watched him looking at his pistol. She was waiting for what he was going to say or do next.

Did she lack something the others had? Could she catch up or put it right if she didn't know what it was?

She thought of Big Leopolda Kulikowa's advice to accept everything as normal, even the most unexpected and the most eccentric. Hadn't the Madam told them that people satisfied themselves in any way they could, even with ducks, sheep and bitches? She must hold on to what she could.

She fixed her gaze on his eyes. She didn't know what would happen next. He was lying on his side, supported by his elbow, holding the gun with his finger on the trigger. Before her eyes was the whiteness that comes to those sentenced to death. Did it matter whether he shot her as a Jewess or as a whore with whom he had failed, or both? In her mind she wrestled with that invisible difference.

At the same time, she felt like that little girl she had seen on the ramp at Auschwitz-Birkenau, under the arc-lamps, which were swinging in the wind. The girl had been separated from her parents and her brother. Crowds of people walked past her. Then a woman invited her to join her. The little girl didn't move. The woman took her by the hand and included her with her own family. All four of them came up before the doctor in the middle of the ramp. With a jerk of his thumb he sent them to the gas chamber.

What was going to happen now did not depend upon her. In her mind she backed away, into some kind of tunnel, where she might hide, where she might escape. The whiteness before her spread out like a fog, white blossoms on unfamiliar shrubs, a kind of warming light snow. The Obersturmführer confused her. She didn't understand what he'd meant by a test of cowardice. She was as bewildered as the people on the ramp after arriving in sealed wagons at Auschwitz-Birkenau. He was holding his gun – his finger on the trigger, aimed at her chest. If he was trying to scare her, he had succeeded.

"Head up," the Obersturmführer instructed her. "Sit straight. Lean against the bed. Don't slouch. Pull your legs up, so you keep them to yourself and not near my toes. I want you to see the whole of me."

She did as he told her.

"That's better."

They were now like pictures on a playing card, one at the top and the other at the bottom. She tried to lower her head so she wouldn't seem taller than him. She was looking at his chest, not his face. Was he going to shoot her now? She could see the cubicle window out of the corner of her eye.

"Do you see me?"

"I see you."

"Why are you lowering your eyes?"

She raised them.

He held the pistol out to her.

"Take it."

"Why?"

"Do what I'm telling you. It's only a piece of metal. It won't bite."

"I don't know how to handle it."

"*Not kennt kein Gebot.*" Needs must when the devil drives.

What need was he talking about? Why did he want her to take his pistol? So he could accuse her of something she hadn't done?

"Do I have to beg you? Do as I say!"

She was afraid. If she extended her hand would the Obersturm-führer change his grip on the pistol, slip his finger through the trigger guard and pull the trigger? Did she have to do what he demanded so he could shoot her when she reached out as if she had wanted to seize the pistol? Was it to be like in the camp when Rottenführer Schratz snatched the caps off prisoners, tossed them to the fence, and shot the prisoners when, on his orders, they ran to retrieve them? Did Obersturmführer Sarazin know which camp she had come from? He could have found out from The Frog.

He leant forward with the pistol. She knew it was a trap, that she would not live to play the scene out to its end. The livid scar on the Obersturmführer's forehead had turned the colour of blood. He was concentrating on something that must be important to him, some-thing that accelerated his pulse. They would know just as little about her as they did about Krikri. Just as nobody knew who Big-Belly was. Suddenly she felt close to both of them. She thought of Captain Hentschel's green pullover. Of his – now her, though not for long – 30 marks. Those who might mourn her were no longer alive. Above all she felt weary now.

"We are both cold-blooded," he said. "We are all cold-blooded animals."

Had he changed his mind about his game with the gun or was he merely prolonging it?

"Do you hear me? Take the pistol."

Her back was pressed against the wood of the bed. Were his eyes getting moist?

"Do as I'm telling you!"

"I'm doing what you say."

"I'm not used to being argued with. Take it!"

He spoke as if he were giving orders to a dog after throwing it a bone. She half shut her eyes. She pressed her hands to her chest. Perhaps he would shoot her in the head and not between her legs. She felt the fatigue of her father. She felt something going numb inside her.

She reached out her hand and took the gun. He didn't snatch his hand away. He didn't fire. His arm sank down on the sheet. Her hesitation had made the gun heavy even for him.

His scar was swollen. The Obersturmführer was aroused. She felt more and more confused.

"Very well," he said. "It would have been worse if you hadn't taken it. Now I'll turn you into a killer."

She had never held a gun before in her life, never held such a piece of metal, shaped for just one purpose.

Only then did it occur to her that she could shoot him. And that perhaps this was what he wanted. Was the gun loaded? Had he used the last round when he was firing at the wolves?

"Listen to me."

"I'm listening."

Then she whispered "Yes", although he had not said anything. Was the Obersturmführer letting her make a decision that was not hers to make? Was he treating her as if she were an Aryan? Should she shoot him? And what would happen then?

"I'm waiting," she said.

"You know what I have in mind?" He was stressing every word. She tried not to move a single muscle in her face. "*Die Sonne bringt es an den Tag.*"

Could he read her mind? Was the pistol loaded?

"Are you afraid of me? Do you despise yourself?"

She knew that she must not reply. Did he want to be killed or did he know that the pin would strike an empty chamber?

"Speak up!"

"I don't despise . . ."

She did not say who.

"You're lying."

"I'm not," she said softly.

Her exhaustion muted everything inside her. She was telling the truth when she said that she did not know how to fire a gun. In her head she heard an echo of *Die Sonne bringt es an den Tag*. Squeezing the trigger would not be difficult. She thought of all those who had been shot before her.

"You can do what you want," he said. "You're holding all the cards."

He was savouring the sound and meaning of each word. He associated with them images of which she had no inkling. Did some words, whose sound fascinated him, carry him to regions where no-one had ventured before him? Where only people like himself were admitted?

"I don't want anything," she replied.

"You don't know what you want?"

"No."

"Is there a heart in your breast? Or just ice?"

She weighed up his words.

"Hold the pistol by its butt. Like this." He leant forward and reversed the gun in her hand. She needed both hands to hold it up.

"That's it," he said. "Release the safety catch."

"I don't know how to."

"That's your fault. If you thought you'd be bored with me, or that you couldn't learn something from me, you were mistaken. Every one of us is only what he's good for. We'll see. You need to have one hand free. You might at least become a better shot than you are an army whore."

She studied the black surface of the pistol. The butt was rough, grooved and cold. Her heart was thumping. Was the Obersturmführer, even without a gun, stronger than she was with one? His scar stood out, blood-red.

"I'm counting to five," he said. "Today's number is five. Do you believe in numbers?"

"Sometimes," she said.

She was afraid his scar would burst and blood would stream from his forehead. She was holding the gun pointing down. She did not touch the trigger. She examined the stiff mechanism to find the safety catch, studied the granular surface, the shallow grooves, the black metal fingered and smoothed by many hands.

Her facial muscles were twitching. She held her breath. With her forefinger she probed the catch. She pressed upwards. It didn't move. She pressed down, the lever moved. It clicked like a light switch.

"At last," he said.

Did he want her to shoot him or to shoot herself? Or did he want her to shoot him and then herself? She no longer thought that he was mad. The mad ones were those who didn't understand, like herself, her mother, her father, her brother. Those who let themselves be put on trains and taken to Auschwitz-Birkenau.

"Hook your index finger around the trigger."

It would all make sense if there was a round in the pistol, even if the magazine was empty. She remembered how he had slipped the magazine in earlier.

"Finger on the trigger," he repeated.

She slipped her finger through the guard. Trembling, she felt the most delicate part of the gun, the metal of the trigger. She dared not move her finger. Would she get cramp in it?

"Aim at me. At once. Can't you aim?"

She steadied her wrist with her other hand. She dared not look into his eyes.

"Finger, trigger, aim. Eye, barrel, sight. Higher! At my heart!"

He pushed his chest out.

"Here," he pointed where his heart was.

She raised the gun to a horizontal position, extending her arm, her wrist still supported by her left hand. With her eyes she measured the distance between the barrel and the Obersturmführer's heart. She lowered her eyes to the sight. She no longer looked like someone who did not know how to handle a gun.

"Shoot!"

She raised her eyes. She met his clouded gaze, his eyes like watery milk, threads of blood in the corners.

"Look at me. Shoot!"

"Fire! Squeeze it!"

Skinny's eyes had become bloodshot. Her green irises were floating in a reddish sea. She was trembling all over. At the same time she was sweating. She was afraid diarrhoea would get the better of her. Her muscles did not feel strong enough to control it.

"I wasn't born to kill," she said. "I've never killed anyone."

"Fire!"

"Why?"

"Because I command you to. Haven't you got the strength to squeeze the trigger?"

"You want me to?"

"It's an order."

"I can't."

"Why?"

The Obersturmführer's forehead and hair were wet with sweat. Did he want to prove to her and to himself that he disdained death? Or to punish her for what he could not achieve in bed? Sweat was trickling down his upper lip into his mouth, down his chin, into the hollow between his throat and his chest. She saw black before her eyes. The sweat coming from his hair was caught in the groove of his scar. She was aiming at the heart of Obersturmführer Stefan Sarazin on his orders.

"I give you five seconds. I'm counting."

She counted with him.

"One."

She was waiting for him to say five. She did not know what he would do then.

"You're made of sawdust. I will decide what happens. You can't miss. I'm your enemy, German blood. Fire!"

She sensed the pain in his voice, masked by willpower. For a moment it reminded her of Tight-Lips and the NCO who had shaved her crotch and laughed. She preferred not to think of what had happened afterwards.

He did not take his eyes off her; she was afraid he might hypnotize her. She felt in his eyes the blood of all those he had killed. She let her hand sag, so that the gun was now aimed at his stomach. And then lower still. In the end she aimed to the side, past him.

"There you are," the Obersturmführer said after a while, but without his earlier determination or urgency. "You could never be one of us. It's obvious you weren't in the Bund deutscher Mädel."

He looked at where the gun was pointing. He smiled slightly. *Die Sonne bringt es an den Tag*. The commanding tone had been replaced by geniality with a touch of contempt.

"I knew you wouldn't fire. Now I know everything about you."

Did he know she was Jewish? Had he seen the invisible, the place where there were no secrets?

"That wouldn't have earned you the Knight's Cross."

He took his pistol back. Had there been a last round in the gun or had it been empty? Had he really run that risk or had he merely pretended? What part in it all had been played by the retreat of the German troops and by the Einsatzkommandos' retreat from glory, which he was both admitting and denying to himself?

She would never know whether she would have shot him through the heart if she had pulled the trigger. He didn't bother to take out the magazine.

"Maybe you'd make a Brown Nurse," he said. "You'd have to volunteer for the support units. You're a different clay from us."

He spoke with contempt. He caressed his gun. If he had a bullet in the magazine he might still shoot her. Her fear had not left her, but shame had joined it, not only because she was naked.

"I must see to the fire or it'll go out."

"If you've got some more fuel, why not?"

She got up. Relief had made the blood course through her veins again. She crammed what was left of the firewood and coal into the stove and raked the grate. The gale howled in the flue. She did not look at the Obersturmführer. She was aware of how close he was without seeing him. She wondered how much longer he would stay.

"No-one reproves a victor. I'll bring you some soap next time. Come over here. Sit by me."

As she sat next to him she involuntarily touched his sweaty hand but she did not want to move away. She sat motionless, her legs crossed, her arms crossed over her breast.

"I am by no means the worst," he said. And then seeing her drawn face, "I don't want to hurt you. You're still a lamb. You need time to grow into a sheep."

She mistrusted his friendliness.

"You're trembling, or am I imagining it?"

She remained silent.

"Am I imagining that you're trembling?"

"I'm cold," she said.

"Perhaps you should dress now?"

"Perhaps."

"*Die Sonne bringt es an den Tag.*"

She kept her knees together as if she were sitting on a bench at school, her hands were still folded over her chest, and she was red with fear and shame.

"Maybe you want to tell me something you haven't told me yet?"

"There's nothing."

Evidently he had not yet finished with her. Would he let her dress now?

"You keep surprising me with one thing after another," the Obersturmführer said.

She did not understand. She was afraid of diarrhoea. She realized that this did not depend on the degree of danger. Fear was corroding her inhibitions, her judgement. It probably was not just cowardice. She felt sick again, but did not want to throw up.

"You are neither rose nor thorn," he said.

A pity no-one saw him here, he thought. He was Knight's Cross material; indeed the Knight's Cross with Oak Leaves, Swords and Diamonds. He would bet his right arm on it.

He got up. She had to move to make room for him. He began to put his clothes back on. He complained, just to keep the conversation going, about a commission that was due to arrive. They didn't like the killing of the circumcised. Damned snoopers, sticking their noses in where they had no business. He pulled on his tight, wool-lined gloves. On his hands they looked like artificial limbs.

Obersturmführer Stefan Sarazin strode out in his hobnailed boots. He slammed the cubicle door behind him.

Seconds later, still in her black underwear, Skinny stepped into the icy water of the tub, with the suds and the dirt of the officer, goose-flesh all over her, and a heavy weight in her stomach and guts.

Part Three

Chapter Nine

Her talks with Rabbi Gideon Schapiro in Pécs were mostly one-sided. The rabbi would ask questions and Skinny would answer them; often more openly than she might have otherwise out of respect for the rabbi's authority. Sometimes she remained silent and the rabbi went on asking questions, until he fell silent. Ten days and ten nights. She wondered whether rabbinical authority had undergone a change – she had seen rabbis at Auschwitz-Birkenau, where they had been no different from the other inmates. Rabbi Schapiro did not know Czech, and Skinny did not know Hungarian. They talked in German. She felt no surprise at the sequence of events that had brought her to him in Hungary, by a roundabout route, after the war. The war had stirred Europe like a huge spoon stirring a cauldron of soup for 250 million people.

She sensed in him a degree of consideration that she was not accustomed to. He was trying to accept something that went beyond his comprehension, but he was careful that she did not take it personally. He was the only person to whom – for some reason or other, perhaps to get it off her chest – she told everything. She stripped herself bare. She felt relief that it was behind her. Did that mean it was no longer present? It turned out that even what had happened at No. 232 Ost was not irreversible. Nothing was irreversible. She was too tired or too unsure of herself to declare an all-out war on those 21 days. The rabbi was aware of dissonance in her story, but he felt her to be a kindred soul, and they ended up closer than Skinny had originally intended. Rabbi Schapiro had a gentle voice, a little hoarse as if he had a cold, and he felt inside him a second voice prompting him. She noticed that he looked at her as if he were seeing himself. He never raised his voice, but she could hear in it an anger that was not directed at her, an anger that was new to her. It made her believe that he was growing with it. In reality, the rabbi was ducking for cover. He had deep brown eyes which at times seemed wild to her. They had trusted one another from the moment they had met, when she'd been taken to him by two railwaymen whose addresses she had been given in Katowice.

"Child," he had said. This was his first word to her when the men had gone. He didn't have to ask her age, he could tell that himself. And he didn't have to ask how she felt: he only had to look into her face with his brown eyes in which, on several occasions later, she would see tears.

"What are we?" he asked, more into the void than to her, like a rhetorical question. "A lump of flesh and a broken soul."

From her reaction he realized at once that he had made a mistake. And he made many mistakes – but he did not repeat this one.

"You were in a house that God had abandoned," the rabbi said.

That determined their relationship. At times she did not know how the rabbi viewed her; she found no answer in his eyes. He was feeling as helpless as the inmates of the concentration camps; assailed by questions to which there was no answer. One question that the rabbi asked again and again was: where was God? He glanced at the book-case that contained his sacred books. They seemed to him to be running away as though they were made of water, trickling down the shining glass across from the window with its heavy red curtains.

At times she felt that he was expecting her to answer this question, which God did not answer.

"Each one who has survived is a messenger," he sighed.

"I don't know," she said.

She realized that conditions in Hungary had been different from those in Bohemia or Poland. There, the anti-Jewish laws came into force only at the beginning of 1944. Unlike to the Terezín ghetto, Eichmann came to Hungary late, managing to kill only half the Hungarian Jews, some 400,000.

The rabbi had before him a child who spoke of a brothel in the way that a miller might speak of the flour he had milled, filled into sacks and weighed, or a bricklayer of a wall he had built from stones and bricks. Or else she was silent like an animal. He had not seen Skinny on that first Friday in December, when, after her first shift, she had washed off the dried blood from the inside of her thighs. She had been afraid to look at her crotch, which resembled a raw, bleeding gum.

It was all new to him, just as it had been new to her, different then and now. Her erstwhile now refused to transform into a present-day then. She did not know that every one of her words dealt a fatal blow to the rabbi. He thought of concepts like honour, humiliation, violation. He had a vision of scales on which he was trying to weigh that which cannot be weighed or measured. He thought of the right of the stronger and the form into which it had developed before the middle of the 20th century, 40 centuries after his own ancestors had decided to outlaw killing; to outlaw human sacrifice. What had happened to justice, which must be for everyone or else evaporate altogether like the steam from a saucepan? He bore each word she uttered as a reproach, a reproach he accepted for himself. Her experience conflicted with all the sacred and civil codes that he was acquainted with. He searched his mind: what had become of morality? Where did the idea of the worthlessness of human life come from? How did the difference between giving and taking life disappear? How was injustice measured? Fortunately Skinny knew nothing of his thoughts.

They were sitting facing each other. The rabbi had two large comfortable armchairs. She stretched out her legs in front of her, while he tucked his under his chair.

Could he understand the Oberführer, nicknamed The Frog, if he credited him with a twisted brain? With sick ideas? If he likened him to a pig?

"We are like a stone in the swamp," the rabbi said.

She did indeed feel a little like that.

"It was confusion," the rabbi said next. "Evil pretended to be good, the filthy disguised itself as clean. Sickness was proclaimed health and the plague was pronounced fresh air. The decayed pretended to be fresh. The low acted as if it were exalted, stupidity as if it were wisdom. It's all behind you now."

The word "decay" recurred in the rabbi's conversation every day. At night he dreamed of it.

"I could not be a just judge, even if I wanted to be."

"Nor could I," she agreed.

"No-one like you could."

"Probably not."

An understanding grew between them. The rabbi was her confessor and her mirror. She could identify with much of what he said, even though he spoke little. She enjoyed the fact that she didn't have to watch every word or control her slightest movement.

"At first I didn't know what was happening. In Terezín we were living almost normally – it was a transit station. But even in the east, at Auschwitz-Birkenau, I knew only a part of what was going on. No-one knew, except the girls they brought in for clerical duties in the Gestapo offices. They gassed these girls, after no more than six weeks, and then brought in new ones. But eventually I got to know. I felt as if I was in a camp in myself. Everyone who was there must have felt the same way. They left us together, but so that we were alone, separated from one another. I felt that I was surrounded by high-voltage wires, as though I was the last person on earth. And if it was a hill, then I stayed at the bottom. I didn't need a panoramic view, I knew what was waiting for me. Those around me went to the gas chamber, one after another. Sometimes there was a short delay, but all of them in the end. Everything was temporary. There was only the now and the past, nothing that was yet to come."

" . . . on our knees," said the rabbi.

He asked himself whether the soul can refuse something which the body cannot refuse but must accept. In his mind he visited the place Skinny had described for him. He had never been in a brothel and regarded it as a place where men dropped their commitments. He knew what was written in the old books about Sodom and Gomorrah. Now Sodom had acquired a new name – Auschwitz-Birkenau,

Feldbordell No. 232 Ost, Germany, Europe. It occurred to him that the Bible should be amplified by what people like Skinny brought back from the camps. Hadn't the Bible been written by people not much older than Skinny? By ploughmen, carpenters and tanners, after the day's work that was their livelihood? From the experiences they gathered, which did not lose their significance even after 2,000 years?

Yes, the line between good and evil, between the appropriate and the false, has been blurred, he thought. The boundaries have ceased to be clear. There is a long way from yes to no, and the end is not in sight.

He did not speak of the Ten Commandments, because he no longer considered them as all-embracing and all-applying, as the sum total of all that is under the stars, of what is allowed and what is forbidden, what one ought or ought not to do. He discovered the power and the curse of imagination. An inner voice told him that he could trust it. A terrible, sinful thought struck him: was there still a God, and if there was, was he not perhaps powerless?

As they sat in the twilight of the first of those ten days she spent at his house, Rabbi Schapiro said: "I would like to be in your place."

"You wouldn't," she replied.

"We were living in a pagan world," the rabbi whispered, but so that at least he could hear himself. "They had their personal god, their golden calf, their degenerate idea. They wanted to have and proclaim their hoarfrost giants as in their ancient times, and they found one. Their giant of evil."

They both knew who he meant. He avoided uttering the name of the man he regarded as the personification of evil, the evil from which the devil arose; as the sum total and quintessence of all time, looking both back and forward, whose spirit continued to move through light and shade, noise and silence, enveloping them like a dark, invisible but perceptible cloud. Who would in future remember his date of birth in the quiet little Austrian town, feel sorry for his mother and his unknown father, and bless the accident that he had no children?

He saw evil producing the germs of further evil, as when a fire flares up and its sparks light new fires on all sides; a huge conflagration engulfing the whole world. He saw the face of the man with a small moustache, as he had appeared on countless pictures and postage stamps, in school books and newspapers, on posters at every street corner, in the windows of zealous champions of his ideas, a man with a shock of dark hair, with burning eyes almost screaming from their sockets. For a long while the rabbi kept his eyes closed, his eyelids marked by fine blue and blood-red veins, the lids purple from lack of sleep, from anxiety and fatigue, from the burden of evil.

He felt that evil had settled in him and on him, like sweat and dirt from an exhausting journey to a destination he had not yet reached and perhaps never would. The journey of Skinny, Hanka Kaudersová, in that coal-tender to Pécs in Hungary was only one part.

He didn't have to disprove to himself that life was an obscure journey from birth to death, one on which only a handful of the chosen started out, travelled, and departed with dignity. Not many could keep their dignity while journeying. And so he looked at the girl from the army brothel, now in his house, as though through a window onto something he hadn't seen before or perhaps even known existed.

Where were those good people, those strong people, those who knew what evil was when it was still in the bud? What questions will their children and their children's children ask them some day? What will they ask those who did not know? The rabbi put this question to the void.

"Where were those who saw what was happening and closed their eyes to it? Who did not even open them when they woke up? What were they doing?"

No answer came back to him from the void, because the void does not even produce an echo. The rabbi thought of the unforgettable parables and elucidation of the Old Testament he had once admired so much, of the innumerable writings, the records of oral tradition, the wisdom of the wisest rabbis, the proverbs of Solomon, the songs of the Biblical poets, the clarity, clear-sightedness and power of truth uttered, come what may, regardless of those in power, by the prophets. That which transcended time and place with deceptive general validity, a boundless and universal validity.

In his mind's eye he saw a goshawk flying over a field, diving down, from an enormous height that gave it a view far and wide, onto a small fieldmouse which had no idea of what threatened it until it was too late, until it was in the claws of the bird of prey. He could hear the rush of the bird's wings and the squeak of the little mouse.

"Will all those with a conscience now have a hole in their soul?" the rabbi asked in a whisper. "Is modesty still a virtue or is it the false sister of excuse for those I know and do not know, and also for myself, if it relates to what cannot be explained, to what I do not attempt to explain?"

Skinny didn't reply. She was digesting an ample midday meal after an even more ample dinner the previous evening.

"You witnessed the ugliness of the world," the rabbi whispered. Perhaps he didn't even want her to hear.

Had the brutality of children who didn't yet know the miracle of life become the brutality of adults because they never grew up? Had it been due to their character, to circumstances, schooling, youth organizations, the army and the many other institutions which had sprung up all over Europe?

Are those who were sure of themselves confused, or are those who were confused sure of themselves?

Is it a punishment for the fact that too many people allowed just a handful to make the decisions?

Is it possible by the waving of a hand to turn human beings into refuse and the world into a refuse heap?

He could still hear those who proclaimed the New Order; the breaking up of what belonged together, as if it were possible to improve the daylight or the brilliance of night, the brightness of the stars, the song of birds, the colour of a lilac bush, of a lucerne flower amid the clover, the crimson of a wild poppy or the slenderness of a stalk of wheat.

The purity of conscience.

The sweet breath of hope.

The innocence of a two-year-old. The transparency of a tear.

There was no end to it. His soul was like a bottomless pit without echoes, a soundless cry, a deafening silence.

"Why did they do it?" he whispered. "How could they have done it?"

What pleasure was there in killing people whom the killer didn't even know?

What could he invoke, which face of God? The God of infinity? The God of wisdom? The God of vengeance? The God of thunderbolts? Or the God of mercy? The God of goodness? The God of the 30 paths of wisdom? The God of the 50 gates of light? The God with the fiery sword? The God of the Covenant?

He had begun to doubt the God of speech. He could invoke only the God of silence. But wherever he looked, more was concealed than apparent. Perhaps these Gods existed only in his imagination? But were they not written about in the sacred books? Where was the God of justice? The God of right? God the saviour? He who was everlasting, unutterable, glorious, infinite, indulgent, good, incomprehensible?

The rabbi remembered how, as a young man, he had been excited by the three worlds, the higher, middle and lower world, and their relation to the human body which also contained three worlds – head, breast, and the body from the waist down.

It seemed to him improper to reflect on this in connection with Skinny. The body from the waist down and, with the girl before him, also from the waist up. Shell, transient substance and core. Blood corpuscles? Head, nerves, breast, blood, stomach and lymph, spirit, emotions and instinct, the life of the cells? He was not thinking of the second phase of creation, of procreation. She had told him about Dr Krueger's experiments, of how he had sterilized her. About Dr Schimmelpfennig's injections. About the psychological interrogations conducted by Oberführer Dr Blatter-Spirit. He could visualize the soldiers telling her about their families, their girlfriends, mothers and sisters, about their children. The officers, NCOs and men for whom going to war was like going to work. Their daily bread.

He did not see the beginning, he only saw the continuation. He knew now where Skinny had been and what she had done. He tried to see her ordeal in conjunction with justice, so that he would not attribute even a shadow of guilt where it was not due. He could not explain what even religion had no answers to. He was confused and disoriented. He reflected on boundless shamelessness. She had wanted to stay alive, and she could stay alive by undergoing what she had endured. When is staying alive a sin, or wanting to stay alive? When is the mere wish to stay alive blasphemy? The rabbi found himself at a point he had not reached before. There was no longer a yes or no answer. A position of good and bad, of right and wrong. What was a lie and what just an error? What was just and what unjust?

He wished it were simpler, for himself and for her. As wide open as the sea when he stood at its shore; as the sky when he looked up. Not disappearing in a fog as the stars at dawn or a shadow at night. The line between justice and sin, between blasphemy and honour. Not an accusation against those who were unable to defend themselves.

Rabbi Gideon Schapiro felt that in a land without God, in a world without God, among people without God, under the pulled-down pillars of the heavenly vault, an unbearable burden fell upon him, like boulders that would crush even the strongest man.

"Thus the disaster came about," the rabbi murmured. "That's where the devil came from. That's what opened the door and the windows and swept away all barriers."

Then he added: "*Shoah*."

She heard the word for the first time. It was Hebrew. From the rabbi's expression, from his shining brown eyes, the beads of sweat that appeared on his forehead, she could guess what it meant. He pronounced the three Hebrew characters as if he were pulling a rock down upon himself.

On her first day at the brothel she had regarded her pain as a punishment – just as Estelle did. She had committed a sin and her only excuse was that she wanted to stay alive. The rabbi wondered when wishing to stay alive could be a sin. She had not expected the depth of her humiliation, nor the pain, nor her unpreparedness, her sense of vertigo and free fall – until she eventually got used to it. Not that "used to" was really the right term. Had it helped that she had to conceal all the pain, just as she did her origin? She shared with Estelle a tendency to blame herself for something that was not their fault. They were surrounded by a world within which was their private world, invisible to others, a world of personal guilt which became their home.

"There is no more justice," the rabbi said.

Then he added: "It is an unending chain." He was thinking of the injustice that enveloped them. He knew of no book that could teach one how to live in such a time.

"We have learned to die," he whispered. Was he saying that they were waiting for a second heaven? She didn't wish to ask him.

It did not bother her that he was talking in riddles. Perhaps she, too, sometimes talked in this way, even though it did her good to speak openly. She wondered how far she should allow her openness free rein. She was afraid that she might herself become terrified by what she was telling him.

They were waiting for the first star to appear.

"What are we, each of us?" the rabbi asked. And Skinny answered him, just as quietly: "I am just a lump of flesh."

She ate well. The rabbi was a good cook. She left practically nothing of what he put before her or let her prepare for herself. She devoured the soft Hungarian bread with its crisp crust that the baker delivered, and the Hungarian salami the butcher brought. At first, the rabbi paid them in Hungarian pengö, later with gold rings and other valuables, until eventually he had nothing left and the butcher and baker supplied him on credit.

On the third day the rabbi opened a large cupboard. One half of it contained the clothes of his wife, the other the clothes and accessories of his daughter.

"Her name was Erzsika," Rabbi Schapiro said.

She realized they were both dead.

"Take whatever you need. It's as if they were giving it to you," the rabbi told her.

She looked at a cotton nightshirt and a flannel one. The rabbi took them out from the stack of underwear and handed them to her. She did not know yet which of the two she would sleep in, perhaps neither. She had become accustomed to wearing things that had belonged to dead people.

During the night she dreamt of Erzsika, the rabbi's daughter.

The rabbi did not mention them to her again. Not until much later did she ask about them at all. Hints were sufficient; she worked out the rest for herself.

On the fifth day they kept silent. Skinny rested and ate. She spent hours in the bath, immersed to her chin, in hot, then tepid and finally cold water – as she was accustomed to. It was unbelievable to feel clean. She divided her day into two halves: during the first half she remembered the faces, hands, feet and bodies of the girls from No. 232 Ost, Madam Kulikowa, the guards and the officers, while in the second half she planned how she would live her new life. At first these ideas were vague but gradually they acquired a sharper outline. No. 232 Ost was always in the background for these. She lay in the water and talked to the girls about what the day held in store, she saw herself passing the guards, recalling individual faces, uniforms, and cars. She was still afraid of The Frog, as though he were just round the corner, instead of the pharmacy, the tailor's shop, the tavern, the baker and the butcher, with its brightly coloured notices in Hungarian. Lying in the bath, staring at the ceiling, she watched the wolves and swept the snow from the entrance to let the vehicles enter and leave the yard of No. 232 Ost.

On the sixth day the rabbi said to her: "You were in a house without God; in a country without God. Under stars where God was absent."

It sounded like an echo. Surely he had said this before?

"Among people who had walked away from the Ten Commandments. You were in a heathen, German land."

"I was in Poland," Skinny said.

"You were in Europe."

On the seventh day Rabbi Schapiro asked her – as if she was the rabbi and not he: "Isn't God everywhere, invisible and omnipresent?"

They were at the end of the circle and back at its beginning.

"He is powerless," she said, as if this were a question one could answer. That was how it seemed to her. Who was she going to confess this to, if not to a rabbi? She did not want to say it again.

The rabbi was ashamed to look into her half-childish, half-adult green eyes. He did not want to see in them a sea of death covered with ashes. She didn't only have sad eyes: she had eyes that saw what she had been through and what was ahead of her. There was in her a primitive awareness that she was alive, in spite of everything. That was quite a lot. She was like a small island of life in an ocean of death. She could not admit to herself that with her 15-year-old eyes she had, during those 21 days, seen more than Rabbi Gideon Schapiro in all the years that he was a rabbi; more than all the rabbis of all generations the world over, throughout the past 40 centuries.

He was looking at her long legs, her thin thighs and childish breasts and resisted the thought of the men she had been with. He hesitated to ask the question, which endlessly troubled him: Was God merciful? Or what was the opposite of mercy. He realized that he was not the first person to accuse God.

He had heard, though not at first hand, how the master race had populated the lands between the Elbe and the Urals by clearing them of their original inhabitants. How the armies of the Herrenvolk had opened the spaces in the east in order to turn them into a home for 200 million Germans by exterminating tens of millions, from infants to the elderly.

He heard from Skinny for the first time how Polish children

thought suitable for Germanization were rounded up in the east, the way weasels were hunted, or badgers – and sometimes even on horseback with hounds and whips, the way foxes were hunted.

The rabbi gazed into her half-closed green eyes. He was filled with a humility he had not experienced before, he wept and felt ashamed. The smoke of the cremated had risen quickly to the sky because it was pushed up by more smoke, but eventually there was so much of it that it sank down under its own weight. Not even the strongest wind could disperse it. It seemed to him that, like people throughout Europe and the world, he would breathe the smoke of Auschwitz-Birkenau for a long time to come.

Skinny smiled at the rabbi. The corners of his mouth turned up while tears were rolling down his cheeks, wetting the collar of his shirt. They understood and did not understand one another.

"When you left home you were a child."

"I don't feel like a child any more."

"A child is not responsible for what it's made to do."

"I knew what I was doing. I chose to do it."

The rabbi was silent. She was tempted to tell something but she didn't have the courage.

"I would have done more if they'd wanted me to," she said instead.

"Was it worse at Auschwitz-Birkenau?"

"I told you what was happening at Auschwitz-Birkenau."

Before her she saw again the German soldiers and men from the technical services, as well as the inmates, all shouting at each other at the railway ramp, the warehouses and around the five crematoria. There were French voices, Yiddish and Hungarian, Slovak, German, Polish and Lithuanian. They were like Martians, like creatures from another planet, but she understood them. They had faces, arms and legs, uniforms or prison clothes. It seemed to her like a gigantic, continuous performance. But soon it would end, not as in the finale in a theatre, after which the audience and the actors go home. This was different. This was real – not a theatrical performance. There was no curtain to go up or fall. Here no secret was made of what was happening. This was what the Germans called Endlösung, the Final Solution. And it was on planet Earth.

Rabbi Schapiro listened, endeavouring to visualize and comprehend, but unable to form a picture of it for himself.

She tried to simplify it for him, to reduce it to concepts by which people communicated. It unnerved her a little that she was facing a rabbi and was unable to convey this to him. How could she make him see? The Germans were no Spartans or ascetics. They had enjoyed the best food while thousands around them starved to death. They lived in villas, even at Auschwitz-Birkenau, in close proximity to the prisoners who were crowded together, worse than sardines, in the wooden huts that had housed Austro-Hungarian cavalrymen. There was no parallel to call on. And it was not something temporary, an emergency situation which the authorities intended to remedy or which (as after the war they tried to do) could be blamed on wartime conditions. This was what they had planned.

She did not say that perhaps the victims were glad they had crossed the bridge which lead nowhere but the gas chamber, that they had reached the end, the Final Solution, after which there was nothing. They had attained their final right or privilege – the right to die.

"There was no heaven there."

"Auschwitz," the rabbi whispered.

"On windless days soot would fall from morning to evening."

"Auschwitz-Birkenau."

"The inscription over the gate was: *Arbeit macht frei.*"

She explained to the rabbi that there had been three camps in one, on the area of eight demolished Polish villages. One of them, Brzezinki, was Birkenau. Aryan inmates gave as their address: Arbeitslager Auschwitz near Neu-Berun.

"Auschwitz-Birkenau," the rabbi repeated.

"Auschwitz-Birkenau," his echo confirmed.

"Feldbordell No. 232 Ost."

"Feldbordell No. 232 Ost."

"How were we born?"

The rabbi let his head drop. He was now smaller than her.

"A child's birth is not governed by his wishes. No-one knows what awaits him."

It went deep, far and wide. He had in his eyes a sea that did not divide. A flood which lasted 40 times 40 days and 40 nights. There was no point in counting the days of disaster.

For a wild moment she imagined inviting Rabbi Gideon Schapiro into her cubicle.

The rabbi had become pale during her stay. He suffered terrible headaches. He didn't eat, and drank only water, occasionally nibbling a crust of bread. He tried to stifle his anger, to dampen it with humility. Flames of wrath were flickering inside him. He was seeking echoes of his lost confidence. He gazed at her as he would into a mirror. He had come up against something that was not in the sacred books – there was nothing in his sacred books about Auschwitz-Birkenau or No. 232 Ost.

On his forehead, at the corners of his eyes and his mouth, wrinkles had appeared which had not been there when she arrived, even though his own life in hiding could not have been without anxiety. His voice had gone deeper, hoarser and more excited. He looked at her with his head lowered as if each day he were seeing her for the first time.

She confided in the rabbi, but she did not complain. She was guided by Madam Kulikowa's advice, perhaps more so than she would have liked. The Madam had taught her that anyone running herself down makes a mistake, anyone apologizing accuses herself at the same time. She was guided by a self-preserving principle, which told her when to draw the line. She did not want the rabbi to feel sorry for her. She spoke more of the other girls than of herself.

"What happened to you is what happened to all who were there," the rabbi said.

"It did not happen to everyone."

"You did what you had to."

"Maybe."

"We've got to live."

"My father threw himself against the electric fence."

"And your mother?"

"I think that they killed my mother."

"As they killed your brother?"

"Yes."

"They didn't kill you."

"I don't know. Humiliating is like killing," she replied.

"You were close to it."

In the end the rabbi said: "I don't want to blaspheme." He was gripped by revulsion. He closed his eyes for three seconds. Perhaps he was praying. He had to pray for 15-year-olds who claimed to be 18. For a God who kept silent. He conceived a prayer which as yet had no text.

"If I asked you whether you've brought back something good from there, would you think I'd gone mad?"

"I would have told you myself: I'm no longer letting anything surprise me."

He was startled by the matter-of-factness with which she had armed herself. Why had God chosen her for the right side on the railway ramp? To be one of 30 army whores? Did He breathe that defiance into her which she had clung to tooth and nail, not allowing herself to die?

"Perhaps," he said.

"Perhaps what?" she asked.

"God is in you."

The rabbi's forehead was like the rucked carpet under his chair. His cheekbones protruded, covered only by thin skin. From Skinny's green eyes sins were looking out at him, legends as old as man, smaller than history and deeper than memory.

On the tenth day she was afraid he might really go mad.

She regretted that she had told him how, on that first Friday, a soldier had planted his body on hers.

*

Rabbi Schapiro knew of children who had knocked at the door of Hungarian people they had never set eyes on, and these people had given them a hiding place. Those were the unknown, the self-effacing, who softened the face of the Christian world.

"No-one is without a face," he said.

"No," she agreed.

She remembered Obersturmführer Stefan Sarazin of the Waffen-SS, the longest serving member of Einsatzgruppe D, who loved to shoot rabbis. For him, one murdered rabbi was like ten murdered Jews. He had shown her a photograph of the unit in which he'd first served. It was like a school photograph, the boys still wet behind their ears, barely unleashed from their mothers' apron strings. They belonged to one of four detachments of Einsatzgruppe D, which, together with Einsatzgruppen A, B and C, had in the course of one year, during their advance from the Oder to the Dnieper and Volga, murdered more than a million people.

Skinny and the rabbi could supplement this picture with photographs taken by the Allies that they'd seen, of the pits, filled with the bodies of people who, before their execution, had had to take off their clothes. Unforgettable scenes, of tumbled, waxwork-like bodies.

To Obersturmführer Sarazin death meant an intertwined mass of bodies whose approximate number he would record, with the help of his book-keeping corporal, and after affixing the unit's seal, forward to Berlin, along with a crate packed with his victims' belongings.

The Obersturmführer had told her: "We are a new culture." They wished to have nothing to do with what had gone before.

The 17-year-olds from her transport had been made to run under a rope strung across part of the ramp, as soon as they had arrived. They had no idea what the test was for. The shorter ones, those who didn't have to duck to get under the rope, like her girl cousin, went straight to the gas chamber.

The hungriest among the others picked up the rats the Hitler-jugend boys had left lying in the mud. Skinny decided not to tell the rabbi – not before supper – what they had eaten.

"What remains good and what is bad?" The rabbi said after a moment.

And then: "What we didn't see didn't exist."

Not for the first time on that tenth day it seemed to her that the rabbi was talking in a confused way.

"Sometimes it's better not to see," she said.

"What makes you stronger – seeing or not seeing?"

He didn't expect an answer from her; or for that matter, from himself. Even so, he felt guilt. Would anyone ever know more? Know the whole mosaic?

She didn't have to tell him that the most credible testimony could be borne only by the dead, not by those like herself who had survived.

"It began a long time ago," the rabbi said.

They had been having this kind of conversation every evening before supper, except that he had not been so feverish before. She urged herself to be patient, so that they could finally sit down at the table.

"Do I want from you something that no-one can ever explain to me?"

"It happened every day," she said.

"You think so?"

"Some things can't be explained," she admitted.

Did the rabbi accept her as an adult? "Child," he had said. That had been his first word to her. She wasn't sure whether she wanted him to treat her as a child or as an adult.

"There are no words for it," the rabbi answered.

Yes, so far there were no words for it, he repeated to himself.

Not once had the rabbi used the word prostitution. It had become for him, over the ten days she was with him, a metaphor for something greater than the fate of just one 15-year-old.

"Even the most sacred was desecrated," he said. "Even the purest was soiled."

Words, he said to himself. For the second time on that tenth day he felt the misery of the world into which they had been born. The darker side of man. That which was in the words and beyond them. The darkness of silence. That which would remain a secret.

"Words such as life, words such as ruin," he said.

"Words can be resisted," she suggested.

"Catastrophe," he repeated.

"Night, darkness, the void," he said.

And then, once more in Hebrew, as though it could not be expressed in German or Hungarian: *"Shoah."*

It was getting late.

"My heart is turning to stone," the rabbi said.

"I doubt that," she objected.

"My feet are turning to stone."

"You should sit down."

"I spent years sitting down."

"I didn't mean it like that."

"Neither did I."

"It's getting late," Skinny said.

"We shall have to learn to speak again in order to understand one another."

Hadn't Captain Hentschel said something similar to her when she didn't answer him – that perhaps she was still learning to speak?

"We shall rake our joys together like last year's dry leaves, those past joys that became memories, and those which we are still looking forward to as a child does to a surprise or a present."

In his head he heard the Song of Songs. He repeated to himself the proverbs of Solomon, but not one of them seemed right for the moment. And the Psalms seemed flat. He was whispering to himself through barely parted lips, which were dry from thirst and fever.

"You are entitled to hate them," he said.

"I'm not sure that's what I want."

"Robbing a person of joy is like rape."

He had not missed what she'd said – that humiliating was like killing.

"I would allow you to hate them," he said.

"I don't wish to."

"No-one would be surprised."

"Even so."

"No-one would hold it against you."

"It isn't in me," she said.

It seemed funny that, while she was desperate to eat, the rabbi was seeking answers to something he couldn't understand.

"You had your back against the wall," the rabbi said.

"My back and my face," she corrected him.

"You are righteous."

"I'd rather be full of laughter."

Before them was the table, the candlestick, its candle still unlit, several plates, the bread on a wooden cutting-board, butter on a little dish, a salt cellar and cutlery. The rabbi wore an old alpaca jacket which was dirty. After supper she would clean it for him. The dark spots on the knife, fork and spoon handles reminded her of the blood-stains on the floor of Dr Krueger's surgery and the four castrated young men standing by the wall, their arms hanging, ashamed and frightened while the doctor photographed them.

"I'm a little confused by it all," she said.

"Would you like to light the candle?"

She didn't hesitate, but picked up the box of matches from the table, took a match out, held it between her right thumb and forefinger, struck it and carefully lit the wick. The flame flickered for a moment, then steadied and grew.

Tears were running down the rabbi's cheeks.

Could he have gone insane during those ten days? She did not regard herself as entirely sane, but preferred not to examine herself too closely.

"It's behind me," she said finally.

"I hope so," the rabbi replied.

"Are we going to eat?" she asked.

"We are going to eat."

Then he said: "Perhaps I believe the way your mother would still believe if she were alive." It sounded to him as if he were really saying that he didn't believe any more. Was he hoping to convince himself or her? What did he still not know?

"Everything and nothing," he whispered. "They took life out of our hands and placed it in the hands of others. They took from us what we knew and let people make decisions about us who did not know us."

"I pretended to be an Aryan, one of them."

"You were under duress."

"I knew I could stay alive as long as I wanted. As long as it depended on me."

She did not want to make the rabbi cry any more, or they would never sit down to supper. "It could have been worse," she added.

"To them we were ants, to be stepped on with impunity. Parasitic vermin. A blood poisoning."

Throughout the past ten days, even though he resisted it, the rabbi had identified her with his daughter Erzika whom they took away when she was 14, nearly 15.

"They robbed you both of your childhood," he said under his breath.

He chased away the image of her being passed from man to man twelve, 13 or 15 times a day. It was not she who had desecrated the Sabbath or any other day. In her place he would have gone mute. In his mind he saw the waters over which she had flown. She had no butterfly wings, only arms, legs and a belly. To him she seemed like a moon which had disappeared for three years and for 21 days and nights before rising again as a slender sickle and ripening into a full moon.

What was the medication the Oberführer had prescribed to the girls? The injections he had given them? Might Erzika face another rabbi the way Skinny was facing him? Might she, like Skinny, encounter the captain and the Obersturmführer? Had fever come upon him to burn away such thoughts? He had been afraid, right up to this tenth day, to answer the question: what had happened to his wife and daughter, to his sister and brother? He did not want to imagine details. Every one of those who had been lost had been somebody, a mother, a father, a daughter or a son, or a child who had died all alone. On the tip of his tongue was another question he dared not ask. Could Skinny have met his daughter or his wife somewhere? Would he wish to meet them himself?

"Just as there was an ice age, a stone age and an iron age, so in the future people will speak of a concentration camp age," he said.

She remembered what her mother once told her – that a rabbi was not a priest but a teacher.

He saw blackness before his eyes. He shut them. He opened them again and still saw blackness.

"Aren't you feeling well?"

The rabbi was thinking of his daughter Erzika, his wife Else and his sister Ella. Of his brother, of his father and mother. Of all his family whom the Germans had killed while he was in hiding in Hungary.

"Maybe their defeat will make them human again," Skinny suggested.

"Maybe. I hope so. Maybe their children."

The rabbi looked into the flame of the candle, which was burning down, and at the slices of bread on the plate. At the foot of the candlestick small piles of wax had congealed.

"What use is an oasis in the desert to those the wind has swept away?" he asked.

She thought this might be a fragment of a prayer. Once she had prayed in No. 232 Ost. She had accused herself of her failings, even though she had not given herself away and no-one had discovered who she was. It was a Wednesday, she was waiting for Thursday. She wouldn't have minded if she didn't wake up the next morning. There were worse things than not waking up in the morning. The bread and butter on the table made her think of her brother.

At last the rabbi realized that she wanted to eat. He blamed himself for what he described as his unfeeling dilatoriness.

"Let's eat," he said.

In her mind she saw the army kitchen at No. 232 Ost, where the girls had peeled potatoes for the Waffen-SS cook during the night. They would eat the raw peelings, wondering if they'd be allowed to take the frozen potatoes away with them.

"They did not know the Commandments," the rabbi said.

"They had their own."

"You were living with the devil," he said.

"Perhaps."

"The devil had twelve, 13 or 15 names each day." The words felt heavy on his tongue.

She could have recited to him the names from her last day.

"The local commander here was called Hans Manfred Wunderkind," the rabbi said.

"They sometimes had odd names."

"Every devil has a name."

"And doctor's degrees."

"Devils with doctor's degrees. With military ranks, birth certificates and citizenships. Every devil has a face."

"I remember some of them."

"Some you will forget."

"I'll try."

"Others you'll never forget."

"No. I hope not."

She found it easier to agree with him. She really wanted to eat now. At last they sat down.

"Help yourself," he said.

"After you."

"Go ahead."

"Thank you."

She took a slice of bread and spread some butter on it, more thinly than the rabbi would have liked. She ate while he thought of all the blood shed during the past six years. He thought of people who no longer needed God, a heart or a soul, who had embraced a new religion. He thought of the problems awaiting those not yet born.

What would they wish to know and what would their fathers not want to talk about?

"Isn't it better not to think about it?" she asked.

"I don't know," the rabbi said, using her well-worn phrase.

"I would have given a lot to eat like this at least once during those days."

"You'll be dreaming of food even when you're not hungry."

"I hope I won't be hungry. But I have nothing against dreams about food."

"Dreams don't forget," said the rabbi.

"And I'd give a lot to be able to forget."

"You are still innocent."

"It would be nice if that were true."

She swallowed another mouthful. "While I have something to eat and a roof over my head, an open larder, food on the table three times a day, a bath full of hot water, and no longer the fear that I could lose all that at any moment, I don't feel I have anything to complain about."

She added: "Here I don't feel envious of anyone else."

"You're a grown-up child," said the rabbi.

"Is that a good thing?"

"It's not a bad thing."

"I don't know, I really don't," she said again.

"Nothing is any longer only good or only bad."

"It's better not to look back."

"Can you manage that?"

"I'll have to," she answered.

He was watching her intently as she ate with gusto. She was pretty the rabbi noted, but too thin. She would grow, he told himself, she was still so young. At the same time she had been damaged beyond what was visible, countless times violated and humiliated and whipped.

He could find no words to express this, or numbers to sum it up. He guided himself by the cabbala, in which the sum of one plus one was three. Twelve, 13, 15, 21 days. Not even the cabbala had a solution for such numbers. They remained a mystery.

"You must be hot," Skinny said.

"I'll undo my jacket."

"You could open the window if we switched off the light."

"Not till it's night."

"I'm no longer afraid."

"That's good. You've nothing to be afraid of."

They both knew that this was not entirely true.

She has beautiful green eyes, Rabbi Schapiro thought to himself. His wife and daughter had had such eyes.

"Go on, eat," he encouraged her, to prove to himself that he could still speak.

"Thank you. I've had all I can eat."

"Have some honey."

"I've had some."

"You've a lot of catching up to do."

"Something, certainly."

"Three or six years?"

She smiled at him like a child at an adult or an adult at a child.

"Our ship sank," he said. "Only some scattered shipwrecks survived."

He looked at her carefully combed ginger hair, parted in the middle and still damp from her bath.

"Our train was derailed," he continued. "The brakes, which used to function, failed."

"Time I went to bed," Skinny said. She would wash his shirts in the morning, she decided, even though it was the Sabbath. She would get it done before he woke.

"You should eat something before going to bed," she said. "It doesn't do you any good to only drink. I saw people in the camp who didn't eat even the little they could have eaten."

He did not ask her why, but if he had, she would not have told him that they had lost the will to live. Was the rabbi afraid that perhaps the war was not over yet, that some part of it might come back? She was looking forward to the moment when she could take off the clothes, underwear and woollen stockings that had belonged to Erzika. Was he waiting for the candle to burn down? Face to face with Skinny the rabbi felt older than the world, older than the stars and infinity. Older than the cabbala and all the sacred books. Older than the hidden meaning of all things. He was afraid to return to the faded meaning of the laws, precepts, customs and ceremonies. To the guiding principle of his religious and civic life. To the exegesis of the great prophets, to that which had not been published in print but which the girl in the tall chair in front of him had gone through.

God, Rabbi Gideon Schapiro said to himself, why have you taken away our pride and exposed us to contempt? Why have you driven us out of the light into darkness, us, your Chosen People? Why did you make the exalted low, the noble rotten, why did you deprive the wise of their reason, the weak of their strength, the desperate of their hope? Why did you permit the enemy we did not know to oppress us like the lowest of slaves? Why did you not let us sleep on that first night they humiliated and dishonoured us, never to awaken again? Why did you make us keep a soul in a dead body?

"It's gone," the rabbi whispered.

He sounded confused to her again. What was gone? She had no idea that the rabbi was referring to his soul. She had seen a lot of people in that state. She didn't say anything, she didn't even move, she just let the rabbi unburden himself.

"I'd like to say that we are rising from the ashes," the rabbi said feverishly, "but we are drowning in them, you and I."

Was the mountain of ashes so big that it had drowned their God?

"I'm free from it," she assured the rabbi.

"You're not."

"Yes, I am," she insisted. "I am with you."

"Perhaps you will be free one day."

"I'm sure of it."

"As sure as there's a heaven above me."

"If that's what you want to hear."

The old grandfather clock struck ten – their usual bedtime. The rabbi blew out the candle.

"It's stopped raining," he said.

"Yes," she said. "It's stopped."

She was happy she didn't have to get up at 4.30 a.m., but could sleep until the light woke her. There would be no Oberführer sounding an alarm.

She waited for the rabbi to rise from his chair and then rose herself. His legs were shaking, but she pretended not to notice. That tenth day with the rabbi had made her see how a person lost his mind, how he could be seized by insanity like an invisible rain falling on parched ground.

He did not want to be locked in a world into which he had been forced by what had happened, yet at the same time he could not get into the world he didn't understand. These two worlds were confronting one another in his head like two tanks, or like two warships sailing towards one another in the dark of night. The line on his forehead had deepened and perspiration was collecting in it. In his dark eyes a madness had taken root, flushed up by tears, but a madness with which one could live. Rabbi Gideon Schapiro was weeping again.

She left on the eleventh day, when she felt she should go and it seemed safe. The rabbi looked on her as on Mount Everest that could not be climbed, as on the Pacific Ocean that could not be swum, as on the abyss of all time. He felt dizzy, perhaps because he had not eaten properly for ten days. She had mostly been eating by herself. He fasted, wanting to starve as she had done. She had put on weight during her stay with him, she had filled out a little, though not much. Her silky, ginger hair had grown again.

He gave her a gold pocket watch on a chain, which played the Hungarian anthem. He had two – one had belonged to Elsa and the other had been his daughter's. The latter he had traded with the baker for bread. He saw her to the door. He had not been out in the street for ten days.

She went to the station, to meet the two railwaymen who had taken her to the rabbi. One of them gave her a pair of high lace-up boots with metal studs. They would last her some time.

"Yes, God is within you," the rabbi had said at the door.

These were the last words that Hanka Kaudersová would hear from Rabbi Gideon Schapiro.

Part Four

Part Four

Chapter Ten

We were sitting in a café in Prague. Skinny was telling her story in bits and pieces.

There had been nights when she couldn't sleep and when she imagined how time had slowed down for people in the gas chamber, when they could no longer breathe and every fraction of a second seemed endless. She would ask herself what right she had to live when all those she had known, including her mother and father, her brother and uncles and grandmothers and aunts and grandfathers, were no longer alive. It remained with her for a long time, as a cry whose echo did not fall silent. She had dark circles under her eyes, as she'd had in No. 232 Ost. She was paralyzed by the shadows cast by what she had behind her and before her.

In the first months after the war she mixed with a small crowd of those who had survived because the Germans had killed someone else in their place. A crowd of daughters without mothers, fathers without sons and sons without fathers, widows, a few elderly women and men, and a handful of children. She became used to a world without uniforms. She had a better memory than she would have wished. She laughed when Adler remarked that he had a memory like Emmental cheese. Echoes, images, words, shouted commands and places and colours chased each other round her head. Snippets of what had happened; where, how, to whom. That selection one Monday morning when it was raining and she was thinking to herself that if they picked her she would get soaked on the truck on the way to the gas chamber and arrive wet through.

For Adler, his past was a cat with nine lives. For me it was a tree protected by botanists, planted a long time ago.

"Are you afraid of the past?" she asked him.

Adler acted like a tiger with broken teeth, still able to tear off a chunk of meat and swallow it faster than he should – so that he never properly digested it.

"I see you're making progress," he replied. "I was beginning to suspect that you were afraid of the present."

He was still trying to decide whether to look on Skinny as a victim or a heroine. He had not yet started writing his book about people in the camps. Evil and ugliness were bottomless; he realized that it was easier to focus on the brighter aspects, but there were many more of the darker ones. Evil was heavy, and good as light as a feather. There were no scales for it, or yardsticks.

"All right, so either we kill the past," Adler said, "or we make it into shackles for our legs."

He regarded the past as a trap. Where instruments of torture were concerned he did not wish to go into details.

When the talk turned to whether we had learnt anything useful in the camps, Skinny said, quicker than Adler or I expected:

"I don't think I learnt anything." She probably hadn't wanted to. "Should I have learnt from Dr Krueger how to castrate Jewish boys? Or choose girls to send to field brothels as prostitutes?" Adler asked her no further questions.

"Well, just look at all the things Jindra Kraus learnt." He pointed at me.

She stiffened at the sight of people in green huntsmen's hats with badger brushes. She thought the items of German Afrika-Korps uniforms, which youngsters were wearing like a trophy, rather ridiculous. There must have been an army surplus store in Prague because so many people wore these uniforms.

Skinny regularly reported to the welfare department of the Jewish Community. People were searching for their missing relations. Each day new lists of returnees were posted up. She hung on to the boots that the railwayman had given to her in Pécs as if to a talisman. She counted her haircuts, gratified that her ginger hair had not been made into mattresses, blankets or rope ladders for U-boats. At night she no longer had to relieve herself into a saucepan or mug to avoid going out in the rain. And during the day, when her turn came, she no longer had to get soup put into a mug, once every 24 hours. Sometimes the soup had been so hot that those who had no mug and had to have it poured into their palms let it spill on the floor. Then they had to content themselves with one helping of soup for 48 hours. She no longer had to hold her nose at the excrement tubs, as in the Frauenkonzentrationslager. Nor did she have to use the latrine at No. 232 Ost. She was living at Belgická 24, in a Jewish orphanage which the National Committee had returned to the Jewish Community. She no longer slept on a three-tier bunk, but in a clean bed with a pillow filled with goose feathers. She no longer had to be either healthy or dead. She did not have to look out on the chimneys of Crematoria No. 2 and No. 3.

Apart from a few clothes, she didn't wish to own anything after the war. It would have been too painful to lose it all again. She thought of little Ramon who, at the age of 13, a fortnight after being accepted among the grown-ups, they had fed on Zyklon B.

"You're pretty," Ervín Adler acknowledged.

"Yes, they called me *Die Schöne*."

"Your hair's coming back very nicely. Can you imagine how many eiderdowns and pillows they could stuff it with? Or line winter coats or insulate houses? Don't say we haven't had the devil's own luck."

"Why the devil's?"

"I don't rely on Heaven any more," Adler grinned. "From each according to his ability, to each according to his needs."

The sky was blue, the weather was perfect. It had been fine for a week. Adler said he had three tickets for a football match. She was thinking how they might have taken Ramon along.

"I've grabbed hold of the future," Adler assured her, as though she had asked him.

"Who hasn't?" she answered. "Besides, we have no other choice."

Adler, like Skinny, had come to realize that his experiences were incommunicable to others. Sometimes he regretted this, at other times he didn't care. He would turn to the written word; it was less recalcitrant. He tried to persuade us to do the same. He wouldn't try too hard to describe physical suffering. He was searching for an eleventh commandment to complete the notorious Ten. Perhaps: *Thou shalt not humiliate anyone.* The Germans did not set up concentration camps in order to concentrate people there. They had killed on a conveyor belt as never before in history. But Adler did not want this to become a straitjacket. He didn't feel like a victim, but he was simply unable to put what had happened behind him.

No doubt there were some things about Adler that Skinny liked. He was interested in the inner reserves of a human being, with the struggle that individuals wage with themselves. The Germans didn't interest him all that much; he tended to ignore them as though Germany was no longer on the map of Europe. He was interested in something else: In what respect could a person be better? Adler looked at pictures of the delighted crowds in Berlin, or at Nuremberg, as they prepared for war – when they believed themselves to be superhuman, a master race. First they humiliated their opponents, hoping that every member of the "lower race" would personally acknowledge his inferiority and be grateful to his murderers. Adler was both fascinated and irritated by certain German words, such as *Endlösung*, Final Solution; *Übersiedlung*, Resettlement; *Sonderbehandlung*, Special Treatment. And also by the articles on the punctuality of the railways, the development of the autobahn network, or how Hitler had been fond of dogs and children. He was furious when one magazine article declared that Hitler and Churchill were tarred with the same brush. It suggested that Hitler might not have known about all the atrocities. Was time blurring the differences between truth and falsehood, between guilt and innocence? Between justice and injustice? Was it all water under the bridge, flowing into the ocean of oblivion?

Over a dish of ice cream we discussed how we would have behaved if we'd been born Germans. Adler was interested less in what the

Germans had stolen from their victims than in what they had offered them to lure them to their deaths.

He would tease Skinny. He could, as he put it, live with her.

"Aren't you lacking ambition?"

"What's that?" She reacted as if an ulcer had burst in her stomach.

In the field brothel she had had to conceal that she was Jewish and now she would have to conceal that she had been an army whore. She could imagine what a lot of people would throw at her. Did she really have no other way? Did she have to be a whore for the Germans? How was that different from Mr Sláma in their block of flats or the barber who, during the war, had been proud to shave German chins? A lot of people to whom nothing had happened in the war would think that she should have let herself be killed.

Fortunately, she looked innocent. It was more than likely that she was the only girl from No. 232 Ost who had survived.

She toyed with the idea of emigrating to some distant country – to America or to Australia. She'd registered for English classes. Then she added Spanish. After three weeks she gave up. It reminded her too much of her father who, at an advanced age, had joined a rapid-study English class.

We strolled on the wooden bridge over the Vltava River. Trams and cars no longer ran over it, it was now only for pedestrians. It was a pretty bridge and we thought it a pity that it would soon disappear as if it had never existed.

I asked her why she was so gloomy.

"Do I seem gloomy to you?"

"You act as if Adolf Hitler were kissing you."

"Adolf Hitler is kissing me."

"Who do you think wrote Hitler's speeches? Did he write them himself?"

"Your worries!" Skinny exclaimed.

"Don't you underestimate it," Adler said. "It's one – nil for us."

"Ten – nil," I corrected him.

"One – nil is enough," said Skinny.

Did Hanka Kaudersová derive no satisfaction from the newsreels shown before each film, showing Hitler in a shabby army tunic, pale and wild-eyed, his head twitching and his left arm dangling helplessly? Wasn't this a long way from 1941, when he believed that he had won the war and so demobilized 40 divisions and ordered industry to start producing peacetime consumer goods? But was it enough to offset Block 18 of the Frauenkonzentrationslager at Auschwitz-Birkenau or No. 232 Ost?

"Something worrying you?" I asked her, as if I didn't know.

"No longer. Not with you. Why?"

Her eyes seemed to say that this was no business of mine.

"Your voice sounds as if you were half-buried in snow."

There was in fact not a single day when she didn't return to No. 232 Ost or to the ramp at Auschwitz-Birkenau . . . 4 a.m., a frosty night, stars bright. The young should make themselves older and the old younger.

The duty squad had snatched infants and children from young mothers and flung them on to the cart with the baggage, crutches and rucksacks, but the women screamed for their children. Some of them were saved only because their children got lost in the crush. Others fought their way against the crowd, and half an hour later finished up in the showers.

"Each man is an island," she said. She had learnt there to do everything quickly. Eat, walk, run. Not to push into the front row. Not to fall behind. From the wooden bridge she was looking at the surface of the river. By the bank, bubbles were rising from the mud. Now and again a fish would splash. A duck was floating with the current.

She was amused when they wouldn't let her into the Kotva cinema to see *Ecstasis* because she was not yet 18. Needless to say, we smuggled ourselves in. All that fuss because of one nude scene blurred by shrubs? Rottenführer Schratz had seen quite different parades. A thousand girls for five hours in the rain, heat or snow.

"It's just like when it rains," she said. "What can you do? You tell yourself that it won't rain forever. Or else you find a reason to like the rain."

The river glistened and murmured. A little way down from us was the weir, where the water splintered and foamed in the dark. On the hill above there were lights in the windows and above the roofs the stars were shining. Below us the water was flowing, under the bridge and onwards. Three old steamers were anchored by the bank. One of them was being converted into a restaurant and another into an hotel. The third would soon be cleaving the waters of the Vltava again.

It came to her like a fly that settles on the outside of your window and, before flying away, reminds you of its presence. Did she envy the water for flowing away into the unknown? Did it arouse in her a desire to share its fate? Or else to throw into it what was not so pleasant?

I watched her, hoping she would not notice. She had a good figure, slim, with an oblong face that remained with me at night when she was not there. Her features, her slim body, her hands and legs aroused in me a longing that was free from desire. Everything I was then yearning for with regard to Skinny was pure – I wanted to take her hand in mine, put my arm round her shoulders, let her put her head on my shoulder or chest – that ineffable feeling from which love springs. She was so pretty, so normal, so healthy.

"The water, just watching it is doing me good."

"Me too," I said.

"Isn't it crazy?" she smiled.

"It suits me."

From the river came cool air and a faint smell of fish. Suddenly she shivered and a chill ran down her spine before she laughed.

"Getting cold? Want to go?"

"All right."

That morning she had met a Czech doctor, aged about 35, who had come back from Buchenwald. As a souvenir, he had brought his striped uniform with him. In 1942 he had supplied his Jewish friends with prescriptions for butter, lard and eggs, tapioca and rice when these were no longer available on ration cards. He offered to examine Skinny.

All three of us went to see him. He kept Skinny to the last. Adler was in the best shape, just undernourished. With me, the doctor found traces of calcification following rickets. This could be remedied by wine containing iron. He kept Skinny back. She was worried that he might send her for x-rays. For a while she was reluctant even to undress. He saw the tattoo on her belly, and inevitably asked questions. Would he keep it to himself? She pictured people somewhere poking fun at her expense. It worried her.

Skinny divided people into three categories. The first were those who created the concentration camps and what went with them, and who operated them. These were the Germans and their lackeys. The second group, the largest, were those who did not give a damn, who wanted to live and work, who went along with it, kept their mouths shut and stayed alive, because – and here they were right – one's life was all anyone had. Finally, the third category, were an infinitesimal minority – those who had the courage to speak up, to stick their necks out.

She had no wish to see again their former concierge who, when he saw any member of her family in 1942, had crossed the street. His wife had her eyes on the furniture, the carpet, the flower-stand or some picture she might secure from their flat before the officials of the Zentralstelle für jüdische Auswanderung got their hands on them. But the Germans made pretty sure that no damned Czech fished their pond dry.

She had gone to look at their old place in Rybná Street. Outside the barber's hung the same ornamental bowl of gilded tin that had been there when they left. Slavomír Sláma, barber and hairdresser, had his flat behind his salon. He welcomed her, one foot in his shop and the other on the pavement, inviting her to step inside. He would trim her fringe. She would look better than Adina Mandlová in *Girl or Boy*.

Instead of the *No Admittance to Jews or Dogs* he now had plaster busts of President Beneš and Marshal Stalin in his window. How were her mother and father? And little Ramon? No doubt all four of them were back again? He would be delighted to give them all haircuts. And no doubt little Ramon would by now also need a shave. In honour of the Liberation the whole Kauders family could have one free visit each. He would clean up Skinny's neck with a new gadget: Swedish scissors. Sweden had supplied more than guns to the Germans. Perhaps she wouldn't believe this, but after the attempt on Heydrich's life he had cut the hair of General Horst Böhme, the chief of police. Two SS officers had stood guard outside his salon. He had sweated, he'd rather not say where. He smiled. It's all behind us now. We all had our cross to bear.

On the third floor of the building was a flat occupied by an actor. He'd always had a friendly greeting for everybody. During the war, on the balcony of the National Theatre, he had been presented with the Eagle of Saint Wenceslas. After the war a woman neighbour asked him:

"Did you have to accept it?"

He had gaped at her, thinking that the woman should have had enough sense to know that if he hadn't accepted the decoration he would have been taken that same night to the firing range at Kobylisy.

The bachelor flat above the actor's was occupied by a student who, together with some friends, had hidden four girls who escaped from one of the death marches. One of them he hid in the corner of his kitchenette, which he divided off with a curtain. His drinking companions couldn't understand why he no longer made them welcome. After the war they asked him if he hadn't been afraid. What was the most dangerous thing about it? That she was so attractive, he said. The Germans tortured nobody more cruelly than those they called White Jews.

In the street she met one of her teachers from Section L 410 in Terezín. He took her to the Café Demín for a cup of coffee. He asked how she had survived. He bought her a rum baba and said that he would write down her answers.

Her old teacher waited, his pencil poised over a notepad. How much did she remember of the time before the war? What had she wanted to do before she got to Terezín? What measure had affected her most? The ban on the purchase of fruit and vegetables, including garlic and onions? The ban on being out in the street after 8 p.m.? The permanent state of emergency where the Jews were concerned?

"Surely that madness is of no interest to anyone now?" she said. "What do you need to know for?"

"I'm writing my doctoral thesis on it."

He asked her if she was more afraid of the past or of the future. And then came the question: "In Terezín, in Auschwitz-Birkenau or in the camps you were in afterwards, did you do anything you are ashamed of now?"

An alarm bell rang inside her, and at the same time she felt furious that shame still trailed her like a shadow. She was even a little offended, but was careful not to show it; after all, it was not his fault. He was working on his thesis. When all was said and done, the era behind them had been unique in many respects; he believed that it would not repeat itself, but that it should never be forgotten.

"Do you have nightmares?" he asked.

"Not really."

"Not afraid of ghosts?"

"I sleep like a log," she said.

"I would like to believe you," the teacher said slowly. For a moment it occurred to her that he might know all about her. But from whom? The doctor might have gossiped. Any concierge in Prague knew as much as the president or the cardinal. Who, apart from the doctor, had seen her tattoo? She might kick off her blanket in her sleep. Her nightdress might ride up.

She clenched her fists. After a moment she excused herself, she had to go to the bathroom.

They stood together in the street for a few minutes. Skinny waited for him to say goodbye. She made her way back to Belgická, deep in thought. The teacher had asked her for her address, but she had avoided giving a direct answer.

She wondered again where she could emigrate. Anywhere she went she might meet people who had survived the camps and had wanted to get as far away as possible from Europe. She would probably run into them even in Tierra del Fuego. Besides, she had heard that Nazis were now getting to Uruguay, Brazil and Argentina; the Vatican alone was said to have obtained more than 5,000 visas for them. Wouldn't it be a joke if she ran into Sergeant Werner Heinz Ziegler somewhere in the German quarter of São Paulo? They could reminisce nostalgically about how far they were from Prague or the Bismarckplatz in Heidelberg.

She also wondered whether her father had frequented the Café Demín.

I tied myself to her as if with a shoelace. I was interested in everything about her and my interest grew stronger every day, until I realized that she had erected a barrier beyond which I was not allowed to venture.

We had all received a one-off financial subsidy, but treated ourselves to five meals a day by eating at the free restaurants. We had our private topography of Prague.

Sometimes Skinny would close her eyes in order to sense from a person's voice whether he or she was lying to her. What she liked about Adler was that he was a good friend and undemanding. I was afraid that I wouldn't seem so undemanding; but perhaps she didn't see me that way. I gobbled her up with my eyes; carefully weighing every expression. When she'd slept well she had big, clear green eyes.

Skinny and I left Prague to spend a week at the Jewish Community's convalescent home in Ostravice in Moravia. It was an eight-hour train journey. Through the window she watched the landscape slipping past – woods, fields and factories as at Auschwitz-Birkenau. We didn't have to speak; we were all in the same situation. The train, the rails;

telegraph posts along the track. Villages with people living their own lives, not caring what was happening in the world. The kind of people we used to be envious of when they moved us from one camp to another. For the repatriated, the railway had abolished the distinction between second and third class. We were sitting in second class on worn green-upholstered seats, with a compartment to ourselves. We were travelling like lords, we knew where we were going and, more importantly, we knew that nothing bad was going to happen to us when we got there.

Skinny looked at me and I knew what she was going to say: "I've not been on a train like this before."

It was beginning to get dark. I tried to touch her, not only like a friend, though also like a friend. I dreamed of holding her intimately. I wanted to kiss her.

"We're here on our own," I said.

"Not yet," she said.

"Why not?"

"I couldn't manage it."

I looked at her close up. That was all she would let me do. Her eyes were gazing at me like two green gates to a fortress I could not capture. I was looking into her eyes; my glance slid down over her face, down to her hands which lay folded in her lap. Suddenly it was difficult, almost impossible, to take her hands into mine. She was looking at me.

Two things merged in me: my longing to touch her body and the recognition that she was afraid of me. I was filled with tenderness. I gathered all my strength and courage. Suddenly I didn't care what happened or what I might wreck.

"I love you," I said. "If I were Ervín Adler," I went on, hearing the awkwardness in my voice, "I would put it differently, but it would still be the truth."

"I don't know what Ervín is supposed to have said to me. He's said rather a lot."

"You should know."

"I don't know." She was hiding behind those little words.

"I could live with you, not just for this moment but for always."

She was silent for a while. Something had calmed her.

"That makes two of you," she smiled.

She looked at me and then dropped her eyes. It was nearly nightfall and I was glad the guard had not turned on the lights. We were immersed in darkness. It was a fleeting moment, then she looked at me from the half-shadows and behind me she must have seen the dimming landscape, the telegraph posts and the sky. These seemed to carry her back to where she didn't want to go.

"What's happened?" I asked.

"What should have happened?"

"The way you're looking at me."

"How should I look at you?"

"Are you afraid of me?"

She remained silent.

"Are you afraid of . . . something?"

"Perhaps."

She was 16, I was 18.

"I know what you're afraid of."

I don't know if she turned pale or blushed, because it was too dark, but she didn't say anything. Suddenly she was vulnerable: there was an ocean of shame in her. She did not know the saying: If we want to keep a secret we must not tell it even to our closest friend.

"I don't want to rush anything. I'm happy as things are."

"We can draw a line under everything that's been and start afresh, together," I said.

This was what she had wanted to hear. In her eyes was the darkness that was falling outside. A white expanse and a quarry deep in snow. For the first time since I'd met her, there was irritation or impatience or fear alternating with gentleness in her gaze. She was looking at me as never before.

"I love you," I said again. I knew that it was true – more than true, the words seemed inadequate. But I said it because there are no other words to describe how I felt, and she must have known from my eyes that it was the truth. I heard a trembling in my voice that I had never heard before. I hardly recognized myself, the colour of those three little words.

"I'm not as mature as you think," she said.

"I would do anything for you," I said.

"Perhaps it'll happen if you don't hurry things."

"You think I'm in a hurry?"

"I need you to be patient."

"I am patient."

"No, you're not. Not as much as you think or as much as I need."

I did not know what to say.

Wasn't it enough for her that I loved her? If love includes respect, then I respected her, and if it includes anguish, then I felt that too. Surely she realized what it cost me to say those words.

"What I'm telling you is the truth."

"You should give me time," she said.

"Surely there are things you don't have to explain," I said.

She didn't seem to understand what I meant; she was clearly alarmed at what she could not explain to me.

"I'm not a rabbi," I said. "But I could do with a rabbi for what I need."

"Don't exaggerate," she said.

"I'm telling you the truth," I said weakly.

She remained silent for several minutes. All I could do was repeat to myself a hundred times that I loved her, that some things could not be invented because they were more true than truth itself. I saw her as half of my own being, but there was nothing I could do unless she felt the same.

"I'm losing you in the dark. And do you know why?"

"Because it is dark."

I see the estate from an icy height. The two bridges over the River San, the circle of the quarry, khaki figures in bulky greatcoats, and trucks in the yard. The long low building of the brothel, the army kitchen, the vehicle parks. I am with Skinny, Hanka Kaudersová, that first Friday in December, when she feels like the flesh of an exotic fruit from which strange hands pluck the kernel twelve times a day, sometimes 14 or even 15 times. I can hear Oberführer Schimmel-pfennig shouting that in other brothels the girls were serving as many as 50 men. I have Skinny's dark circles under my eyes. I am standing there, with no clothes on, for hours, in front of the bored SS men.

I am in Terezín with her parents; they are still alive. Her mother is splitting mica for the cockpits of Messerschmitts, Heinkels and Fokkers on Bastion III or on South Hill. Later she works with Skinny in the tailor's shop, adapting German uniforms destined for the eastern front by spraying their backs with white camouflage paint. Skinny's father is working in K-Produktion (Kistenproduktion), assembling diesel engines for U-boats in a large circus tent in the square outside the Catholic Church. Ramon is attending the so-called substitute school and helping out in the carpenter's shop in the former riding school.

In September 1943 the Dienststelle allowed the children to do gymnastics in preparation for the Makabi Games on Bastion III. A Protectorate Newsreel team came out to film them at it. After their exercises the children were packed off to Auschwitz-Birkenau by Transport DL.

I see her again on the ramp at Auschwitz-Birkenau, where soon her brother will be cremated. What amazes her father is that some-body has had to think all this up, to plan it, put it on paper, convert it into a thousand memos and instructions and orders, all worked out to the last detail. Do any of these people, as they shuffle forward in single file, suspect that one and a half million people have already passed in front of the doctors on this ramp?

The new arrivals were greeted by the prisoners' band playing a French musical hit in German. Come back to me, I'll wait for you, you are my happiness. "J'attendrai". The band also played it for those who had tried to escape as they were being hanged. No-one could say that there wasn't a sense of humour at Auschwitz-Birkenau. Come back to me before I've searched the world for you. For the first time in her life Skinny encountered a force for which she had no name, a force stronger than any individual. Until then, evil had been a sweet offered by a stranger, which might be poisoned. She was on a boundary line, among the dead even if they were still alive. Suddenly happiness lay in becoming a slave, a whore. The crematoria looked like brick kilns or baking houses. Where was that virgin soil, still untilled, which, allegedly, they had come to settle? They had been promised that families would not be separated.

Now I see before me the night when SS men are using their whips to drive onto a train some Aryan girls chosen to work in field brothels. Skinny knows by then that there are worse things than a whipping, but she clambers onto the train as fast as she can to avoid further lashes. An SS man slams the wagon door. They have an escort – 60-year-old Scharführer Franz Ordentlich, who never utters a word.

I am standing in front of Madam Kulikowa at a roll-call taken by Oberführer Schimmelpfennig. Madam Kulikowa is preparing the girls for tomorrow's batch of soldiers, men exhausted from their withdrawal under fire. The troops come here shaken by the battering they've received, confused by defeats for which nothing has prepared them. They no longer look like the flower of Germany, as they had after defeating Poland and France. They no longer believe that nothing would stop them until they had reached the foot of the Urals. Now they were a master race with sore bottoms, inflamed foreskins and swollen feet, with water on their knees, with prominent varicose veins. Their eyes are bloodshot with fatigue. They come to the brothel as if to a field hospital. The members of the Waffen-SS do not seem so crushed by the retreat. They have the same uniforms as the Wehrmacht, field grey, except that on the right sides of their helmet they have a white shield marked with the SS insignia and on the left side a swastika in a white circle on a red background.

I can see Skinny, feeling like a piece of raw meat on a butcher's slab after the first time she has intercourse. I see them cross the threshold twelve times a day. Faces, bodies, boots, trousers, puttees. Every day except Sunday, and sometimes even on Sunday.

I am gazing into the wasteland through her eyes. I see a roan horse struggling through the snow, jerking its head around, terrified of the wolves. Scharführer Wolfgang Strupp drives the leader of the pack away by firing at him. The silver wolf, his tail up, is clever. He will not let himself be shot. Scharführer Strupp calms his mount by lightly patting its flank. He slips his rifle back under the saddle.

Even when compared to the British and French servicemen the Americans were well dressed and well fed. They got as far as Plzen – the Russians would not let them advance further. At that time we did not yet understand why, we were in favour of anyone who drove the Germans out. The Allies had behind them an unquestionable victory. No-one spat on them. They didn't have to beg favours from anyone. But they also had some costly operations behind them. For every mistake, for every underestimation of the Germans, as at the bridge of Remagen, they had paid heavily. They had truth on their side, and honour, and the kind of humour and lightness that we associated with America. Now they were on leave in Prague. People were a little envious of them, perhaps because America was so rich and also because it was so far away. They had been in Normandy, in Alsace and in Berlin, and on their side of the Elbe. They seemed self-assured, whether they were looking out for a taxi or asking the number of a tram, the name of a street, a tavern or a nightclub.

Skinny examined the faces of passers-by as we walked. Suppose Ramon hadn't died in the gas chamber but had got lost? What if her father had lost his memory and was now trying to find out who he was? Maybe he had lost his sense of time and place? Imagine if it wasn't true that her father had flung himself against the wire in Birkenau? The people who said they saw him die could have been mistaken, and by some miracle he might have survived. She almost forgot that she'd seen him herself. Was her memory playing tricks? The same might be true of her mother. If she was still alive three days before the end of the war, then perhaps she was now walking about, searching, as so many others were.

We had one advantage: we did not pity one another, we had everything still ahead of us. All of us lost practically everybody to the murderers – nine out of every ten people. Pity for the fate of others only came a lot later. At that time, the band in the café, a decent meal and a clean bed were worth a lot.

"*Tabula rasa*," she said to Adler one day.

"What's that?" he wanted to know.

"A clean slate."

"That I am not," Adler said. "Are you?"

In the kosher restaurant at 18 Maislova Street we met an American officer.

"Eighteen is my lucky number," Skinny said to the doorman as we entered.

"Why?"

"I was in Block 18 in Auschwitz-Birkenau."

"Eighteen is the Jewish number of life," the doorman told her.

"What does that mean?"

"That you're still alive," said the doorman, who had lost his daughter. "Run along and eat, Number 18. You're luckier than you know."

Just then the American arrived. The next table was occupied, so he asked whether we minded if he joined us.

"Not as yet," Adler joked.

We frequented Maislova 18 because it was free for us. The American had come from Subcarpathian Ruthenia. He was trying to trace his parents. He had seen Germany on its knees. Anyone in Berlin wishing to buy a coat, a pair of trousers or a pullover needed a special permit, and as a rule they were turned down. One Chesterfield cigarette cost 100 marks, one-third of a worker's monthly wage. For a bar of chocolate the Germans were offering young girls or their mothers. They were searching the refuse bins for unfinished American, British or New Zealand tins of food. Everything was in ruins. The black market was flourishing. He had been looking for his father's brother, his three sisters, his grandfather on his father's side, the first Jew to receive the German Iron Cross for heroism in World War I. He had found no-one, not a single member of his extended family.

The American was looking at Skinny. To him she was a person who had come back from that secret German-Jewish war, in which only one side was armed and the other not at all. Within World War II there was another war, an even greater one, concealed.

The American believed that Europe needed re-education. Skinny laughed. Was he going to send Europe to school? Adler, holding up his soup spoon like a pointer, said that he had attended a re-education lecture in the Buchenwald camp near Weimar. He tried to explain to the American that we had jettisoned the old morality and acquired a new one as early as in the first form of our primary schools. It was a more accurate and certainly a more flexible one. Higher was lower, nearer was further away, black was white and right was wrong. The only things that remained unchanged were day and night; because those were difficult to exchange. Our education had continued in the east. There, no-one complained any longer, as the people in Lodz still did when they had to eat rats.

The American was silent. There was decency in him, as well as sadness and an echo of something that he couldn't grasp. He was clearly searching for a key to us and did not find it. His name was Rex Weiner; he was married, lived somewhere near Chicago and had a small daughter by his American wife. He was an airforce colonel. We guessed that the rank of colonel was not dealt out in the US forces like a hand of cards. He watched us finish our soup and we realized that he hadn't touched his and that it must be quite cold by now. He noticed that all three of us were looking at his plate. If we were not offended, would we allow him to order for us? All courses – starters, main course, dessert. Fruit and lemonade. We did allow him.

Skinny, unexpectedly, was all smiles. Rex Weiner's story pleased her. He questioned his own motivations; he didn't interrogate us. She would have liked to help him to understand. There was nothing worse than mistaken beliefs. Her wish was a wish for justice tempered by retribution, and for retribution tempered by justice.

Colonel Weiner's war philosophy was simple: kill anyone who tries to kill you. Adler identified with it enthusiastically. He omitted to say that he was rather glad that so far he hadn't had to kill. When the time came he would not hesitate. And never again would he get on a transport so obediently.

A moment later the smile disappeared from Skinny's face. On one of the Japanese-occupied islands in the Pacific, a young man whom the colonel knew had tried to escape from a prison camp. The Japanese guards forced him to drink one glass of water after another, until his stomach was inflated and rigid and he couldn't get another drop of water down. Then, with drawn swords and threatening to cut off the heads of anyone who didn't obey, they ordered the other prisoners to kick the young man in his stomach. They were allowed to stop only when the man's stomach burst and he died.

Rex Weiner spoke almost in a whisper. Infamy, though it had no name and seemed inconceivable, nevertheless existed.

Were we not alone? Was it not ridiculous that men should invent a hell with everlasting fire in which sinners would burn until Judgement Day? You didn't have to see it. Imagination was enough.

Adler would not find it easy to write his book about the concentration camps. All around us there was a tinkling of forks and spoons, a clatter of plates, a hum of words, snippets of conversation. It was a fine sunny day, the war was over.

"You can share our bread, boots or cigarettes," Skinny said.

Colonel Weiner was taken aback. "We share the terror of death," he replied.

Skinny thought of her father and mother, and of her little brother who, in her mind, would always remain little, never grow up and never grow old. She thought about what she had shared with him.

Slowly, as if we had known each other for years, Colonel Weiner said: "Terror, but also hope."

He called the waiter and paid. He left a tip on the table. We felt close to him and distant at the same time without being able to explain why. He got up, politely said goodbye and walked out. We never saw him again.

We tried to laugh at everything one could laugh about and at everything that suddenly seemed too much. Deep down perhaps we laughed at ourselves. A trap for ourselves and others. We kept bandying proverbs about; possibly because we believed there might be some wisdom in old sayings. It occurred to Adler that we would not find it easy to use words now because it was doubtful how much validity each of them still had, even though a word might sound reliable.

Wasn't it ridiculous that 10,000 years ago people believed that the soul resided in the teeth? Later they thought it was in their shadow. The Jews discovered that the soul was in the blood, including the blood of certain animals, which was why they should not be eaten. This was not something we worried about in the restaurant of the Jewish Community. But as far as Adler was concerned, or myself or Skinny, they could, as a memento of the good old days, have served us boiled or fried pig's blood – even in tins with German labels – and we would have polished it off.

Adler began to think that a person's soul was in their words, in the events they had lived through. In communicated and uncommunicated experiences or what was left of them. Perhaps for all three of us this was the case. Our talks often turned to memory. How long did reminiscences survive? Would one cancel another out? Was it possible that after some time a person no longer knew what had happened to him, what had happened to others, or what he had merely heard?

"So we haven't learnt anything?" Adler suggested.

Did we at times have the feeling that we hadn't escaped the camps at all? Skinny must sometimes have imagine that what caused her itchiness on a hot summer's day was not her sweat or the fierce sun, but the ashes of her little brother Ramon, getting under her blouse or into her lungs.

I went dancing with her at the Blackbird's Nest in Národní Street, next door to the Adria building. We paid five crowns for admission and then sat there until 3 a.m. over a single glass of lemonade, scarcely even sipping it. The head waiter had plenty of paying customers and the musicians couldn't care less. We always had a table for two, with a vase of artificial flowers, a cut-glass ashtray and a snow-white table-cloth, just like a palace. She was bound to see the shadows of her parents on the dance floor.

"In a little while I'm off to bed," she said finally.

"It's like it was in the Electrician's House," I joked, referring to our dances in Terezín. The music at the Blackbird's Nest was the same as the Germans had played in their officers' mess and the Kamerad-schaftsheim, which we used to listen to secretly from a distance, as if it were forbidden fruit, even though it was behind a timber wall separating the ghetto from the road leading out of it.

The head waiter was very friendly, he never passed our table with-out a smile. He must have been in his forties.

"It's nice here," she said.

She was afraid that the authorities or the school would investigate her past until they dug up what she was not willing to tell them. She tried either to forget about it or, at least, to distort it for herself. She fashioned her own world.

"What did you tell that rabbi of yours?" I asked.

"I didn't tell him everything."

"It would have been too much for him?"

"What would have been too much for him?" she asked cautiously.

"We both know what."

"I don't."

"Don't you feel corrupted?"

198

She looked at me questioningly, and then a little smile appeared on her lips. For me, it was a beginning after the end of the world. It was a smile of helplessness, embarrassment or shame, but at the same time one of hope, determination, a decision to live, perhaps not as before. A page torn out from the Book of Destruction which Rabbi Gideon Schapiro had told her about in Pécs. The rabbi was a new milestone in her personal history, and hence also in mine. Unlike the Book of Good Deeds, which writes itself, the Book of Destruction is written by many hands.

She needed to get it off her chest and this was the evening.

"Do you know what shocks me? The way I simply accepted the death of so many people, including my family. Losing a brother was as natural as Sunday following Saturday. Maybe it was just fear that it would break you otherwise. You put it away somewhere, even though it pressed on you from all sides. You promised yourself you'd mourn later, when you had more strength. Where did this hardness, this indifference spring from, this numbness or whatever it was, when you knew perfectly well that you'd never really be able to come to terms with it?"

She paused for a moment before continuing.

"I'm afraid I may be capable of watching one person after another die. Am I sick? Infected? Has it corrupted my soul? I don't want to kid myself that it's a question of strength. The death of one, two, thousands or even a million people no longer means what it once did. To me it's more important that I'm still alive myself. So someone dies, even someone very close to you, and you just go on. You must always go on. And this is where I have got to."

"Amen."

"Yes, amen."

"It's also where I have got to."

I was reminded of an ancient saying, dug up by someone – what reason cannot cure, time will.

We went out nearly every evening, dancing, to the cinema or the cabaret. They were playing wartime hits – "Under the Old Lamppost",

"Ciribiribin" and others. Skinny was startled when the girl announcer said that the arrangement had been sent from Terezín by Fricek Weiss of the Ghetto Swingers. It had been passed on by a friendly gendarme. That was in 1944, the year that the Germans prohibited dancing in Prague. Fricek Weiss died in a gas chamber because he wore glasses, the announcer said.

Chapter Eleven

Twelve: Hermann Ritter, Tobias Zluwa, Dieter Schramm, Ebergardt Massner, Edward Petzina, Uwe Deutsch, Joachim Arnheim, Oswald Funcke, Ernst Jensen Bessel, Otmar Strasser, Kundar Jäckel, Peter Heiden.

Twelve: Norbert Grünn, Bruno Jechmann, Martin Klause, Edmund Baumgartner, Franz Gregor, Hannes Bäck, Ewald Herder, Quido Haasse, August Keitel, Ernst Traurig, Matthias Dofleben, Lothar Kemnitz

Twelve: Rudi Schlaff, Wolf Köhler, Fritz Dimmel, Heinrich Fresser, Hans Dorpmüller, Wilhelm Kleinmann, Gund Kleimer, Fritz Seidel, Albert Steinfuss, Marian Schulte, Hans-Peter Schullmann, Walter Pechvogel.

"My mother was killed by a car last year," Beautiful said. "Forty-three days later my grandmother died. Forty-three days after that my aunt, my mother's sister. Soon I will have been here 43 days."

Skinny did not know how to answer her. Was a person's fate determined before they were born? They were sitting in the latrine, suffering with diarrhoea. Beautiful saw herself differently from the way the soldiers saw her, or Madam Kulikowa, or the other girls, who were all jealous of her and watched whom the Madam sent to her. There was insecurity in her blue eyes.

"I've got enteritis and I'm cold," Skinny said. "I don't want to sit here longer than we have to."

They had been eating frozen potatoes for three days running.

"It's one of my bad days," Beautiful said. "But I don't want to blame myself for having been born."

"Not a good day for me, either," Skinny said.

The sentry was circling the boarded hut at a decent distance. They could hear his footsteps, his hobnailed boots. After a snowfall, before the snow was cleared, the sentries walked noiselessly. They waited for him to pass. The military censors had held back a postcard sent to Beautiful because it had a grease stain on the stamp carrying Adolf Hitler's face.

"I never was a virgin," Beautiful said.

Skinny was listening to the wind. It came from the north; there had been no snow for two days.

"I don't want you to be afraid of me," Beautiful continued. "When I'm with a soldier I think of a tree whose sap is oozing out. Or a stone from which someone is trying to squeeze blood. I feel like a garden where no-one plants anything, they only pick the fruit. And it's not that tree in the Garden of Eden. I think of gardeners who don't tend the soil. I think of my mother before she died."

She handed Skinny a carefully folded square of newspaper.

"It's what they kill the Jews with. Don't spill it. It comes as a powder like this or in crystals. A Scharführer gave it to me. He explained that it's a mixture of hydrogen and hydrocyanide. They call it Zyklon B."

"What did he give it to you for?"

"He had nothing else to give me. He probably didn't want to carry it about with him."

"What am I to do with it?"

"I've got some for myself. I carry it in a sock."

"You think I want to kill myself?"

"Who doesn't sometimes?" Beautiful smiled shyly.

The latrine stank of quicklime. When they talked or breathed through their mouths the stench was not so overpowering.

From the bridge came the clanging of a train. A military transport.

"Always reminds me of the train which brought me here," Beautiful said.

Skinny rolled the folded paper into her sock as Beautiful had done. She too thought of the train on which she had arrived.

From the waiting room came the sound of music – works of the Strauss family. Skinny thought there was too much blood even in the waltzes: "Vienna Blood", "The Emperor Waltz" and "The Blue Danube". Madam Kulikowa played "Vienna Blood" at least five times a day.

The guards were singing "Heimat, deine Sterne" from the film *Quax, the Pilot without Fear or Blemish*. It was a marching song for hobnailed boots.

In the officers' bathroom used by Hauptsturmführer Hanisch, the commandant of the guard detachment, stood an earthenware bathtub on cast-iron lions' paws – booty from a Polish home in the early days of the campaign. The water was heated by oak logs; the beech had all been burned. The guards had chopped down trees far and wide.

Their tour of duty was coming to an end; they were getting ready for the front. They were half drunk. Now they bawled "Alte Kameraden". The Waffen-SS, the most Aryan breed under the stars. They felt like stars themselves. They would shine in the sky long after they were extinguished on earth. They were putting up a Christmas tree in every room.

The River San shimmered under the light of a low moon, like a herring gradually vanishing in the distance. The wind changed its force. Its howling reminded her of those she had lost. Father, mother, Ramon.

The guards were singing "Muss i denn, muss i denn . . ."

The ravens by the gate attacked. The biggest of them hacked the tail of the dog that had snatched some food from the kitchen. Another tore meat from its teeth.

The soldiers in the waiting room were watching the winter lightning. "You count the seconds between the lightning and the thunder. Then you divide by three to see how many kilometres away the thunderstorm is," one soldier said.

*

Twelve: Uwe Biheller, George von Zucker-Kreiss, Robert Albert Altmann, Gustav Leibnitz, Franz Kraft, Hannes Czech, Andreas Heismeyer, Konrad Engelbert Schiese, Jennings Hörbiger, Jochen Hütter, Hugo Henschel, Karl Haasse.

Twelve: Hubert Schiller, Theo Zander, Udo Wulff, Schenk Kraut, Gerry Schödl, Axel Alfred Röhm, Wolfi Wolf, Henning Wegeberger, Adolf Winter, George Sonnenglass, Rudolf Remnitz, Hans-Jochen Hauser.

The cold did not let up even on Twelfth Night. An SS man, Hauptsturmführer Wolfgang Tropp, was approaching the gate. His horse could scarcely drag itself along. With his heavily gloved hand the SS man stroked its mane. Suddenly the horse sank to its knees. The Hauptsturmführer only just managed to get his feet out of the stirrups. The horse was dying. For a moment he hesitated. Then he drew his pistol.

"All right, boy, all right."

A shot rang out. The Hauptsturmführer slung his leather bag and rifle over one shoulder, unbuckled the saddle and laid it over his other shoulder, and then the canvas blanket which had covered the animal's back. Without another glance at the animal he strode to the gate.

The wolves came bounding out of the quarry. The SS man dropped his load. Legs apart, he emptied half of his magazine at the wolves to drive them away from the dead horse, but it was useless. He kept the remaining bullets in case the wolves attacked him. They began to tear at the flesh of the horse. The snow beneath the animal's body turned red.

At 2.30 a.m. the brothel was awakened by a huge crash and the crunching of metal against metal, followed by the sound of twisting steel, crushed metal and splintered glass. The front locomotive had turned over, the one at the tail end of the train had jumped the rails. The carriages rose up and settled on their sides. The steam whistle didn't stop even though the engine lay like a wounded beast rooted to the ground. The carriages looked like toys flung down by a child. Steam was escaping from both engines with a furious hiss.

The guards ran out into the darkness with rifles and stretchers, their dogs on leads. The maintenance crews followed them. Into the shouting of military commands and the barking of dogs came the explosion of a second charge. The fire, the smoke and the shouting were carried beyond the river by the wind.

Searchlights went on at all four guard towers. They lit up the train, and you could see far into the wasteland. The sidings were a huge lighted target.

Oberführer Schimmelpfennig blew his whistle. The sound mingled with the hooting of the railway engine. The cook struck the iron rod by the kitchen. When the train's steam whistle fell silent there was the sound of screaming, crying and shouting.

"Bandits," Ginger said hoarsely.

"You really must be stupid," Long-Legs said.

Stars stood out in the sky. Eight carriages had left the rails. They were piled end to end. The carriages were green, red and blue. The sleeping car carrying Waffen-SS Obergruppenführer Walter Rudi von Kammers was crushed. He'd been on his way back from a conference at the Führer's headquarters. In his locked briefcase were the directives of the commander-in-chief of the eastern front forces, Heinz Guderian, and in his head he'd carried the echoes of futile concerns: Germany would bleed to death unless troops were transferred from the west to the east. His body, as much of it as could be extracted, was carried out by the guards. Both charges had been detonated before the engine reached the bridge, which was undamaged.

Oberführer Schimmelpfennig was assigning tasks. The Dirnen, the field whores, were transformed into nurses under the direction of a group of Brown Nurses who had been travelling in the blue carriage.

"I'm not ruling anything out," said The Frog.

The Brown Nurses, whose carriage had been attached to the train at Festung Breslau, were under the command of a woman officer, an Obersturmbannführer of the Medical Corps, Mathilde Kemnitz. She looked like a hospital matron.

The air was filled with the moans of the injured. Smoke was rising from a tanker, lit up by flames. The nurses, along with servicemen, guards and maintenance workers, carried the injured out of the train and put them on stretchers and blankets. The less seriously hurt clambered out of the carriages themselves. Now and again the flames soared up, illuminating the catastrophe with shades of light which redoubled that of the searchlights.

Skinny had never seen anything like it. The plain had acquired a different appearance. She could not equate the death of Germans with that of her own people. The pain perhaps. But there was a connection missing. The train had been going to the front. She realized that she had to move if she was going to keep from freezing. All around her she was aware of a tremendous effort: she would join in it only to the extent she had to. She had the impression that The Frog was rather pleased to be faced with such a challenge, with a disaster. Perhaps this was the moment when he could cover himself with glory. He was continually in motion, not stopping for a second.

To move meant helping those whom she would have preferred to help to their graves. That was how she felt until she looked at their faces.

The guards and maintenance men came along with oxygen cylinders, cutting gear and more blankets. The searchlights focused on the accessible side of the train. The burning tanker proved impossible to extinguish. There was a northerly wind, but mercifully it was not snowing.

"Heil Hitler!" The Frog greeted the officers. "Heil Hitler! Heil Hitler!"

"I heard you the first time, colonel," one of them grunted.

Schimmelpfennig organized the sidings into an open-air field hospital until the ambulances, summoned by radio, arrived. He believed that every test would further temper him. This knowledge imbued him with furious energy. He wanted everyone to tremble before the wounded majesty of the Reich. In his hand he carried an axe. He thought of the opportunity that now presented itself to him – to emerge from the twilight of No. 232 Ost. He made himself visible to ensure that there were witnesses to his prowess. He did not want his involvement to slip into the shadows or to be forgotten.

Behind the train stretched the wasteland, full of treachery and the still untamed strength of an enemy that seemed to have launched a personal attack on him.

"Those weeds will be eradicated" he proclaimed, but he was not sure that anyone heard him.

Red was everywhere. The little curtains in the shattered carriage windows were billowing in the icy wind. He saw a dead body with a stony face, in an impeccable uniform. That was how one should die, he thought to himself. He caught sight of a plump colonel with an engagement ring, a wedding band and a ring with a large stone on his fingers.

"They have honoured us with a visit. We are fighting an invisible army," said an officer – one of those The Frog had just greeted with an enthusiastic Heil Hitler.

"Of bandits," the Oberführer completed.

The officer asked who the girls were. The Frog looked at him as if he didn't understand.

"Feldhuren," he said. "Sex partners serving the army."

"Disgusting," the officer said into the freezing air.

"Quite so," the Oberführer said.

It occurred to him, fleetingly, that the weakness of some officers possibly extended right into the Führer's bunker. It was not just a physical weakness but equally a psychological and moral one.

The frantic bustle of the guards was largely due to their anxiety not to get frostbite. The Frog wondered how many cases he would have to treat in the morning. He divided his attention between the activity on both sides of the train. It was a frightening thought that it took just two or three guerillas to stop a Herrenwaffe train on its way into battle. A general had been killed and they'd had to carry his broken body out like split logs. By the nearest carriage on the floodlit side a young officer was standing, but almost at once his knees gave way and he collapsed, hitting the back of his head against the carriage steps. For a moment he looked like a juggler.

The Frog went on assigning tasks and supervising their execution. He issued orders for amputations of arms, legs and fingers to be performed in the tent that the guards had erected by the outside wall. It looked like a Turkish refreshment kiosk. The patients were exposed to the wind, but there was nothing that could be done about that. The male nurses worked efficiently. They knew, even in the dark, what they had to do. The Oberführer made the girls' cubicles, the guards' dormitories and even his own office available. He ordered more tents to be erected.

"Looters will be shot," he shouted at Madam Kulikowa.

Within five minutes Long-Legs had given Skinny two warm flannel shirts from an open suitcase. Next to it lay a woman with a smashed head. Long-Legs was unmoved. The dead woman was too heavy for the girls to lift. Her white face was spattered with blood as if powdered with sand. The blood had immediately frozen and congealed. The woman's eyelids were closed; darkness hid her death's grimace.

Skinny left the shirts under the carriage.

Two hours later a rail trolley arrived from the Wehrkreis with a repair crew, doctors and the Gestapo. Behind the trolley a locomotive was pulling a field hospital. They came to a halt as close to the wrecked train as possible, where the track was still undamaged.

The Gestapo men quickly strode around the train. With them was a Waffen-SS general. The Frog was exhilarated at being in the vicinity of the top-ranking army and Gestapo officers, and he had good reason. Proximity to power like that and promotion were twins. He must not fail even the greatest challenges. He reminded himself that the army was retreating. He prepared himself for what he would say if the general addressed him. They were not hard enough; that was the prime cause of all troubles. But he was not sure they wouldn't criticize him for letting his searchlights provide targets for enemy aircraft. Heavy guns were rumbling in the distance.

By the track the wounded were laid alongside the dead. Those rescued were stumbling about. The amputation tent was full. Amputation at that temperature, even though the tent had warmed up a little, was no fun for the doctors, the nurses or the auxiliary staff. The surgeons from the hospital train – accustomed to working 18, or sometimes 24 hours without a break, without a thought to the quality of the operations they were performing and exhausted to death – had their hands full. One of the doctors from the hospital train looked like Klaus Schneeberg, Dr Krueger's assistant. The Oberführer thought of his friend from Mauthausen, an amputation specialist, and of his wife-to-be, now a doctor at Buchenwald.

Skinny was terrified of blood. It made her dizzy, and she closed her eyes. Even so, she felt excited, full of a secret joy, not triumphalist but no longer defeatist. Madam Kulikowa had assigned her to the matron of the Brown Nurses, Obersturmbannführer Kemnitz. The woman got her to soak patches of gauze in aluminium caprylate. The basin soon froze over, making the task difficult. Skinny straightened the blankets of the injured who were taken into the estate or the hospital train. Now and again she slowed down and faced the burning tanker to warm herself. It burned with countless flames, big and small, constantly changing colour and yet remaining the same. She felt weak.

"Keep going," Long-Legs said.

"Yes," she replied.

It was impossible to be amid the blood of the others and not absorb a fraction of their pain. She passed the stretchers of battered women. They looked at her as if she was one of them.

The matron scrutinized her for quite a while. She had tired watery eyes, and she was about the age of Skinny's mother. At the moment of the train's derailment some of the Brown Nurses were dozing, while the others had been singing about the Führer, and how he loved Berlin. "Mein Führer", the song addressed Hitler like a prayer. It spoke of that promise which must not and would not be broken. A spiritual glow. A difficult operation from which eternal peace would spring. Of humiliation and of honour regained. What Germany was in the eyes of the world and in its own eyes. Then, abruptly, the explosion.

When dawn came they were exhausted. Heavy guns were still roaring in the distance as if they had nothing to do with what had happened on the railway track. The fire at the back of the train had burnt itself out. The area, as the Obergruppenführer informed the Oberführer, was being searched by Einsatzkommandos of the Einsatzgruppen, by their best Jagdkommandos. They would leave not a single stone unturned in the quarry. The weather was in their favour, it was a clear day. The meteorologists did not expect a snowfall for the next 24 hours, there was just a hideous wind. With these observations the Gestapo general departed, along with the hospital train pulled by a diesel locomotive and followed by the rail trolley.

The Frog's report stated that there were 78 dead, 327 severely injured and 83 slightly injured. The train and its engines were almost totally destroyed. Both engine drivers and three firemen were among the dead. Most of the damage was repaired within six hours of daylight. The track was expected to be back in operation in another six hours.

The repair work was directed by Obersturmführer Xaver Kinkel, a dwarfish man in a colonel's uniform which made him look like a green gnome. He wore fur boots and a woollen ski mask on his face. A little man of indefatigable energy and organizational talent, he wore several Nazi decorations. He appeared to have sprung straight from a Dr Caligari film. All one could see of him were his bespectacled eyes.

Obersturmführer Kinkel knew how often similar disasters happened on the Ostbahn, the eastern track whose repair and maintenance – but not its security – he was responsible for. Not one of them had been an accident. He claimed no other merit for his work on the Ostbahn than that which a clockmaker would claim for repairing a broken timepiece. Those who threatened the Ostbahn threatened Reich property, the spirit of the Reich. Germany's railways now seemed to him like a wounded, bleeding beast.

The matron organized blood donors. The Brown Nurses all volunteered. So did servicemen and women who'd come through the disaster unscathed. The matron got Skinny to bring out some chairs. Who knew their blood group?

Ginger, Maria-from-Poznan and Smartie had already volunteered. The matron noticed Skinny's tattoo on her forearm. A number? Feldhure? She was shocked. Only then did Obersturmbannführer Mathilde Kemnitz realize where they were. This was the estate they'd heard about. She stopped being impersonal.

"*Schämst du dich nicht?*" Aren't you ashamed of yourself?

Skinny shook her head at the nurse.

"She's not one of us," the nurse said.

"She passed my screening," Oberführer Schimmelpfennig intervened. "She has Aryan blood."

At least I hope so, he added to himself. In the chaos of Auschwitz-Birkenau or Festung Breslau the right hand didn't know what the left hand was doing.

"*Jawohl, Herr Oberführer,*" the matron said.

The Frog hung up an acetylene lamp by the gate. Out of the corner of his eye he saw the gilded tin eagle. A truckload of army engineers pulled up. They had come for sex, but the truck did not even enter the estate. Operations were suspended. The men could dismount, the truck would stay. They could wait in the waiting room. Was it warm in there? Yes, warm and there was music.

The Oberführer took the matron on a tour of the estate. He showed her the latrines, the kitchen, the guards' dormitories, and where she would find drinking water. Skinny helped her until nine in the morning. She could scarcely stand. Finally Obersturmbannführer Kemnitz allowed her to go and lie down. The dormitory was full of soldiers.

She stretched out in Cubicle 16 and fell instantly asleep. She dreamt that she was a Brown Nurse and that her train had been derailed. When a Hitlerjugend boy saw her blood he shouted that she was a Jewess. Her blood turned to water. Rats were crowding round her. She screamed when the heat from the fire got under her skirt. Her heels were burning, she was afraid she might lose her legs. Her stomach was aching. She tried to fight off the rats with her hands.

She was woken by the matron, who had heard her scream. The woman gave her a plate of tapioca pudding with a scattering of sugar and chocolate and a topping of raspberry juice. She put a little jug of milk before her. The first thing Skinny was aware of was diarrhoea. Was that why she'd had a bellyache in her dream? She ate faster than she wanted to in front of the matron.

"What are you afraid of? Do you have diarrhoea?"

"Sometimes."

"From the food or from the cold?"

"I don't know."

"No wonder, in these conditions. All of us have it, out east."

Then she said: "It happened so suddenly, in a matter of seconds. A colossal bang. Cases were flung about, people screamed. We were thrown from our bunks and seats, hitting other bodies. There was shattered glass everywhere. People were pushing and stumbling, stepping on each other. And at last the train came to a halt. We were lucky it didn't happen on the bridge. Perhaps we were moving too fast. If it had happened on the bridge we would all have been drowned in the icy water." She paused. "We came to the east to bring them civilization," she continued. "To teach them German, get them used to German laws."

Her voice broke. She watched Skinny eat, licking her plate clean and drinking the milk in big gulps. It was the first milk she had had for three years.

"No-one's going to take it away from you," the matron said. "And look what they've done," she went on. "We were on our way to the front. They ought to shoot anyone getting close to the track. Surely the Ostbahn is ours? Who's going to make up the loss? Doesn't anyone guard the track? Where are our aircraft?"

"I am full of misgivings," the matron said.

She raised her eyes to Skinny: "So few like us."

Skinny needed to belch.

"It is Germany's fate," the matron said. Her neck wrinkled into folds that seemed to Skinny like a many-stringed necklace. Lines appeared on her forehead. In spite of her ample figure she was a good-looking woman.

Then she added: "Would you want it to happen all over again, seeing that you're not German?"

After a while she asked, with her eyes on the ground: "How many?"

Skinny did not understand. Her short hair was stuck to her neck with sweat. She felt different now to how she had at the beginning of the night, more like an uninvited guest at someone's feast. Or someone's wake. She was aware of the pudding and milk in her stomach. Small amounts rose now and again to her mouth. It was pleasant, reminding her of food and of being full.

"How many soldiers each day?" the matron asked, explaining her question. "Those poor boys. My name's Mathilde – Sister Mathilde or Frau Mathilde. On duty they call me Obersturmbannführer Mathilde."

Her voice and gaze echoed the numberless sick, wounded and dying she had seen.

"Twelve," Skinny said.

"Twelve?" Sister Mathilde repeated.

"Sometimes more."

"Every day?"

"Except Sunday. But sometimes on Sunday too. Not today."

"I saw the troops arrive. Will you have to catch up?"

"I don't know. Perhaps."

The matron reflected on the different lives that people were born to, how their fates differed. Her mother had also been a matron, just as her mother's mother was before her. The Kemnitz matrons. It was a family tradition, a dynasty.

She looked at Skinny. Might she have become a nurse? She did not wish to know how a 15-year-old had become a whore in Germany.

"I wouldn't have the stomach for it." Then she asked: "Didn't the Lebensborn organization have this place before?"

"So they say."

It seemed to Skinny that there was distaste in the matron's well-fed voice. And Skinny was right, the matron had a rather bourgeois view of fallen girls and of marital fidelity. She would not allow a man other than her husband to have anything to do with her body.

"You must have started early. You look very young. Fifteen?"

"Eighteen," Skinny said. "Getting on for 19."

"You did a good job," said the matron.

Skinny didn't answer.

Skinny had gulped her food down like a sick animal, afraid that someone might snatch it away. This aroused both suspicion and compassion in Obersturmbannführer Mathilde Kemnitz. And when, earlier on, she had kicked off her blanket and screamed in her sleep, the matron had noticed a festering sore on her bottom. For a moment she considered enrolling the girl in the Brown Nurses. Was she in the brothel as a punishment?

"Lie down on your tummy," she ordered.

With her fingertips she probed the wound.

"Has the doctor seen this?"

"He gave me some sticking plaster."

"It's not healing too well in this cold. How long have you had it?"

"A few days."

"A couple of weeks?"

"About that."

"Do they beat you?"

"Only as a punishment."

"Punishment for what?"

"For a complaint."

The matron squeezed the pus out of the wound. With skilled movements she covered it with a piece of sterile gauze. She said something about how helpful the prostitutes had been during the night. For a while she looked into the girl's eyes. This young army whore had the same green eyes that she herself had had in her youth.

Chapter Twelve

Twelve: Kurt Fischel, Norbert Peltz, Helmuth Brünnich, Max Joachim Klein, Bruno Bartels, Ottofeld Bader, Fritz Urban, Hans Markvart, Hans Feldmann, Sutr Johannes Schulhof, Anton Mahler, Alex Roubal.

The girls got up at 4.30 a.m. They shared their reveille with the guards, and then the cook struck his iron bar. The guards had their roll-call, morning exercises and breakfast, and then began their duty. The first shift ran until 8 p.m., the second from 8 p.m. until 8.00 a.m. the next morning. In the evening they had Party lectures on racial hygiene. Every day they had an air-raid practice, in which The Frog included the girls, though not all at once. For the slightest infringement of discipline the guards got three days of severe-regime imprisonment. The essence of the Waffen-SS was discipline. It was sufficient for a guard to be caught wearing a scarf in the blizzard for him to end up in the "glasshouse". They learned to patrol around the estate with their chins pressed against their throats so that the wind did not blow down their collar. In a blizzard they wore motoring goggles with green-tinted glass. Any infringement was a disgrace for the whole of the Waffen-SS. For a second disciplinary punishment an SS man was sent to the front. But some of the guards had had their application for transfer to the front rejected.

At breakfast, Ginger told them that, if it came to it, she could look after the entire backlog of soldiers. There was no upper limit where she was concerned. Fasting did not do her any good. Her body was like a fish, it needed water, or better still a river, even a lake. She felt like a sponge, if they knew what she meant. The choice was theirs. With a full stomach she could do wonders. Long-Legs ate the sugar she had received for giving blood all in one go. They had been given sausage, which smelled, and potato salad made from frozen potatoes.

Twelve: Fritz Knoll, Raymond Stoll, Gerd Hartmann, Adalbert Neustadt, Hugo Brill, Karl Rek Neumann-Zaneski, Igor Vogel, Paul Scheer, Wolf Neugebauer, Siegfried Sessendheim, Marcel Seebauer, Jens Lindauer.

The girls' latrines were surrounded by a partition made of rough planks covered with tarred paper. The paper was held only by a few nails and was regularly torn off by the wind. From outside it was possible to see the figures moving about inside. Occasionally a guard would peep in. The girls sat next to one another, wrapped in their coats and with kerchiefs round their heads, leaving only a gap for the eyes, each holding a stick for driving away the rats. At 25 degrees below it was difficult to maintain personal hygiene. The soldiers had inflamed backsides, brownish emissions, rashes, eczema and blisters, but from the girls they expected total cleanliness.

"I had a bellyache with all of them today," Long-Legs announced. She kicked some rats away from her. What were they trying to do? Bite off her nose? How could such disgusting creatures be considered sacred in India? She had an aristocratic nose – experts on Aryan features had drawn her attention to it. Her legs and her high, foal-like ankles were as slim as her nose. When there was nothing she could steal from a soldier she would make do with twisting off his buttons.

"I'm passing blood," Skinny said.

"Maybe it's only diarrhoea."

"Perhaps it's from drinking melted snow."

"You've got to drink something. I can't get that general in the train off my mind. He was crushed by the walls of the carriage. The compartment was lined with purple plush, with windows that had little dark red curtains with gold braid bands. Those bandits must have had God on their side. Maybe the Jewish God. Before they made me a whore I had a Jewish boyfriend. My family weren't exactly ecstatic about it, but I would have run away from home rather than give him up. The Jews have hard heads. They'd sooner have their heads cracked like a walnut than give in."

She remembered how her lover had prayed, also for her: *Baruch ata, Adonai:* Praised be our God, king of the universe. She'd liked the fact that he never hurried to climax before she got there. He waited for her. She didn't want to know where he was. Or was not.

Beautiful was pouring water into the tub.

"I'm not ashamed of anything I do. I haven't done anything so far that I couldn't admit to my mother, although she's no longer alive. The nuns told me that a good girl waits. You can wait as long as you like, but you don't escape that face above you."

Beautiful had a voice that enchanted everyone, not just the soldiers. Her words floated liltingly, as if she didn't want to wake from a dream. With the sleeves of her sweater pushed up, she poured in more water. There was passiveness in her eyes. Helplessness, perhaps, or a kind of chastity. Madam Kulikowa had given her perfume and glass earrings.

"Your voice is like a balm," Skinny said to her.

Beautiful spoke as though she were interpreting. She immersed herself in her own resurrection, somewhere between consciousness and unconsciousness, an errant soul, almost languid, in contact with her mother. She was wearing a trace of lipstick.

"Can't appear on roll-call all pale. Maybe I'll tell him I menstruate 31 days a month."

"You're stooping today," Skinny said.

Beautiful hunched, making her shoulder blades stick out from her back so that her breasts would not be too prominent. One soldier had told her that she had a bosom like the waves of the sea.

The tub was now three-quarters full.

"Ever thought that you might die by the side of a soldier?" she asked.

218

"Perhaps."
"Or he at your side?"

Twelve: Fritz Rattenhuber, Rudolph Mansfeld, Karl Kersten, Hans Lammers, Heinrich Zeitler, Kurt Wunderbar, Julius Scheller, Karl-Ludwig Woos, Dietrich Stahl, Arthur Mengerhausen, Erich Kruger, Hermann Junge.

Twelve: Markus Frotzinger, Joseph Gruss, Bertram Hahn, Franz Prochaska, Roloff Frankenberger, Kurt Boskowski, Willi Titzelm, Juppe Schwartz, Nicolaus Ebner, Jürgen Pazzeller, Bruno Rahm, Ferdi Kranz.

Twelve: Peter Drier, Dutrow Tello, Franz Hase, Egon Stolzfuss, Benedikt Bergmeier, Bartolomeo Stein, Martin Luther, Edmund Bernard, Franz Dietel, Dietrich Blumenbauer, Siegfried Ripke, Sepp Springer.

"I can't rinse that soap off," Estelle said.
"Rub yourself with your towel," Skinny said.
"My skin gets all dried out in the cold."
The noises of the night were carried away by the wind. Now and again a searchlight cut through the darkness. Another train clanged over the bridge.

"What astonishes me is that I hate myself almost as much as they hate me," Estelle said. "They want a world without you or me. So that only they are left. The noble race. This morning a lance-corporal told me how two Judenweiber had been hiding out in a coal shed by the depot. He caught them as they were trying to get rid of the tattooed numbers on their forearms. One of them was cutting her skin off with a knife; the other was trying to burn the numbers off with a candle. War to the Germans is a vendetta. The honour of the knights must not be diluted by Slavs, Jews or Gypsies."

*

Madam Kulikowa looked drunk, but wasn't. There were dark rings under her eyes and fine red lines formed a pattern on her eyeballs after the thrashing she'd received. The Oberführer was not one for kid gloves. Her long fur coat was torn at the seams and on the sleeves. Skinny offered to mend it for her after evening roll-call. The Madam noted, without comment, how quickly Skinny had learnt Polish.

"I know what I'm saying. And I know, unfortunately, who I'm saying it to." The Madam spat out a tooth. "Defending oneself isn't always as fine a gesture as one might want it to be."

At roll-call the Oberführer yelled at them.

"Maybe someone promised you you'd have a ball here every day?"

The Oberführer had forbidden the dormitories to be heated. He had been up all night, planning urgent measures. If there was the slightest unrest, he informed Madam Kulikowa, he was prepared to nip it in the bud. The back wall was still there.

The Madam had no illusions. The Frog's severity probably signalled the coming end of No. 232 Ost. The approaching gunfire spoke for itself. She had no doubt that he would unhesitatingly hand them all over to the execution squad.

In the yard, Skinny was pushing with all her might against the stiff gate. It was 3.40 a.m. The oiled iron hinges yielded with a squeak. She swept the snow in the driveway. The previous day a truck had skidded there, smashing its headlights and right-hand mudguard and buckling the door.

She raised her eyes. A wolf cub was standing about 20 metres from the gate. It had long thin legs and a yellowish, almost white, fur. The snow was turning blue in the dawn. She lifted her broom, and the cub jerked, turned and ran away. Twice it looked back as it fled. In that first moment when they had looked at each other she'd seen in the cub's eyes the look of a brother. Finally she saw herself. The wolf cub would turn up at daybreak, when the night ended and the mists gave way to daylight. The first time it came was on the day of Captain Hentschel's visit to Skinny, the last time on the day when Obersturmführer Stefan Sarazin of the Einsatzkommando der Einsatzgruppen turned up again. While still in the doorway he had informed her that they'd caught the saboteurs who had derailed the train. They had executed them on the spot. He regretted that they couldn't have executed them twice, a hundred times, a hundred thousand times. A dead man cannot carry another, said a German proverb. These punitive actions rarely failed to be effective. Every spot at which an enemy was killed would one day be declared sacred. Fools, all those who believed they could destroy the Reich! In the Obersturmführer's squeaky voice she heard unassailable conviction.

In her mind Skinny ran with the wolf cub along the river down to the snow-covered quarry and beyond. The cub ran to where all wolves were equal and were allowed to breathe the same air. Where that was did not matter.

Beautiful swallowed the gram of cyanide at the moment that artillery corporal Fritz Möhlen — one of Major von Kalckreuth's men — lay on top of her. A snowstorm was raging outside. From the start they had not spoken a single word. She had undressed, opened her legs and waited for the corporal to come to her.

Now he was hammering on Madam Kulikowa's door.

"Is anything wrong?" the Madam asked.

"Not with me," he replied.

Big Leopolda found Beautiful in Cubicle 7 with her head turned back and her legs drawn up as if she were sitting while lying down; her lips were parted and already stiffening, her glassy eyes slowly getting darker. Like a frightened fish, the Madam thought. There was some raspberry-coloured lipstick, badly applied, on Beautiful's lips — the lipstick which the Madam had given her that very morning. Over her face fell the shadow of the dead. Her arms were flung wide open, her hair slightly dishevelled as if she were half a sleep. Her naked throat was like that of a pigeon. Her breasts had begun to sag, still fresh and at the same time already those of an old woman. On her face was a mixture of sadness, pain and horror.

It struck the Madam that if the corporal had called the doctor, and if the doctor had used a stomach pump on the girl, there might have been hope. Who could tell what the Oberführer would have done? Finally, as if she felt it her duty, Madam Kulikowa picked up the girl's lifeless hand. For the first time in her life she felt that in the girl who had taken her own life she had lost a piece of herself. In the dead girl's expression there was an unanswered question. But even if they had saved Beautiful's life she would only have gone to where she was already, via the wall. The Frog would have pumped her stomach so he could have stood her up against the back wall.

For some reason Madam Kulikowa could not tear herself away from the dead girl's face. She was like a drowned body pulled from a lake. Beautiful had not just been a pretty girl; her attractiveness lay partly in her ability to resist subjugation: it implied more strength than most other women have, a special female strength. Would this puzzle the Gestapo?

The Madam drew a deep breath and let it out with a wheeze. No doubt I'll get it in the neck, she thought to herself. But she could not delay reporting to Oberführer Dr Gustav Schimmelpfennig.

"There must be no disruption of operations, you bitch!" the Oberführer screamed at her. He interrogated Corporal Möhlen. He took notes. His first instinct was to hush it up. He got the man to sign the standard form about keeping official business secret. The corporal signed without even reading it. Then The Frog went along with Madam Kulikowa to look at the dead girl.

One of her hands was resting on her stomach, the other was flung out to the edge of her mattress. Hadn't she had both of them on her chest before? The Madam was not sure. They were long girlish arms, now turning bluish, with slender wrists. She looked at the girl's tattooed abdomen as though she were seeing it for the first time. At the spot where Beautiful had felt the coiling snakes.

"Where did she get the poison?" the Oberführer wanted to know.

Even though Feldbordell No. 232 Ost enjoyed an exceptional reputation among brothels, without Oberführer Schimmelpfennig having done anything to enhance it, he feared that Corporal Möhlen's encounter with the dead girl would not help his standing with his superiors. It was sickening that a corpse should detract from the merits he had earned. In his mind he saw himself retreating, just as, in the larger picture, the Herrenwaffe was on the retreat.

"Damned sabotage!" he growled.

He was about to slap the Madam's face. "And that applies to you, too. Not a word to anybody. This is a military and police secret. She left this place under escort, you understand? I'll make sure none of you lives to a ripe old age here. At roll-call you'll announce a punishment. Three strokes of the cane for everybody, without exception. You won't say what for. One day and night without food. If they ask why, you don't know. The heating ban to be extended for another three days. Not a single shovelful of coal, not a single log. Do you hear?"

"Yes. Three strokes for everyone tomorrow."

"No, today!"

Then it was as if a sharp razor blade had run down her cheek, drawing blood. Her face twisted with pain. It was the most powerful blow she had ever received from The Frog. He nearly lost his balance, and had to steady himself, legs apart, and even take a step or two back. Madam Kulikowa shut her eyes. The corners of her mouth hung down.

Slowly she opened her eyes, as if even the half-light hurt them, and under her lids she turned her grey pupils on the Oberführer. Before her she saw an executioner.

"You'll lock up this cubicle. How the hell could you have left it unlocked? You'll hear about this later. We'll carry her out when it's dark. You'd better make sure operations proceed normally."

The Oberführer spared her the second slap. But she could bet her life that he wouldn't forget it.

In the waiting room Corporal Möhlen was listening to Strauss waltzes, a lecture on racial hygiene, and then more waltzes. He had been waiting three hours for the Gestapo. He studied the posters stuck up in the waiting room. They included the one with the big ear: *Feind hört mit!* The enemy is listening. The soldiers waiting their turn suspected nothing. Ginger, Long-Legs, Smartie and Maria-from-Poznan each got two extra men. A prostitute had fallen sick. Corporal Fritz Möhlen had been with her.

They could hear the artillery barrage. It seemed quite close. The bursts were continuous, no longer like the distant rumble of thunder.

"I can't go to sleep," Estelle whispered. "My eyelids are heavy."

"You'll fall asleep in a little while."

"Do the roots of your hair hurt?"

"No. I haven't got much hair, combing's no problem."

"I only spoke to her this morning. We've been here the same time. Forty-three days."

With no heating it was cold in the dormitory. They were covered up to their chins, their overcoats on top of them. Estelle knew that if she got no sleep she would be looking at the soldiers with lifeless eyes. She bit her nails in the dark.

"Have you ever been to Galicia?"

"No."

"It seems to me that each one of those 43 days I've shrunk a little."

"Better not shrink any more," Skinny said.

"It's already three o'clock. It'll be foggy," Estelle said.

Madam Kulikowa put Beautiful's belongings in a sack and tied it up with string. The gold coin bearing the head of a Russian Tsar went into her own pocket. What plans did the Germans have for them?

Twelve: Robert Kaiserhof, Günther Bomber, Friedrich Ochse, Siegfried Jawornik, Kamil Ficke, Johannes Bonner, Fred Spirit, Hans-Fritz Beyer, Jeremias Archer, Klaus Landmann, Jürgen Mihalek, Adalbert Schönfeld.

Twelve: Jochen Reitmann, Hans Deutermann, Maurice Snagenberg, Willy Steyer, Heinrich Streber-Munte, George Bittner, Hannes Schlafrock, Helmut Winkler, Karl Sachsenberger, Arthur Rota, Frederick Gaube, Thomas Binder.

The Madam massaged the major's shoulders, the muscles below his neck and around his shoulder blades. The major liked this, just as her cat Rosina had back at Kopernik Street. She told him how, in Warsaw, they used to dance the cancan for special guests. They would not have been ashamed even in front of professional dancers. Good Lord, the things you can express with your body! They wore high-quality black tights which did not wrinkle, which showed not the slightest crease even during the wildest movements, high-laced boots of the finest calf leather, long full skirts whose hems they would hold raised between thumb and forefinger from beginning to end, and white lace panties made even more dazzling by the spotlights. She could still hear the deafening applause, the flourish of the band, the air electric with desire, the readiness of the best of them to come up to all expectations. She still heard the clinking of glasses, the popping of champagne corks – the most expensive and sometimes also the cheapest – and the shouts of "Bravo, bravo!" – that went on so long that they had to repeat the number. And shouts of "Sto lat" and "Živijo, živijo", until these were replaced by German "Prosits", but not for long.

Major Karl Maximilian von Kalckreuth screwed his monocle in place in order to see her better. He too remembered a cancan, in Germany, at the Salon Kitty. The girls right by the footlights, almost above you!

Madam Kulikowa proceeded to massage the major's thighs with a dedication and strength he did not expect from her. She was thinking of the hairy legs of the 60-year-old lover she'd had when she was 14. To the Germans all hairy men were gorillas

*

Long-Legs was executed three days after Beautiful poisoned herself. Present at the execution were The Frog, three soldiers, a doctor and Madam Kulikowa as witnesses. Maria-from-Poznan and Ginger held the Madam responsible.

An Unterführer in the Waffen-SS, 37 years her senior, had complained about Long-Legs. He had asked where the Polish rivers, the Oder, the San and the Vistula ran. The answer he had wanted was "to the German sea". Germany was everywhere. Her answer instead was that she couldn't care less. She wasn't here for a geography lesson. He told her she looked like an emaciated mare and she retorted that his face was like pork schnitzel, already hammered but not yet breaded, whereupon he spat into her face that she was a sea sow. Finally, during an unsuccessful *coitus interruptus*, she reached out and stole a ten-mark piece from his trousers on the chair. She was not co-operative – the most common complaint at Feldbordell No. 232 Ost. She created a hostile atmosphere, he claimed. She made inappropriate jokes. This should not be tolerated. She had disgraced his uniform, his self-assurance as a soldier, his honour. He had been fighting since 1939. He deserved more than this.

"You're a whore if you give them what they want, and a whore if you don't. The bastard. He kept talking about the battles in Flanders in the First World War, when men died like flies. He said that their bodies manured the soil. The old bastard even talked about them in his sleep," Long-Legs told the Madam.

That morning a sapper sergeant had said to her that if her legs were just a little shorter and her wrists a little slimmer she could be an actress. He had seen *Lady of My Dreams* and had sung her a hit from it.

But none of this mattered any longer.

Long-Legs undressed by the back wall. She was allowed to keep her boots on. She folded her clothes and underwear into a neat bundle, as if it was important to her. She held the bundle under her arm; it warmed her side a little. The crash of the salvo, which she heard, and the flashes, which she barely saw, went through her like demons of grief. The bullets smashed her teeth, as they were later to smash those of Big Leopolda Kulikowa. At the end came the sharp, clear report of the Oberführer's Luger.

That same morning Ginger was taken away by the Gestapo. A letter from her had been found on the body of Sturmmann Manfred Bormann. She had got him to pass on 632 marks from her to someone else.

Chapter Thirteen

Maria-from-Poznan told them how the local population would organize hunts for people who escaped from concentration camps. The Gauleiter, she said, announced rewards to be paid by the municipal office. For proof of capture it was sufficient to produce the ears, the nose or you know what. People were making a tidy heap of money. The girls imagined bloodstained noses and black wrinkled skin.

"People take what they can," she explained.

She also told them how she had come home one day and her father had welcomed her with the words: "You look terrible. You'll end up as a whore." That was the first time that she had been paid for it. Her father had searched her and taken every last penny.

"My father was always right," she said.

Why didn't the Jews straighten their noses with a hammer? On a Saturday, so she was told, a Jewish woman would not wash her child even if it dirtied itself up to its ears. If their roof went up in flames over their heads on a Sabbath, they would not throw even a bucketful of water on it. She did not care a damn about what they considered holy. They were the most opinionated people in Poland. And at the last moment they suddenly declared themselves to be Poles. A Sarah suddenly became a Nada, a Rachel or Rebecca became a Natasha or Elizabeth. A Cohen would become a Medzurecki. Some Poles would give them shelter – her neighbours Irena and Janek Komacki had hidden a deaf-and-dumb Jewish child and now they had lost five of their own. They had been taken to Germany, five fair little boys with blue eyes. They would turn into Germans. When they grew up they would not know anything. They had been hanging them publicly in Chopin Square, and soon the Jews would no longer creep through Poland.

*

Twelve: Gert Harlan, Heini Rothmund, Max Huber, Kurt Prestell, Richard Knoll, Fritz Salzburg, Volker Horn, Hanspeter Jasper, Valentin Heinzle, Balder Spert, Hansi Weizmann, Rudolf Hasenfratz.

Twelve: Berndt Junghans, Ludwig Wagner, Hannes Kerl, Fritz Lochner, Karl Jorg Owerger, Horst Beckenbauer, Karl-Dietrich Dolfuss, Sepp Gruber, Heiden Heyst, Julius Stack, Heini Forstmann, Gerdhard Streicher.

The guard detachment of Hauptsturmführer Peter Hanisch-Sacher decided to hold a party before their departure. At first The Frog wouldn't even consider letting the prostitutes take part. But the Hauptsturmführer persuaded him at the card table. He would forget about the debt of honour of the previous evening, when The Frog had lost 150 marks. Why shouldn't the girls have some fun for once, regardless of the situation at the front? What about the inspectors from the Wehrkreis who recovered two Junkers aircraft the day before? He'd been told that champagne flowed in rivers before they started the propellers the next morning.

On the night, the prostitutes were made to parade in the guards' gymnasium, which had been created by joining the former stables and the cowshed. The radio technician had installed some equipment, and the music came from Festung Breslau and Radio Flensburg – the bands of Peter Kreuder, Eugen Wolf and Barnabas von Geszy-Huppertz. They had to go out into the fog to visit the latrine.

Skinny was snatched up by Obersturmführer Stefan Sarazin. She tried to dance a waltz with him, but the Obersturmführer had no idea how and she was not much better. He told her, as he stepped on her toes and got his rhythm wrong, that in Bremen he had seen U-boat crews fraternizing with Czech, Italian and French singers and dancers. Also with some Viennese. The Austrian girls enjoyed socializing.

"That would probably suit you too," said the Obersturmführer.

"Perhaps," she answered.

She lit the candle in her cubicle. They had not yet been told to pack up. She lit the stove. How long before it got hot? About ten minutes, she said. He wanted what he had wanted before – that she tie him to the bed. He was almost apologetic. With his squeaky voice this sounded ridiculous.

"Nothing human is alien to me," he croaked, aroused. In his gaze, somewhere deep down inside desire, there was an uncertainty, something he didn't understand himself, something he could achieve only in a brothel. It was a child's and at the same time an old man's request for something that he wasn't sure he was entitled to. She knew that she must look at him as if at a beast, a worthless beast, to make him want her at all. She must place him on the lowest rung of the ladder.

"Surely you're here for me?" he demanded. "Or aren't you an army whore?"

She had noticed earlier, in the gym, that he'd been drinking. His eyes were sunken, his chin hung down almost to his throat, to the hollow where his chest began. He seemed exhausted. He lay there, stripped to the waist, as emaciated as before. His misty irises and pupils had lost their brightness. His eyes looked lifeless. She felt the sudden tension, almost a spasm, in his body. He tried to find a more comfortable position, and opened his mouth. He squirmed, as if overcoming the spasm, before raising himself and trying to tear free from his fetters. Then he went motionless.

"Now," he croaked. There was insecurity in his voice, anger, something between shame and insolence. He was breathing heavily. He assumed that she'd realized what had happened. His chest was rising and falling, his ribs sticking out. The corners of his eyes were moist.

"It's my birthday today," he said.

He was 27. He felt as if he had disgraced himself, but it had only happened in the presence of a whore. If it came to it, he could easily order her to be flogged or put to death. If he wanted to, he could shoot her dead without another thought.

They could hear the dance music coming from the gymnasium. In the background was the thunder of heavy guns. They could make out the croaking of ravens, the howling of wolves and, as always, from the corridor the squeaking of rats.

She waited for Obersturmführer Sarazin to free himself from his bonds, remembering him telling her that a friend had taught him how to tie and untie eight kinds of knots.

"Don't say anything more," he ordered, although she hadn't spoken.

"You know me by now . . . you know me quite well by now. But I don't know you so well."

By the light of the candle the scar around his forehead and his hairline had the colour of garnets. He was lying on the blanket. He left the cords on the bed by his side, unlike the previous time, when he had immediately wound them up and put them in his pocket.

"Lucky for you that you obeyed me. Everything I want is mine. Now, here, at once."

He looked at her clothes. Madam Kulikowa had fitted them out with the best things she could find in her boxes, including brightly coloured silk squares, the kind she herself wore round her neck to conceal the wrinkles of her throat. The Obersturmführer was resting. He did not care for chatter with prostitutes. He liked her underwear, her revealing bodice when she leaned over him. Again he noted that she had half-childish, half-adult breasts.

Obersturmführer Sarazin came from Garmisch-Partenkirchen. He showed her a photograph of him standing in front of a tavern with a wooden crucifix and the letters I.N.R.I. on the spot where someone had been killed. He was seventeen then. He was wearing embroidered lederhosen and hand-knitted socks. On the snow there were black patches, maybe wine.

He held her fingers between his lips, from one corner of his mouth to the other.

They had used dogs against the saboteurs who derailed the train.

Each member of the Einsatzkommando had his own Alsatian or Dobermann. The Jagdkommando had been provided with a reconnaissance plane, a Storch, which had been fired on with rifles. He told Skinny that he and his animal had followed the tracks through the snow. They had been three days on the move, not allowing themselves to rest. He had lived on dry salami, bread, and a few pieces of fruitcake he'd received for Christmas. He had washed it down with schnapps from one flask and water from another. He always stuffed his side pocket with food before any action, as an emergency reserve. He was obsessed with hunting these people down. Once he had caught them he was gripped by melancholy. He could not explain it. Close up, the saboteurs were a pitiful sight, in spite of their frightening appearance. They were like lamps with tiny little flames about to go out. They stank of vulgarity: unwashed, uncombed, in sweaty rags. Their equipment was enough to make you weep. And that rabble had been chased by the foremost élite units deserving of a worthier adversary.

He must have been drunk still. He claimed that the cubicle looked different from last time.

"Your shrine," he observed. "Your sphere of repose. Your place of thanksgiving."

He had brought her some amber beads; he would not wish her to think him mean. She had better not ask whose neck he had snatched them off. He laughed. How many welts did she have on her behind? It would give him pleasure if she kept the beads on. Amber reminded him of ash wood.

She turned away from his breath, the sour smell of a smoker. His body smelt of dry sweat. She felt the presence of those he called saboteurs.

"Even if they hadn't confessed, their time was up," he said. "Always sentence them, never pardon them."

"Move over to the window," he ordered. She was afraid he might fire at her, as last time he had on the wolves.

"Your back to me." She did as he ordered. "Now turn round and face me."

"You should be proud of your white skin," he told her. "You promise a good seed." Some tribes, he explained, could be admitted to German blood. They were working on it at the Office for the Consolidation of Germandom. Detailed plans had already been made. "In the right proportion inferior blood – so long as it's not in the majority – dissolves in pure blood."

She was thinking of what Beautiful had done. And how ridiculous it was that she had survived even Long-Legs.

The Obersturmführer explained how, from spring to autumn, he fished the Polish rivers. He no longer felt quite so much in a foreign country; he had come to feel at home. Eels did very well in rivers with dead bodies in them. They grew fat even from dead horses. As for bream, perch and carp – one of his friends called them the rats of the rivers – a hand grenade was more effective than any fishing line.

He told her about a transport of French Jewesses from Drancy near Paris. The French police had rounded them up, 2,000 of them had been under 15 years of age. A man in Bordeaux had given them false papers. She would not believe how many Jews there were in France, but their arrogance would encounter German thoroughness. Those girls had been too weak for work. Guided by searchlights they had gone into the darkness. The sheer force of the crowd had pushed them into the underground rooms. They had looked like a monstrously large flower of a water lily, with 2,000 blossoms, soon to be devoured by a carnivorous plant. They had stood for a day and night on the square before being sent to the gas chamber. They had arrived in the morning and their turn had not come until the evening of the following day. Some had fainted; some had wet themselves, or thrown up. Fortunately, the Jewish Moloch devoured itself.

He asked her to clean his uniform. And could she sew a button on the pocket in which he carried his emergency rations? He liked everything neat and tidy. He would wait in bed.

"The world is divided into Jews and non-Jews, into a pure and an impure race," he said. "That is the only boundary human history acknowledges. That's what future anthropologists, philosophers and astronomers will write about."

The fire was going at last, the flue turning red-hot. She went to get a needle and thread, then sat down on the edge of the chair on which he had put his clothes. The Obersturmführer remained lying on the bed, whistling to himself.

She didn't know that a Moloch was a Phoenician god personifying the creative and destructive force of the Sun, he thought. But at least she knew about the poets. *Die Sonne bringt es an den Tag*. Nothing new under the sun.

"*Es kommt der Tag*," he said. The day will come. "One thing you should know, a thing the whole world should know. Even a defeated Germany will not fall upon its knees."

She had learnt to sew on buttons while still at home – with a little shank so that buttoning up would be easier and to stop the button from tearing off. She caught sight of the lines on the Obersturmführer's face and around his mouth. He shut his eyes. He was sleepy; the music worked like a lullaby. They were playing a Strauss waltz, one that started softly and went on for a long time. Violins, a zither and clarinets. An echo of warmth, domestic comfort and everyday worries. "Tales from the Vienna Woods".

Once Skinny's mother had danced with her father to it. She finished wiping clean his uniform. The button was sewn on. The waltz swayed on for ten minutes or more. The Obersturmführer was snoring. From her sock she retrieved the screw of newspaper. She did not have to hesitate now; none of them would be there for much longer. They would not leave the prostitutes behind without guards. She had to be careful and quick.

Skinny looked at the Obersturmführer's closed eyes, his purple lids, his depraved features. She shook some of the powder into his schnapps flask and the rest into his pocket, taking care not to touch the cyanide, the Zyklon B. She pictured Obersturmführer Stefan Sarazin of the Einsatzkommando der Einsatzgruppen from Garmisch-Partenkirchen standing near the tavern by the wooden crucifix. She saw Beautiful,

Ramon, her father. The waltz was coming to an end with a roll of drums. She imagined the Obersturmführer in the middle of a punitive action, taking some bread out of his pocket, some salami, and washing it down with schnapps for courage. Or in a camp, watching those young French girls.

She stoked the fire. The scrap of paper flared up, the letters on it burning first. She closed the stove door. The clash of cast iron against cast-iron woke the Obersturmführer.

"What's the time?"

"I don't know."

"I can hear music, so it can't be very late."

"No."

"Have you finished the job?"

"It's been finished some time."

"That was quick. Let me see."

She handed him his tunic. He was satisfied.

"Why didn't you wake me?"

"You didn't tell me to."

"You should guess what I want and what I don't want."

"Yes."

"You're working for Germany."

He laced up his boots with their 38 nails in each sole. Casually he smoothed his greasy hair, and put on his cap to hide his scar. "We're in a war of races," he said. She watched him dressing.

"I'll tell you one thing and you'd better remember it," the Obersturmführer declared. "I didn't know what beauty was till I came out here to the east. To find you're allowed everything. That there's nothing at all that you can't do."

"Beauty is beyond morality," he went on. "Beyond good and evil. Beauty is Germany, the Waffen-SS, the Einsatzgruppen, the Jagd-kommandos. The bomb that drops on an inhabited site. A town consumed by flames. Anything that dissolves into nothing. A captured enemy division turned into ashes like those vermin at Auschwitz-Birkenau, Treblinka and Majdanek. The hand grenade we

235

thrust between the legs of that Jewish prostitute. I pulled the pin and watched from a distance as she lay there, with her hands tied, screaming, and then turned into a firework."

He remembered the smell, the burnt flesh, the incinerated skin and bones, the hair flying in the wind like an old man's beard.

"A pity those scribes weren't present, the ones we burnt at the stake along with their books. Beautiful is whatever dissolves the ugly, the unnecessary, the subversive."

She assumed that he expected no reply from her. It was one of his outbursts. He was intoxicated by it.

"You're young. Beauty is not just a picture. Beauty overturns what we've become accustomed to. Nothing we've known before can withstand it."

She kept silent.

"Beauty is death," Obersturmführer Sarazin said. "My lover. The most faithful of all. If I didn't know what death was I wouldn't know what beauty is."

She could not avoid his eyes. She felt as if she were sinking into dense fog, the end of which she couldn't see. She was desperate not to arouse his suspicion.

Some of the girls were busy in their cubicles. The Oberführer had had to turn a blind eye. Skinny returned to the party. Estelle was missing. It was just after 11 p.m. and "The Emperor's Waltz" went on and on. She didn't even notice which of the guards she danced with.

"Let's get back to our posts," said Oberführer Schimmelpfennig finally.

During the night a truck from the Wehrkreis arrived with a barrel of salted herrings. Later that night the Oberführer was visited by a liaison officer from the head of the Gestapo, Heinrich Himmler. The officer was Himmler's personal representative in the region. He brought The Frog his evacuation plans.

In the morning Skinny watched a guard stripping his rifle on a green blanket spread on the snow. He cleaned every single part, then oiled it and reassembled the weapon. He looked at it lovingly.

Major von Kalckreuth was with Madam Kulikowa in her room. He remarked that the high command in its bunker in Berlin was like the crew of the *Titanic*. The ship was down at the bows, but the band went on playing military marches.

"We're waging a war of cannibals, my dear," the major said.

His remark caught the Madam by surprise.

"We were close to victory, and that made us giddy. It made our heads spin. The worst people are those who think themselves invincible to the very end."

Twelve: Hjalmar Steinbruch, Hubert Donnerstag, Haraki Trinkiewitz, Jürgen Heck, Horst Geuss, Dieter Fritzen, Ulrich Kohl, Manfred Kollmann, Hannes Lurke, Bragi Kleist, Otto Fest, Adolf Eiermann

In the afternoon the weather cleared. Later, there was a blood-red sunset before the sun disappeared in the patchy clouds. Dark mountains seemed to tower on the horizon, with a fire burning on top of them and spreading towards both sides. Skinny had not seen a sunset like this before. The wind was howling outside the window. She listened to forces she did not comprehend. The sky had dropped lower. Darkness fell on the plain and in the cubicle. Ice was forming on the window and on the grille, white at first and almost transparent, but slowly darkening. She felt a fear that she couldn't name. At the moment when her twelfth soldier, Adolf Eiermann, pointed to the bed, the wind suddenly dropped. She closed her eyes, sensing that there was something in the air, new and unknown, something imminent.

After they'd had sex, the soldier dressed. The slightest sound could be heard – the rustle of the cloth, the scrape of his puttees, his bootlaces being tied. Snowflakes began to fall into the silence, a heavy snowfall.

The Madam called them out into the corridor and announced that there would be no more men. None had arrived.

The Oberführer did not bother to tell them the next day why their rations were being reduced. There was no need to speak of blocked roads, bombed-out supply depots, ambushed military convoys. The Third Reich was on its knees. If they had practically nothing to eat in the fatherland, why should they feed parasites such as the army prostitutes? He'd regarded them as vermin from the moment he stepped over the threshold of the brothel.

"It's only a matter of days before the fortunes of war do an about-turn again," he said at roll-call. "Hitler has a miracle weapon."

Chapter Fourteen

On the twenty-first day of Skinny's service, before the sappers blew up the two bridges, The Frog, the commandant of Feldbordell No. 232 Ost, Oberführer Dr Helmuth Gustav Schimmelpfennig, put Big Leopolda Kulikowa up against the wall.

He ordered her to undress because frozen stiff she would not resist. He knew what the frost did to a naked body. The condemned woman would prefer to get it over with. He had worked in the camps and knew why inmates so rarely rebelled; starved, frozen and helpless people did not revolt. All that was required was to starve them for a few weeks, not allow them to sleep, make them do heavy labour on not more than 242 calories a day, as at Auschwitz-Birkenau.

"Keep your boots on!"

He approached her with his Luger drawn. If she flung herself at him he would finish her off. He recited to her in a businesslike manner what she was being sentenced for. A hostile attitude to the Reich, proven by a series of acts of sabotage. She had bitten Corporal Mussel's hand when he thought she was going to kiss it. She had cut a fistful of Corporal Broder's hair off when he asked her to shave the fine hairs on the back of his neck. At that moment Madam Kulikowa realized that she was feeling as so many before had in this situation – like a Jew. That was how the Jews must feel, she thought. The last people on earth.

The morning was exceptionally clear, with only a faint haze. At daybreak the best marksman among the guards, Horst Witzleben, had succeeded in killing the silver wolf. There were no shadows yet. The Oberführer glanced at his watch.

On her way to the wall Madam Kulikowa remembered a fortune-teller who had told her that anything that was important in her life would happen in daylight. She had assured her that she would not drown or be burnt to death.

Madam Kulikowa no longer saw the sun. She looked wearier than weary. What she had lost was not just a struggle against fading or ageing. She had long suspected that she would not leave the estate alive. Her knees had given way during air-raid practice and she had twisted her neck as if rocks had been piled on her. It occurred to her again that she should have had a child. When she was 14 she had dreamed of a white wedding and a grand feast. Now she was to be punished, but not for infertility. Perhaps for having stolen the bread, salami and margarine intended for the girls. There was a taste of salt in her mouth. The Oberführer avoided her eyes. They were smoky grey and had bewitched many men. In them was a gleam of feminine longing. She had as much strength in them as she had between her thighs. During the night she had shared out sugar, margarine and bread among the girls. She made them tie all the brooms together. She was not permitted to tell them anything, but this spoke for itself.

Rigid with cold, she gazed through the open gate towards the white plain. She had heard the shots that killed the silver wolf. In the distance the overcast sky met the wasteland and the frozen river melted into infinity. The guards were getting ready to depart. Three of them still had their firing squad duties to perform, and then they would join the rest of the evacuating personnel, except for the prostitutes who would walk in the direction of Festung Breslau. The men were singing the Horst Wessel song, "Die Fahne hoch", as they fell in below the inscription proclaiming *We were born to perish*. No. 232 Ost and its guard towers would be blown up.

Skinny was the last person to speak to Big Leopolda Kulikowa before she was collected by Schimmelpfennig. The older woman's voice was gravelly.

"I've known from the start what you were. I kept my fingers crossed for you. In the beginning we try to survive with dignity. Later, we just try to survive. Someone must describe what happened.

Hardly anyone will believe you. Look after Estelle. I rearranged her name – she's really Esther."

Her suitcase was packed, with a leather strap around it and with a label: "Kopernik Street 19, Cracow".

"At the end there's nothing," she said. "To everybody comes his day. I will always have Cracow." As her grandmother used to say, when you are old and sick there's only one thing left for you. To die in your own way. She had been a woman at twelve, a bride at 22, and at 32 she certainly had no need for a gravedigger.

The painter who had kept Leopolda when she was 17 had shown her the Pole Star, around which the other stars turned. She had been fascinated by the dawn when it came. She saw the vastness, the transience of everything. The eternity of transience. Now she thought of that Pole Star. Of the wild geese it guided to safety.

Through her mind flashed a memory. As a young girl she was standing at 19 Kopernik Street, in the former convent. It had a staircase with a handrail of polished oak. The interplay of light and shadows provided the décor: twilight, dawn and nightfall, the bright sun, the moon and the stars. She was waiting for her 60-year-old lover. She would have married him at 14, regardless of the years between them. When she was 15 he told her that between her legs she was like a valley where it was always evening. In her mind she heard his declarations of love. Love of my body, love of my soul.

"It's annoying that I should die without ever having learnt the names of flowers, or of more trees." She stroked Skinny's gingery hair. It had grown a little during those 21 days.

Madam Kulikowa had long resolved that when her time came she would accept it with dignity, elegantly, like those women they'd sung of in Cracow. She doubted that anyone would sing about her, but once she had dreamed of it. It seemed to her that the wall against which they were going to stand her up was nothing out of the ordinary. Nor was what would happen next. The knowledge that she was ready filled her with a great calm. Her eyes softened. She was looking at Skinny, but she saw something else as well, or somebody else.

"That swine, the Oberführer, is right. You need Arschaugen here, eyes on your arse. Eyes in front and behind," she said.

Ravens were strutting along the top of the wall, forming an irregular, glossy black line. They turned their heads to the inside of the wall. Suddenly they rose up over the estate. A fraction of a second later came the explosions of the dynamite charges. Three times the birds circled over the cloud of dust. They flew over the carcass of the silver wolf, which the rats were gnawing at. Then they wheeled towards the wasteland, towards something that humans had nothing to do with.

The evacuation had proceeded quickly. The alarm had sounded, and within minutes they were away.

Skinny escaped the night after the SS men shot Smartie because she had laughed. She had muttered something about the clouds being high and the mountains even higher, even higher than the sky. She came from a little town called Ub on the Tamnava River.

Maria-from-Poznan was shot by Sturmmann Friedrich Zeitler. There had been something between them at one time. The group had been given orders to march at a fast pace. Those who couldn't keep up were to be given a bullet in the back of the neck. Sturmmann Zeitler had ordered her to walk faster. He didn't do so twice. They were sinking into the snow, exhausted even when they'd set out. They were given nothing to eat. The column waited for no-one, the SS men were in a hurry. They could sense the Russians at their heels. It was Skinny's worst day. When night fell they were still walking. Now and again a shot rang out. She didn't have the strength to look back, to see who it was this time.

During the night she and Estelle used the straps from Big Leopolda Kulikowa's case to tie themselves to each other. The Madam had bequeathed them her warm underwear, 2,000 marks, 10,000 Polish zloty and a gold coin bearing a Russian Tsar's head. They waded together through snow, ice and mud, walking on the railtracks and tripping over the sleepers. They were like sisters. They had no strength to talk. The thought of the Einsatzkommandos floated through Skinny's mind. She was lethargic, but she did what she had to do. One of them dragged the other and then they changed places every half an hour. They remained somewhere in the middle of the column before they separated from it. The SS men did not bother to stop them from looking for a place to sleep.

Near Katowice Estelle was torn to pieces by Dobermanns. Skinny hid in a coal truck at a railway station, under a tarpaulin she'd found in a railwayman's hut. She did not know what would happen. The brothel was behind her. In front of her was nothing.

Chapter Fifteen

That was the story of Skinny, Hanka Kaudersová, or the part of it which stood before me as if it had happened to me. In Prague after the war she wore a smile on her lips, a smile fed by embarrassment, the incredibility of what had happened, a sense of both shame and guilt, but also of innocence. It was not easy to explain. Perhaps one lives with a certain time-lag, like a clock that is slow. Or an echo. One could say that our bodily "I" moves forward, while our mental "I" has halted yesterday or the day before yesterday. She retained her eyes in front and at the back – her *Arschaugen*, to use the Madam's expression. What lay behind her was like a landscape speeding backwards past a train. Sometimes in sleep she would see a pair of colourless clouded eyes. It was not only Obersturmführer Stefan Sarazin who had made her accept the morality of the age – kill or be killed. Those who were in the first war, like her father, had brought it home with them. When it came to a bayonet charge it was either you or me.

No-one ever told her of Stefan Sarazin's death and she made no attempt to find out what had happened to him. The war had buried him like so much else and so many others. Sometimes she would see herself sitting with her back to the stove, sewing his button on, or pouring the powder into his flask. Now she no longer cared.

In the street she would return people's smiles, like a person greeting neighbours. Good morning, good afternoon. She was like a boat floating on an unfamiliar ocean, drifting from a darkness that only she knew into the light that was common to all.

She wanted to believe that she came from a world which was already gone. From a nameless land to which only she had given a name. A mirror in which she alone saw her face from the other side of time.

In its reflection she also saw Wehrmacht Captain Daniel August Hentschel. He had already left Cubicle 16, and was walking down the long flagstoned corridor which stank of rats. He hadn't promised her anything he could not fulfil. In retrospect, if she dismissed a lot of things, he now seemed to her better in some ways. She did not wish to seem unjust, and gratitude had something to do with it.

She was always meticulously dressed and made up, the sleeves of her blouses always down to her wrists, and she was determined not to show her stomach to anyone.

It would be simple to say that she survived with the help of her body, that she reached down to the roots of her strength to overcome herself. She was lucky that she was young, healthy and tough, capable of any work including the hardest, that she had had the presence of mind – if one can put it that way – to make the ultimate effort at the right moment. That was all. The body. But the body was never on its own, just as the soul was not. What was a person to do if, having been born into this kind of world, she wanted to survive?

Even in the lives of the happiest of us there is a touch of despair. Even from the worst a seed might spring. But a seed of what? We all have in ourselves contradictory tendencies – for self-destruction and for survival. Explicable tendencies, conscious and subconscious ones. She knew that anyone might cross over, from one day to the next, to become one of those in misfortune. Morality might turn into a labyrinth. She had been through a lot and she was young. It appeared as if her life was still ahead of her. Only yesterday she had stood on her own against a great Reich which had no place for her. A Reich which had confronted the world and which had tried to exterminate those who, through some mistake, had already been born.

She found it difficult to ensure that the echo of the words German or Germany did not immediately conjure up a panorama of burnt villages, devastated towns, shattered families and countless humans murdered, tortured or crippled in the name of racial purity; not just a vision of brothels in the east and in Festung Breslau, or wherever the Herrenwaffe set foot. She realized, as the rabbi had, that to condemn all this in words would not be enough. She absorbed it as the liver and kidneys absorb substances, and she tried to pump it out of herself again as the heart pumps blood into veins and cells. Like the rabbi she was not sure if there was any point in talking about it, in bringing back those echoes, because it would be equally ill-advised and criminal to forget even the smallest part.

She sometimes remembered how Captain Hentschel had walked out to his Horch. She was standing by the frozen window of her cubicle. He had walked to his car with cautious heavy steps, over the swept but ice-covered stones. Before taking his last step he had turned. He could not have seen her. Or was she mistaken? He had aroused something in her. It was only a glimmer of something. Perhaps if he had not turned she would have wiped him from her memory. He would have vanished from her life just as his Horch had vanished into the blizzard. She had stood by her frozen window, almost invisible, and his look remained with her. Why?

I never formed a clear picture in my mind of Obersturmführer Stefan Sarazin of the Einsatzkommandos der Einsatzgruppen. I didn't really want to. But Adler knew why he wanted to be a judge when they were in short supply. Skinny, of course, was entitled to be both judge and executioner.

She felt in her bones that it was better not to know certain things, not to remember certain people. That was easier said than done, as she'd once remarked to Estelle. She remembered Sarazin yawning and telling her that this was how the world would yawn one day if anyone who survived told their story. But what about his eyes, I wanted to know. Did they really have no colour at all? They did, Skinny told me. She just could not remember now. Lies had been like the clothes she put on, like the water she quenched her thirst with, a handrail she held on to. She had not forgotten her fear, just as she had not forgotten her diarrhoea.

Had she been afraid of Sarazin? Yes, certainly. He'd personified for her a Germany that she had not imagined before. In Terezín, the

Germans in SS uniform had still seemed comparatively civilized. But they had two faces and they quickly revealed that second face, in the first seconds at the ramp at Auschwitz-Birkenau. That was a world without masks. Sarazin's eyes remained deep inside her like devil's eyes gazing at her through the mist, through the night, between valleys and mountains, through the lowlands and wastelands of her soul.

I reflected on the nature of the love that caused such anxiety to both Skinny and me, but at the same time, gave sense to everything. At 16 few people talk about beauty, they just let it warm them, as if in sunshine. With Skinny I felt as if I were on a raft on a turbulent river. Ahead was the bank, where we would land and tie up. To begin with, a small wooden hut would be enough for us. We could sleep under the stars before the dew came down or the frost bit. Then we would see.

When he realized that I'd fallen in love, Adler thought I had gone out of my mind – although he did not criticize my choice. I asked myself the question, on Skinny's behalf really, how so many people could have lived in safety, out of the wind, when those colourless milky eyes were fixed on her.

"If you add it all up, we were lucky," she said.

"Who'd add it all up?"

What we call luck has a thousand faces. Who can tell how much it consists of other people's bad luck? She had created armour for herself, a shield close to her chest, the way gamblers hold their cards to prevent others from peeping.

Adler thought she was tired. He had his own explanation for her reticence. Like the rest of us she was suffering from an incurable disease which one must live with. After the war it was important to forgive others for that very thing we hoped they would forgive us for. Skinny, Hanka Kaudersová, was 15 and six months when she got to Feldbordell No. 232 Ost and she was still two months short of 16 when the war ended. She could not forgive what was unforgivable. She did not get free of the net in which they had caught her.

Looking back, she tried to sort out what had been important at No. 232 Ost. She had arrived there unprepared, and survived. She had asked her body to hold out, and it had. She had asked her soul and conscience not to condemn her. But how could she have talked to, lain with, breathed the same air as, her murderers, the murderers of her parents and brother?

She soon discovered that life belonged to the living. For the dead, there was only honour, all the honour she could give them. The soul, too, was an empty place, like that place in her abdomen which her mother had told her about three years earlier. No-one would get to it if she did not let them, no-one without a key. Never mind how many bodies had forced themselves on her.

There were days when I felt I might be given that key, even though I had doubts about it on that train ride to Moravia.

"You know," she said to me. "They say that when Big Leopolda Kulikowa was about to die she shouted at the execution squad: "God is my pimp!"

The whole time before and afterwards, Skinny, Hanka Kaudersová, later my wife, was flesh and blood. A soul in which remembrance and oblivion contended. Her eyes had looked on the devil twelve times a day or more, as had the other girls – every day except Sunday and sometimes Sunday as well. Her eyes had seen good and evil.

When Skinny was fifteen, getting on for sixteen, she had clear skin, shiny hair – carefully brushed and growing long again – and lovely green eyes.

BY ARNOŠT LUSTIG
ALSO AVAILABLE IN VINTAGE